Praise for *The Si...*

"A well-written portrait, not just of grief but also of the pain of realizing you didn't really know someone you thought you were close to… A heavy but powerful read that tackles big topics without letting them drag the narrative down."

—*Booklist*

"The story reads like *Go Ask Alice*… As Allie learns the many sordid secrets of her sister's concealed life, she begins to understand the powerful influence her sister had on her and, a talented painter, struggles to find her own voice."

—*Kirkus Reviews*

"A powerful story of redemption, forgiveness, love, and the ability to persevere."

—*VOYA*

THE

HOME-

COMING

Also by Stacie Ramey

The Sister Pact

THE HOME-COMING

STACIE RAMEY

sourcebooks
fire

Published by Sourcebooks Fire, an imprint of Sourcebooks, Inc.
P.O. Box 4410, Naperville, Illinois 60567-4410
(630) 961-3900
Fax: (630) 961-2168
www.sourcebooks.com

Library of Congress Cataloging-in-Publication data is on file with the publisher.

Printed and bound in the United States of America.
VP 10 9 8 7 6 5 4 3 2 1

This book is dedicated to JKR, who is my beginning, my end, and all of my in betweens, and who has given me the world.

CHAPTER 1

Standing on the high school's lacrosse field in the town I never thought I'd go back to, I wait for my turn to do suicides. The sun blazes, and I take a drink from my water bottle and try not to chew myself out for landing here instead of getting to stay in Chicago with Uncle Dave. What would Leah think if she saw me now?

"Strickland!" Coach calls. "Line up."

It's not my turn to run again, and the unfairness starts a flame in my stomach, but I line up anyway. No way I'm gonna let Coach see he's getting to me. Or let the team know how out of shape I really am.

"Get your legs up!" Coach Gibson screams, and I think he's talking to me, but I can't be sure, because six of us are racing, and I'm losing. Bad. Guess the last few years of smoking weed hasn't helped my stamina.

Matt, a guy from my neighborhood who I used to play lacrosse with and one of two people Mom fought like hell to keep me away from, yells from the sidelines, "Wheels, Strickland, wheels." But he laughs as he says it, and I know he's just giving me shit.

I knew they'd go hard on me. Payback for moving away. For

not playing lacrosse since fifth grade. For hanging with the druggies instead of the jocks. I'm one of the new guys on the team. An honor not usually given to seniors. So I'm treated to Hell Week like the freshmen and sophomores. I don't mind. That's just the way it is.

Coach Gibson points to me. "Just Strickland this time."

Bodies collapse around me, and I hear their sighs of relief as I crouch in the ready position, sweat pouring off my chest and arms and legs while I wait for Coach's whistle to launch me like a bullet from a gun. I run from the end line to goal line. Goal line to end line. End line to box line. Box line to half field.

"Push, push, push," Coach yells.

I do what he says, push my body. Pump my legs. It sucks, but I do it, because with each stride, I feel my body taking over and my mind being left far behind. Maybe this time, Dad was right. Lacrosse is just what I need.

"Again." Coach points to me. He clicks his stopwatch, and I race again. He shakes his head as he documents my time. Like I don't know how bad I suck. Like I don't get how much persuading Dad must have had to do to get me on the team. Thinking of Dad fires me up to tap into my beast. I bend over. Try not to puke. Take a drink of my water and hit the line to run again.

I don't actually mind this part. Whenever I run full out, push my body past its limit, those are the times I'm not thinking of Leah.

"Again." I run my route one more time, my body failing a

little more with each step. When I'm sure I'm going to fall to the ground, I make myself think of Leah. How I was supposed to save her. How I didn't. And that's enough to propel me forward. At the end of the run, I bend over, spit on the ground.

The other seniors and juniors start their Indian drill. They jog by us freshies, run their rhythmic jogging and even breathing, reminding me that they are warriors, and I am not. Matt yells out, "Damn, Strickland." Then laughs as I lose this battle and puke on the ground.

Brandon, another guy from the old team, joins in the hilarity. "We got a puker!"

I look at each exercise as a brick in some mythical wall I have to build before I can earn my walking papers. That makes it easier to face. One step. One drill. One minute. One hour. One week. One month. More than one year since my girlfriend Leah died. (*Killed herself*, I remind myself, careful to make the memory hurt as much as possible.)

Probably thirty minutes left in practice. Nine weeks till my first report card. Nine months of probation, ten months till I can graduate and move on with my life to California. The farthest place from my family I can go without getting a passport. Where I can cash in on my one and only talent: growing and selling weed. Legally there.

Finally, Coach calls us in. The juniors and seniors have already been sent to the locker room ahead of us, so he's only addressing us wannabes. "You guys didn't totally disappoint me today, so tomorrow, you can bring your sticks."

Some of the guys pump their fists. I don't even have the energy to do that.

"Now hit the showers and head home."

I'm turning to leave when Coach calls me over. "Hey, John, I wanted to say I'm sorry about your brother. And your girl."

The dragon roars. Flames engulf me. People just can't let an accident like Ryan's go, even after all these years. But Leah? That's too much. They didn't even know her. I don't want to share her tragedy, her life, her memory with anyone.

"You've had some tough breaks for sure."

Dad and his stupid mouth.

Coach shifts his stance, crosses his arms—his clipboard with all my times now clutched to his chest. Numbers that for sure say I'm not good enough to be on any lacrosse team—definitely not the varsity team at East Coast High. "I don't want you to get discouraged. Coach Stallworth told me about you. Said you used to be a hell of an athlete. You can be again, I'm sure."

His stare feels like he's trying to figure out what I'm made of. I want to tell him not to waste his time. I'm happy to tell him exactly who I am. I'm the kind of guy who doesn't mind taking whatever physical punishment he wants to dish out. But when it comes to my emotions? Coach is going to have to understand that that shit's off-limits. Emotions are for idiots. Feeling crap doesn't change what happened. Good weed works so much better. Hell, even bad weed beats feeling any day.

I gulp more water. Spit on the ground. Look him square in the eye. "Thanks, Coach. That all?"

I guess Coach picks up on my noncommunicative status, because his eyes go back to his clipboard. "See you tomorrow."

I give him a nod and jog to the locker room so Coach'll see I've still got a little juice in me, even after everything.

———o———

Last one in the locker room also means last one out. I sit on the bench, lean over to close my locker as Matt and Brandon head for the parking lot.

"Later," Matt throws over his shoulder, the *er* reverberating as the door shuts behind him.

Matt and I've got some history to get over. It was his big brother, Pete, who hit Ryan. Seven years later and that still hangs between us. Not that it was Pete's fault exactly. When it comes to those things, fault hardly even matters. It's called an accident for a reason.

Besides, Pete hasn't exactly gotten off scot-free either. Some people might think becoming a high school dropout, working pizza delivery while feeding a major drug and drinking problem is not as bad as Ryan's deal, but I say that nobody has a right to judge. I stayed in touch with Pete even after I moved away. Nobody understands that, but it was like he was the only one who got the nuclear fallout of that accident.

I'm stuffing my sweaty clothes into my bag and zipping it up when I hear my cell chirp. I grab it, hoping it's one of Pete's connections I reached out to today. Someone who can help me with my little sobriety problem.

But it's not Pete's connection. It's Uncle Dave. Hey, just checking in. Hope you're settling in OK.

I text back. Yeah. Fine.

How was practice?

Somehow, that kills me. That he's still checking on me. Uncle Dave. Not Dad or Mom. Him. This warm spot inside me lights a little every time he calls or texts.

He texts again. When someone you love dies, it changes you. Remember that.

He means Leah for me. My perfect big brother for Mom.

After Ryan's accident, Mom didn't change so much as reduce, like the sauce that Uncle Dave made for my filet the last night I was living with him. He explained how a little fire under you can intensify whatever's inside you. After the accident, Mom got more intense for sure. Driven. Focused only on Ryan. With me, I just got more angry. Just the way I am, I guess.

Uncle Dave always tries to turn simple moments into lessons. Not preachy ones, just different ways to look at life. His texts aren't meant to pry or annoy, but I can't help wishing he hadn't. I screwed up the best living arrangement of my life, the one Dad said I needed after I told him about Leah. But I killed the whole deal by hanging with a bunch of thugs and acting like a punk.

There's a mass of activity around me in the locker room that doesn't include me. Kids banging fists. Giving each other shit. Nodding when the others ask if they've got a ride. Then it hits me: I'm completely ride-less.

The guys on the team have picked up on my not so subtle *I want to be left alone* signal. I know teammates are supposed to male bond or some shit like that, but that's not what I'm here for. I'm here to finish probation. Live according to Mom's rules. Then get out and go away. And never come back.

I text Uncle Dave. I'm exactly the same jerk I used to be.

He texts. Nice try.

As the door bangs shut for the last time, I realize my being a selfish ass and ignoring everyone means I'll have to walk home. *Great work, Johnny.* I almost laugh out loud at what an idiot I can be.

The phone chirps again. This time it's Dad. Picked up your Jeep from the compound. Cost me a fortune. Show me you've earned it and I'll bring it to you.

Always pushing. Uncle Dave is so much cooler than Dad is that it's hard to believe they're even brothers.

The door opens, and a janitor leans in. "You done?"

"Yeah. Sorry." I look around the locker room one more time. I am completely alone, even on a team of thirty kids. Classic me.

CHAPTER 2

'm only two steps out the door when my cell rings. I almost don't look. Then I'm glad I did. My little sister, Livy.

"Hi, maniac," I say. "I'm just leaving practice."

"Oh my God," she says. "Mom's making meat loaf, and she says we can't eat until you get here. I'm starving, so hurry!"

I can't help smiling at Livy's theatrics. She's my favorite person on the planet and way too cute for her own good—and mine. It would be a ridiculous understatement to say I spoil her. But honestly, that's my right. She hasn't had enough of anyone's attention since the accident.

"I'm doing my best," I say, switching my bag to my other arm so I can keep talking.

Livy's called me on the iPhone I gave her so she could always get me. Livy was the first in her class to have an iPhone, and since I pay the bills every month, there's not a thing Mom and Dad can do about it.

"You're walking?" Livy's voice gets this weird sound to it, like she's annoyed but not with me. Maybe with everyone who's let her brother down. It's nice to have a warrior to protect me, but it won't help with Mom.

"Too tired to jog," I joke.

"I'll take care of this."

"No." I stop walking, try to use as stern a big brother voice as I can muster, knowing there's no point, because Livy is untamable. Still, I fill my words with as much intensity as I can. "I don't want to bother Mom. Want to start off this visit on good terms, OK?"

"Visit?" Her voice gets sad.

"I'm here for at least nine months," I offer, knowing it's not what she wants to hear.

I do worry what it will mean for Livy when I move out again, but she could come out to Cali for her winter and spring breaks. I could come to Connecticut sometime in the fall. I'll help her understand that it's no good for anyone for me to be here long term.

"Tell Mom I said to eat without me. Tell her I had to stay after to talk to the coach and I'm gonna be a little while."

"Mom insists we eat together for your first family meal."

My stomach sinks at the thought of the whole family sitting around the table.

Then Livy says, "Only not Ryan. Rosie and Mom gave him his dinner already. Mom says it's too late for him to eat."

I breathe out. I have to remember that this version of Ryan is a person too. New Ryan may not be the same big brother I had before the accident, but he is *still* my brother.

The counselor I used to see when I lived here, Steve, used to say I had to stop looking at things like that. Old Ryan. New Ryan. He said labeling was just a way of distancing myself from the guilt. No shit. Steve called it survivor's guilt, and *that* label pisses me right the eff off, because after Leah, I guess I've got a double dose of it. Awesome.

But then Livy's voice shifts into her practical tone, the one that kills me, because at ten years old, she shouldn't have to worry about taking care of me or anyone. "I can get you a ride. I've got an idea that doesn't involve Mom."

Before I can say anything, she's hung up. I pick up my pace so Livy won't have to wait so long. I've only made it to the front of the school, our house still a good two miles away, when a Camry makes a U-turn, drives back into the school entrance, then stops.

"Hey," a girl yells out the window. "Are you John?"

"Um, yeah…" I don't recognize the car, but I walk over anyway.

"Livy sent me. Said you might need a ride."

I rub my hand across my stubble. "Livy sent you?"

She shows me her cell. Even from this distance, I can make out Livy's name with some kind of text. "We're neighbors."

I can't help smiling. What a pest my little sister is. "Oh. Right. I'm sorry. Livy can be a little…"

"I babysit her sometimes. She's awfully protective of you, so she texted me to see if I'd look for you."

My hand on the window, she points to the back of the car and a bunch of field hockey equipment. "It's no big. I was just leaving practice too."

"Thanks." I'm not about to turn down a ride home, especially not from a girl.

"I'm Emily," she says as she shifts the car into park and puts on her flashers. A kid in a Mustang behind us beeps. I shoot him a nasty look. Being mean to girls totally gets my beast going. I walk around to the passenger side and stare at the pile of textbooks on the seat of her Camry.

"Sorry. Just throw them on the floor. I wasn't expecting company."

I almost do as she says, but something about how neatly the books are stacked makes me think that she's pretty fond of these textbooks, which amuses me. So I line them up carefully on the floor. I'm not sure if she's pleased by my actions or is the kind of girl who smiles a lot, but she shoots me a nice one right after I do it, revealing super white and straight teeth that make me want to get her to smile all over again.

"Livy can't stop talking about you. I mean, even before you moved back. It's always John this and John that."

I shut the door and give her a nod, letting her know I'm in and we can go. She waits—actually waits—until my seat belt clicks closed before putting the car back into drive. "She's a good girl," I say, trying not to give her one of those cheesy up-and-down looks, because I'd hate for some guy to do that to Livy one day. But I can't help notice a ton of little details about her. Like how her olive-toned skin and dark-brown hair is completely different from Leah's. How she's got these leather bracelets that are really cool. How she has a nice body.

"I live next door." Emily breaks the silence. "Sometimes I sit for Ryan too. Or I used to. Maybe not anymore now that you're back."

It's weird to hear someone who never knew Old Ryan talk about New Ryan. New Ryan has a head injury and uses a wheelchair, and New Ryan is in that condition largely because of me. No wonder my family is so messed up.

"I wouldn't worry about losing your gig." I almost add that Mom doesn't usually leave me alone with Ryan but think better of it. Instead, I say, "Lacrosse is going to be my life for the next few months anyway."

"Field hockey." She gestures at her gear again, seemingly noticing that she's sweating in front of the new guy, because she tips the rearview mirror to check out her hair and forehead and ends up fiddling with the vents, which blow a ton of air into the car that is mostly warm. Which is fine with me, because the temperature's dipped since practice ended, and it's dark. September in Connecticut. Emily blushes, and she picks at the headband she has holding back her hair. She looks pretty, and it kills me when girls worry about all that superficial stuff. God knows I don't. She turns to smile at me. "You're not what I expected."

"What were you expecting?"

"Livy's painted you like a bad boy guardian angel. With all the stories she's told me, I was kind of imagining a *Sons of Anarchy* type."

"What stories?" I ask.

"All kinds." Emily gets a text and peeks at it while we wait for the light to turn green. Her face scrunches up like she's read something she doesn't like. She puts the phone back in its holder on the dashboard. It's white and shaped like that owl from Harry Potter that Livy loves. Emily drums her fingers on the wheel. She looks to me, her eyebrows raised as if she's expecting me to contribute to the conversation, then back at the road, but I can tell her mind is occupied by whoever texted her.

Small talk is always awkward. I could take the edge off by contributing some larger-than-life story. Get her to stop worrying about whatever that text said. It's not that there isn't a reel of movies running through my head about *that* time after the accident. I just don't think it'll help anyone to talk about it.

Most of those stories start with New Ryan screaming his head off, Mom and Dad fighting, and me trying to distract Livy. Like the time Livy and I jumped on my bed with screamo music blaring in the background. I cranked it loud to keep her from hearing them yell at each other.

"Go higher!" I told her.

"Like this?" she asked as she jumped.

"Higher!" I shouted. "Higher! Higher!"

The bed frame broke, but I caught her, and we just kept jumping and laughing. Jumping and laughing. Finally, we collapsed on the mattress, sweaty and laugh-crying until Dad came to check on us. I was so glad it wasn't Mom. She would have completely lost it with me.

Sitting in the car with Emily now, I sum up my blatant disregard of the house rules, as Mom liked to put it, for her the best I can. "I guess you could say I wasn't the best role model."

"All I know is Livy adores you, and that has to mean

something. You're a good big brother." She nods as she says this, as if she's deciding to believe in the John Strickland urban myth, even though she only knows the hero part of my story.

As we pull into her driveway, I ask, "You wanna know a secret?" because I can't help myself.

The car goes into park. Lights off. Engine off. She turns to face me, an amused look on her face. "Sure."

"I had my SAMCRO back tat blacked in when I left California."

She smirks. "Knives or flames?"

"You weren't kidding about being a *Sons* fan, were you?"

"Just did a Netflix binge last weekend. It was serious." She raises her right hand as if she's testifying and laughs this sweet little laugh. Man, she's adorable.

"I guess." Part of me wonders if she realizes she's just told me that she's looking for a safe bad boy. That's exactly my MO. Part of me thinks she did it on purpose. But that's probably just arrogant guy shit. Probably. "Thanks for the ride," I say.

"I can take you in tomorrow," she offers. "Bus comes at six thirty. I leave at seven."

"That would be great. Thanks." I step out of the car, let my bag fall to the ground, and gather up her books for her, which are a considerable stack and super heavy. Her haul is impressive, and we're only in the first quarter.

"Thanks." She hugs the books to her body.

I take one last look in the backseat of her car at her field hockey gear and know everything I need to about this girl. It's studies first, sports second with her—exactly the kind of influence I want for Livy. But she's got this nice ass, which I realize is not cool to look at, but honestly, I'm behaving better than I have with any other girl, so maybe my little sister has already been a good influence on me.

Emily turns to face me one more time. "Seven sharp. OK? I hate to be late."

"Yes, ma'am."

She stares at me, measuring me up, but this time, I wish I'd been less smooth and more real with her, because she looks slightly disappointed in my flip remark. Like maybe she's used to being treated as if she's not relevant.

"Thanks again," I say. And this time, I really try to act like I mean it instead of being the sarcastic idiot or player I usually am. This girl is different, and that makes me want to be too. Plus, she's important to Livy. So I tell myself that Emily and I will have a completely platonic relationship. That would be a first for me. Well, besides Leah's little sister, Allie.

I'm digging in my bag for my house key when Livy opens the door and screams, "Johnny!" Livy wraps me in a hug and starts to pull me inside the house I'm never ready to enter. I glance back at Emily's house.

Livy smacks me in the arm. I rub the area and pretend it hurt. "What was *that* for?"

"You can't date *her*," Livy says as if I were considering it.

"Why not?"

"She's my favorite sitter and a really cool person. She's totally off-limits!"

"OK." For Livy, I will just be neighborly.

Definitely.

Probably.

Maybe.

———o———

The smell of home-cooked meat loaf hits me as soon as we walk through the door, and I have to admit, one of the things I missed about living here was Mom's cooking. Especially her meat loaf. She claims its some Food Network person's recipe, the one whose name Livy and I were always laughing about. Ina Garten. Like she's in a garden and using that as a really poorly thought out alias. We used to go around the house making up other equally entertaining names like Ina Shoe or, my favorite, Ina Pickle.

Mom never found any of that funny, because Mom was a journalist and it's the lady's actual name, but Livy and I laughed all the same. Besides, Mom gave up her journalist credentials after Ryan's accident. She said her job was to get *him* better.

As I walk to the kitchen, I see that Mom hasn't changed anything since I left, including the Benjamin Moore eggshell walls that I spent a fair amount of time fixing after punching holes in them. Most of my outbursts were brought on by Ryan's fists on Mom's face, a fact that was never discussed, because he couldn't help it and I could. It amuses me that my spackle jobs started out terrible but got much better as I went, like Mom unintentionally taught me a trade.

Livy tugs me harder, maybe because she senses me tense up. I let her navigate me past the first memory minefield in our house.

Rosie, our housekeeper, comes forward. The crinkling around her eyes and her outstretched arms show how happy she is to see me. "John. John. John." She wraps me in a hug and rocks me a little. "Are you OK?"

"I'm fine, Rosie."

"When they told me about your arrest…"

"It was nothing. Just stupid guy stuff."

"So stop being stupid. Eh?"

I nod. If only it were that easy.

Everyone gets silent as Mom walks in the room. She stands back, her arms unsure where to be. First she brings her hand to her chin, as if posing for a picture. Then she folds her arms over her stomach. Her dark-brown hair is pulled into a messy bun, and her lips are painted apple red, which accentuates how pale and tired she looks.

Rosie takes my bag of lacrosse gear out of my hands.

"No." I grab the strap. "Coach says we each have to be responsible for our own gear."

She wrenches it away from me. "Not when you just got home."

Home. I look around. I'm really here. My plane got in so late last night and I got up so early this morning, I've barely had time to register that.

Mom stretches a hand out toward me. "Come on. Let's eat before your sister drives us crazy."

I trudge toward the dining room table, which is set like it's a special occasion. Not with the good plates and glasses but with the white linen tablecloth Livy and me got Mom for Mother's Day one year, flowers in a vase, and napkins rolled in the napkin holders Livy made in kindergarten, the ones with shellacked leaves.

Salads sit expectantly on plates. Livy dives into her salad, but I take my time to put my napkin on my lap and eat slowly like Mom likes. She takes in my efforts with a small nod, and it feels good to have a small truce so soon.

"How was practice?" Mom spears a piece of greens and brings it to her mouth slowly, as if she were at a tea party with the queen.

Livy makes her eyes cross.

I try not to laugh, but it's hard. "It was fine."

This time, Mom actually returns my grin. "I remember how much you love small talk."

"It was OK. I'm the new guy on the team, so that means I have to prove myself. My times suck, and I gotta get better quick."

"Then we better get some protein in you." Mom motions to Livy. "Go ahead, clear the salad plates."

Livy shoots out of her seat and gives a little "Yes!" with a fist pump.

I start to feel really happy that I'm home until Ryan shatters the silence. "Mommommommommom!"

Mom's eyes fly to the ceiling. She looks back at me. "Let's see if he stops."

Livy comes in carrying the meat loaf, oven mitts on her hands.

Mom heads to the kitchen, even though I can tell she wants to go to Ryan. Settle him down. I push away from the table and follow her into the kitchen.

Mom passes me with the potatoes, and I grab the string beans and rolls. Livy comes back for the butter. Ryan screams louder. "Mommommom!"

Livy's eyes meet mine. Guilt settles over me. I wonder how many times she's been left at the table alone. She's ten years old, for cripes' sake.

"I want to come down!" Ryan yells. "Momomomom!"

"Maybe we should let him?" I ask. "I could bring him down."

Mom's eyes wet, but she shakes her head. She blinks a few times and says, "We're not supposed to give in when he's like this. If he has a good day, he can eat with us tomorrow night."

Rosie pops her head in the kitchen. "I've got all your pads sprayed and laying out to dry, and I put the practice uniform you wore in the washer. I'll dry them tomorrow." She pats the gear bag. "I've put a fresh practice uniform in your bag. OK?"

"Thanks, Rosie."

She blows me a kiss. "So glad to have you back." Then she goes out the front door.

I go back to the table where Mom is holding the knife over the meat loaf. The muscles of her face tighten, working hard to act like none of the commotion is happening. My heart softens for her. It's gotta be hell always having to choose between your kids.

"You want to go see?" I ask, my voice so even and normal that I'm kind of proud of myself. "We can wait for you."

Mom looks at the knife in her hand as if she'd forgotten she was holding it. She straightens in her chair and cuts the meat loaf. "No. He's nineteen. He needs to learn to go to sleep by himself. He needs to follow the rules."

The words slice into me. *Can't you follow simple rules, John? Simple fucking rules?* How many times had she said that to me?

Mom puts out her hand, and Livy extends her plate so Mom can place a piece of meat loaf on it. I offer her mine, and she gives me two helpings, smiling as she does. "You need to eat better."

Bang. Crash. "Damn. Damn. Damn. Shit!"

Mom's hand shakes, sending her own piece of meat loaf flopping off her plate and onto the tablecloth.

Livy sucks in a breath, and I'm not sure if she's upset about Ryan or about the tablecloth. We bought it right before I got kicked out of the house.

I scoop up the meat loaf and put it back on Mom's plate.

Mom stares at the stain like she can't figure out how to fix it.

"We can soak the tablecloth," I say to both of them.

Livy nods, but I can tell she's trying not to cry.

More banging. More screaming. Mom puts down her fork. "I'll just be a few minutes."

"Don't expect us to leave you any." I wink at Mom so she knows all is OK and for Livy's sake too.

"Table for two?" I ask my sister, hoping to lighten the mood. She looks worried, so I add, "We can take our plates in front of the TV and watch whatever horrible show you like but shouldn't be watching."

20

Livy says, "I think he's getting worse."

"What makes you say that?"

"He's always so mad. He yells all the time."

"Maybe he just wants to be with us." I am amazed I say that out loud. "Maybe we should talk to Mom about that."

Livy nods. "I think he really does."

I feel a little lighter. Which is weird but cool at the same time. Then Ryan screams again, and there's a thud.

I force myself to take a bite of meat loaf, except it's hard to chew since my mouth has gone dry.

We hear Mom soothing him. "It's OK, Ryan. It's just time to go to sleep."

"She has to stay with him most nights to get him to go to sleep," Livy says quietly.

"She doesn't give him meds to sleep anymore?"

"She says they don't work and that they're bad for him."

I remember when Mom brought Ryan home from the hospital. He came in an ambulance. All our neighbors gathered around while the medics unloaded my brother from the back. Even the kids got off their bikes to watch. It was like a freak show.

Ryan had stitches all over his head like some sort of monster. His eyes didn't focus. He didn't recognize me. He didn't seem to know anybody or anything. I tried to stay away from him as much as possible those first days after the accident, but the worst was at night. He woke up screaming almost every single night. The sound was horrible. Mom went to him. Tried to calm him. Dad too. Livy started crying, and no one tried to help her. So I went in her room and took her out of her crib. Rocked her, like I wanted to be rocked. Cared for her the way I wish Mom still cared for me.

I rub the palms of my hands together, the friction calming. Chew on my knuckle. I point to Livy's plate. "I thought you were starving. Let Mom worry about Ryan. You worry about beating me at *Super Smash Bros.*"

She smiles a thin smile and forks a green bean. "I thought we were watching TV."

"Changed my mind. It's been way too long since I schooled you."

The sound of a smack. Mom cries out.

My hands clench, and the rage starts. My blood converts to rocket fuel awaiting a flame.

I try not to listen as the monster inside me whispers, *It's always Ryan. He hits her. You hit the wall. Only you get in trouble.*

My gaze falls on the large painting Mom got to cover the massive hole I put in the wall the first time he hit her.

The beast inside me tells me, *You were the one who got sent away.*

"John!" Livy's face is near mine. She's shaking me. I force myself to stop listening to the anger. To get back to reality.

"I'm sorry," I mumble, finally noticing that I've spilled my water on the table and it's dripping into my lap.

"It's OK. It stopped." Livy says. "He's stopped."

I should be taking care of Livy. Not the other way around. "She should give him meds at night," I say.

"I know," Livy agrees.

My eyes go to the mess that Mom and I have both made.

"We can tell Mom you were trying to get the spot out."

I stand, a plate loaded with food in my hand. I grab my glass of water and a napkin. "Let's bounce." My voice is back to normal. I'm totally in control. "What's your fave game now?"

Livy stands. "*Super Mario*. You know that." Her voice is light and jokey, but underneath is a strain that is there because of Ryan and me.

"Let's just watch something. I'm too tired to play," she says.

"Already making excuses?" I lower myself into Dad's old chair.

She's turns on *Switched at Birth*, which I can totally relate to. I try not to think about Mom's uneaten food. How skinny she is. How after everything our family's been through, she's tried to hold on to the appearance of civility, the formal family meal, the salads. All my sister wants is someone to eat dinner with. All my brother wants is to be able to stay up past seven o'clock. And all I want is to be in California, away from all this.

CHAPTER 3

After dinner, Livy and I clear the table and put away the food. We leave the rest for Mom to deal with. Livy disappears into her room. "Homework," she says.

I hold my breath and open the door to my room.

My room is exactly as I left it, and I'm not sure how that's supposed to make me feel. Does that mean Mom wanted me to come back? Or did Ryan take up so much of her time that she never got around to changing it? I decide the first makes me happier, so that's what I'm going to believe. Look at me making good choices. Uncle Dave and Steve would be proud.

I start to unpack so when Mom comes in to inspect, she'll see that I'm doing what I told her I came here to do: starting over. And starting over begins with a clean and orderly room.

I open my drawers and shove sweaters and T-shirts in one. Pants in another. Underwear on top. A place for everything. My eyes trail over the things I left behind when I was ten. Pictures of the family. All of us together. Before. Then after. Single pictures of us. Or forced ones of Livy, Ryan, and me. A small turtle box I'd gotten on one of my trips with Uncle Dave. He always took me and Livy to the aquarium or the zoo or the science and space museum when he visited. Said even though Ryan needed therapy, we all needed to be kids. I lift the lid and am hit with a whirlwind of memories.

I pull out a tiger shark's tooth, a small plaster fossil of a velociraptor's claw, and the silver necklace Uncle Dave helped me make. It has a dragon in the middle and stars surrounding him. I used to call him Maia Cetus. He was my own personal dragon of protection. I named him after one of the dinosaurs we saw, the maiasaura, the good mother dinosaur, and a constellation that Dad showed me once. Uncle Dave laughed when I told him the name. He said I was a really cool kid, but looking back, I was a dork. Still, as my fingers go over the medallion, I feel my dragon's presence, like he'd been waiting for me to come home too. How stupid is that?

I put on the necklace. The leather cord feels good around my neck. I take all the family pictures and throw them in the top drawer. In their place, I put up *my* pictures. A funny picture of Livy and me from the last time I saw her, six months ago, when Dad and I both came in for her school play. A panoramic of Chicago. Some of the buildings there are so big and striking that just standing next to them made me feel like a different person. A better one maybe. One whose heart wasn't always so jacked up and crushed that I needed a constant supply of calm-down pills or drinks—or both.

Finally, I put up a picture of my favorite beach in California. Malibu. I've never been there, of course, but Leah told me about it. She said the water was a permanent shade of aquamarine blue, so pretty it looked unreal. I remember we had just smoked some of my Blue Haze. She was lying on the bed with me, our eyes closed, her voice like a breeze. Leah said the water was ice-cold, and if you walked straight into it without a wet suit, it would take your breath away.

The visions of that beach stay with me as I hang my jacket and a few shirts in the closet. My foot bangs into a box that's been shoved toward the back. I bend down and trace my fingers over Mom's writing. She must have packed this box after she kicked me out of the house. *K'NEX. LEGOs. Transformers. John.* The words punch me in the gut. These weren't just my toys; they were Ryan's too, but after the accident, Ryan never wanted to play with them anymore. And then I realize why I am persona non grata in my house. I killed everything good. There's no coming back from that.

I sit on my bed, my head in my hands, and try not to cry like a baby. Honestly, sometimes, it's too damned much.

My phone beeps. Uncle Dave. The important thing is to keep moving forward. Keep your eyes ahead of you. Stay in the now.

It's eerie how that man gets me, how he knows just when to find me.

Beep. Nothing is ever as cut and dried as you think. Stay open to the possibility that you don't know everything.

I rub my eye with the heel of my hand. Text back. I don't think I know everything. I just think I know everything worth knowing. One of our inside jokes.

He sends me one of those stupid emojis. A dog holding flowers or some shit.

I text back. Wtf?

Trying to get my emoji on. The ladies love that.

To which I text, Save some for the rest of us. Another Uncle Dave joke.

I lie back on my bed and try to erase the image of that box in my closet. I picture that beach Leah loved. I pretend I'm walking out into the ocean, letting the shock of the water numb my body. I'd float for as long as I could take it and then bake in the sun on the beach. Maybe I'd stop feeling everything. The Ryan stuff. The Mom stuff. Even the Leah stuff. I'm exhausted from lacrosse practice, worn out from being back here with all my family's issues, and I close my eyes and fall into a dark cavern of sleep.

CHAPTER 4

I wake up five minutes before my alarm goes off, my mind still full of Leah from my dreams. I don't remember what they were about, but I'm happy until I remember it's not real. She's not here, and she never will be again. Boulders pile on top of my chest and then more on top of those. It hurts to breathe.

I thrust myself out of bed and drop to the floor. Do twenty-five push-ups. One hundred and fifty crunches. Twenty-five more push-ups. My form sucks, but I'll take it for now. On my way to the shower, I'm already planning my next workout when the sound of the coffee grinder jolts me. *Coffee.* How can something as simple as homemade coffee completely unhinge me? I grit my teeth and swallow the memory as the freezing cold shower punishes me for being weak and trusting that good feeling when I woke up.

I'm dressed in no time and down the stairs, where I find my lacrosse bag packed and ready for me.

Mom sits on a barstool at the counter but swivels to face me as I walk into the kitchen. "You want me to take you in today?" She sips her coffee.

Mom sitting, serenely drinking coffee, is such a surreal image that my mind has trouble making sense of the scene. Toast pops up in the toaster, and we almost bump into each other as I reach for the butter and jelly. She knocks me with her butt, like she's playing around with me, like she used to before Ryan's accident. I'm almost convinced I've walked through a wormhole or had a seizure in the shower or something.

"John?" She snaps her fingers in front of my eyes. "I asked if you wanted me to take you in today. I don't mind. Rosie'll be here soon, and I'll be back in time to see Livy off."

My heart is leaning toward her, hoping for some maternal sign, but now her face is concerned and annoyed. "John?"

"No. I'm good. Emily said she'd give me a ride."

She brings her coffee to her lips. Sips without making any noise. Her voice is throaty and small, as if she'd been up a lot last night. But she's got this sarcastic little smirk on her face. "You always were so damned self-sufficient."

Part of me wants to answer Mom back, all smart-aleck, but then she says, "Wait." I turn to find her with a to-go cup of coffee and a bagged lunch. "Your dad said you like it now."

She means the coffee, but my heart jams at the sight of the lunch. Dad used to hand me money in the morning. Every morning. An insane amount usually. It was how I financed the start of my little drug-dealing business. But he never, not one time in the seven years, made me lunch. And for, like, the hundredth time, I'm a mess of emotions.

"John? You OK?" Mom puts her hand on my forehead like I'm a little kid. "You're freezing." She rubs my arms like she used to when I was younger. I'm stunned silent. For a second,

I let myself want my mother's comfort as if it's OK for me to be weak around her. She moves the hair out of my eyes. "I've missed you." Her eyes well. "I know this isn't what you wanted or how you planned things, but I'm glad you're back."

Emily honks, breaking the spell. My eyes go to the door, and I get up to pitch the rest of my toast, but I feel the need to offer my own truce.

"Hey, Mom, I was just thinking about the coffee. You know, like mother, like son."

Her eyes hold me in place. She nods with the hint of a smile, making me feel like a good son for once. "Like mother, like son."

I'm almost out the door when I stop. "Hey. Did Ryan have a bad night? I didn't hear him."

"No, Sweetie. He slept. Have a good day at school."

Her answer confuses me, because she looks so ragged, but maybe she's paying for the cumulative effect of sleepless nights. And for all the stressing about me. Before. And after. And now. I push through the front door, convinced I can make life a little easier for her by doing well in school. Even though it sort of shocks the shit out of me that I want to.

———◦———

Emily waves as I get closer to the silver Camry. I open the door.

"Hey." She smiles at me, then beats the dashboard of her car. "Stupid fan doesn't work."

"Beating it helps?"

"No, but it's my only play. Thankfully, it's not cold yet. We are going to be icicles if I don't get it fixed before then." She puts the car in reverse, waves at the radio. "Pick your poison."

"This is fine." Even though she's got on some inane talk show where the disc jockeys are doing stupid bits and laughing at their own jokes, which I totally hate.

Emily turns out of our neighborhood just as one of the guys on the radio dares another to let him shoot him with a paint gun. As if that proves how tough they are. I grunt without meaning to.

Emily points to the radio. "They're idiots, I know. But they crack me up."

"That's good." I let the streets slip by, trying like mad not to associate this road with anything. Not with Pete and his brother. Not with Ryan's accident. Definitely not the memory of running from my house, my mother screaming, "John, what's *wrong* with you?"

It's been seven years since that happened. These memories need to leave me alone and shut the eff up or I'm going to need to find a new supplier. Stat. I stare at my cell. Pete's friend still hasn't texted me. I start to hum the melody from *Blackbird*, strumming the riff on the leg of my pants.

Emily's eyes shoot to my hands. "You nervous?"

The answer to that question is a definite yes. But not nervous about normal teenage crap. I'm nervous about messing up again. About being kicked out again. I'm not going to let that happen. I've got to keep my cool.

"It's hard to start over, right? I mean, senior year at a new school." She bites her lip like maybe she feels she's said something she shouldn't.

"I'm good," I say. "How hard could high school be?" I want to kick myself for sounding so effing needy.

"Wow. I'm impressed. Also, thanks to me, we're here super early, so you've got some time to get yourself ready." She shoots me this sympathetic look, as if she gets what I'm going through. Which makes me all edgy and raw.

I stare at the empty parking lot. It's seriously empty. Like *we showed up on the wrong date for a concert* empty. Then she gets a text that makes her chew on her nail.

My turn to be concerned, but I'm not sure it's cool for me to ask, so instead, I say, "Thanks for the ride."

She's still looking at her cell. I wait. A few cars pull into the teachers' parking lot, and the sound of car doors shutting seems to jolt her back to life. "Oh, sorry." She shows me her phone before stowing it in her purse. "My cousin. No big deal." Except her face isn't registering no big deal at all.

She opens her door, and I do the same. The ground feels as if it's moving under me, and I grab that stupid dragon medallion I put on last night. Like a weak little kid, I hold on tight to the talisman that helped me through the days after Ryan's accident.

"You know," I say as we start toward the building, "I could look at that fan for you. I'm pretty good with cars."

"Really?" Her voice goes up an octave in that sweet girl way. "That would be great."

"Sure. We'll do it this afternoon."

"We both have practice or have you forgotten already?"

My sore muscles and huge lacrosse bag should have reminded me. "This weekend?"

"That would be great. Thanks."

"I haven't done anything yet."

"No, but you will."

I smile and sell her on this whole lovable bad boy act; meanwhile, the chemically deprived part of my brain, the seriously fucking jonesing for a little pot or a little Jack part of my brain, is scheming. Because car supply stores? They're usually close to liquor stores and bars that don't look too close at your ID. I think about the fake ID the cops confiscated in Chicago and the one I have hidden in my drawer. I remember the smug look the hard-assed cop had as he told me that he was doing me a favor, disarming me like that. "It's a lot harder to act like an ass without the beer bravado," he'd said, getting a big chuckle out of it. Then the younger cop laughed too, and I felt like slamming my fist in his stupid smirk.

Emily smiles at me one more time as we make our way through the courtyard, and she plants me in front of the main office. Part of me feels like a fraud, but I haven't done anything bad yet. Thinking about doing bad things doesn't count. If it did, we'd all be in jail.

CHAPTER 5

English IV is exactly as exciting as I thought it would be. The class's got three of my teammates in it—Brandon, Parker, and Will—so that means I'm expected to sit near the back with the rest of the lacrosse players.

The teacher is this thin old guy, Mr. Francis. He walks back and forth, a copy of *Great Expectations* cracked opened in his hands as he speaks. I stare at the book as if it's the ghost of my girlfriend. Why did it have to be that book?

"We've got to get our new student caught up," he says. "Who can tell John about this fine literature we are studying?"

Something hits me in the back. Snickers sound behind me. I bend down and pick up the paper wad, shooting the guys who threw it the bird as I do. A girl in front of me laughs. I tell myself I'm totally in control. It's just a book. A stupid effing coincidence. I need to keep my shit together.

"Dominique," Mr. Francis says. "Please share what is so funny about Charles Dickens's classic?"

"Nothing, Mr. Francis." She tries to keep the laughter out of her voice, but it's unmistakable.

"Do you want to come up here and tell us about the novel?"

"Only if the new guy comes with me." She flashes me a smile

that should make my day, but I'm kind of immune to girls coming on to me. Back when I lived with Dad, they flirted with me for my drug connections. Here, it's all about landing the new guy, I'm sure. And in this class with *that* book, I'm definitely not going up there with her or anyone else.

Catcalls. My boys are clapping and whistling for me.

"Nah. I'm good." I hold up my hand, hoping she'll withdraw her proposition. Knowing she probably won't. My stomach tightens. I can't break to pieces in front of the entire class. I force myself to think of the sound of the coffee grinder that morning, right before the accident. The sound. The smell. And just like that, the dragon inside me roars and cauterizes my weakness till I no longer care about Mom or Leah or any girl who's stupid enough to try to get close to me.

Mr. Francis snaps his fingers. "John? We're waiting for you."

When did he walk back to my chair?

I stand up straight, forcing Mr. Francis to back up. I swagger to the front of the room, not because I'm that cool but mostly because I'm incredibly sore from working out. Dominique shines this smile on me as Mr. Francis follows me up the aisle and hands each of us a book. The minute the paperback is in my hands, the feeling of total and complete loss pours into me despite my tough guy defense. I run my hand through my hair and hope I just look nervous and maybe a little annoyed.

Will laughs his ass off, and Brandon calls, "Own it, Strickland."

Mr. Francis shoots them a warning look. "Dominique? You've got something to say?"

Dominique curls the ends of her long brown hair with her finger. "*Great Expectations* is about a guy who's in love with a girl who is way too good for him."

Laughter erupts, and even Mr. Francis cracks a smile. She faces the class, her hands palms up, accepting the crowd's cheers. Which everyone happily gives her. Everyone but me, because I'm super uncomfortable, to say the least.

He shakes his head. "OK, you both may sit. Who can add to Dominique's synopsis?" No hands go up. "How about you, Will?"

Will shifts in his seat. "The guy tries to make himself better for her."

Mr. Francis motions to continue. "Keep going. Sarah?"

"He goes away to become a proper gentleman." A light laughter ripples through the class. "And then comes back for his love."

They are wasting their time trying to catch me up. I've read *Great Expectations* three times. The first time with Leah. Then twice right after she died. (Killed herself.) I remember the feel of her head on my shoulder as I read it to her that first time, both of us lying in my bed. Totally chill. Me flipping the pages. Her warning me, "You can't read ahead. Promise me."

Her hair smelled like mangoes. I'd breathe it in when I read. Would stop to deliver the bests lines slowly, because when we got to the sad parts, she'd let out this soft little breath that made me want to wrap her up and keep her safe.

I bite the inside of my cheek and draw blood, using that

metallic taste to bring me back to the classroom where Mr. Francis is looking straight at me. "John? You with us?"

Laughs again. This class is like a bunch of hyenas.

I clear my throat. Try to think of a smart-ass response, but I've got nothing.

Will comes to my defense. "His head might be somewhere else." He shoots a glance in Dominique's direction, and she pretends to be offended by the attention she clearly craves.

"All right, all right. Let's settle down. Who wants to start reading? We are on chapter ten."

"He calls the knaves, Jacks, this boy! And what coarse hands he has! And what thick boots! I had never thought of being ashamed of my hands before."

The words rip through me. "I'd never hurt you like that," Leah said.

I didn't know if it was the pot we'd smoked or just my mood, but at that moment, my heart was wide open, and I didn't even care. "You're the only one who could."

She looked me straight in the eyes, so dark and secretive, I couldn't bear to look away. "I never will. I promise you, I'd leave you first," she said.

She meant it as some kind of solace, but that was the deepest hurt of all. She did, in the end, leave me. Alone.

———o———

The bell rings, and we all close our books. The halls are a blur of faces I used to know. Some are kids I went to school with but don't recognize—kids who live in the now while I constantly switch between the before and the after, never in one time or one emotion for long.

Parker catches up with me in the hall by my new locker. I'm throwing my books in without really paying attention to what the hell I'm doing when he slaps me on the back.

"What's up, home dog? You should totally hit that." He tilts his head toward Dominique, whose locker happens to be directly across from mine. She is next to it, posing, the way girls do when they think we don't realize they know we're watching.

I direct my attention back to my locker and the choices in front of me: which books I need for my next class.

Will leans in. "What's the matter? She not your type?"

"It's not that. Sex kills my game."

They practically bust a gut. Brandon clutches his hand to his heart. "What game?"

I shut the locker. Lean against it. Can't help but smile. "You're hilarious."

Will whacks me on the arm. "See you later, player."

Dominique and other girls like her are exactly what I don't need. What I need is a little weed or a bottle of Jack. What I need is that chemical checkout that will make me a much better human being to be around. I pull out my cell and text Pete again.

Still waiting.

He texts back. Sorry, man. Will look into it.

The bell rings, and I'm two hallways away from my next

class. Everyone around me frantically rushes to class before the seventh bell rings, making us late. That's the difference between them and me. They still believe there's an order to life, and I know for sure that's not true. Being on time means nothing. Being late means less than nothing—a lecture, a detention, a referral. None of those things scare me. It is all so freaking meaningless. I click my lock closed.

That's when I see Emily. She points to her watch as she passes me and raises an eyebrow in amusement. I sheepishly mouth, *I know.* She smiles and slips into her class. At least I have a distraction from Leah. I know the stupidest thing I can do is start caring for someone after Leah. I have to be careful not to hurt this girl. And that's when it hits me: I've known Emily exactly two days, and already, I think about her more than I should.

I make a mental note to stop that shit. For everyone's sake.

CHAPTER 6

I walk off the field, my legs heavy like they are filled with lead. With each step, my muscles hum. I forgot how good it feels to be in shape.

Matt whacks me on the back. "Hey, man, you're starting to look like an actual player."

"Um, thanks?"

Will is next to me in a flash. Brandon and Parker fall in line.

I see Emily jog into her locker room. She waves and flashes me a smile as she does.

"She's pretty cute," Brandon says. "We'd approve of that."

"Don't remember asking for your approval," I say.

"We do everything as a team," Parker says.

"Yeah. Sorry. There are some ways I am not a team player."

Laughs and smart cracks surround me, and I sit on the bench in front of my locker, enjoying the workout euphoria before I hit the showers.

Matt shows up, towel around his waist. "Hurry up, and I'll give you a ride home."

"Thanks, but I have a ride."

"Hey, man, my brother told me to bring you by."

I haven't looked at my phone yet, so maybe Pete's connection came through. "Yeah, sure," I say.

Matt retreats around a bank of lockers, then circles back. "I'll give you a ride, but I've got to say, anything that takes away from your game on the field is not cool."

"Nothing takes away from my game. Anywhere."

He rolls his eyes. "Still such a hotshot. Be ready in ten, or I leave without you."

I grab my cell and text Mom. Going out with the guys. Team building. It's Friday night, so she won't object. Plus, she'll think me spending time with the team is a good thing. Me making friends, forming relationships. She'd be part right, except I'm talking about drug connections. It's semantics.

Next, I text Emily. Going out with the guys. Text me tomorrow when you want to get that part for your car.

Finally, I send one to Livy. Gotta take care of something. Going to be late.

Three texts. I've made more social connections here in two days than I had at Dad's in seven years. Associations are not good. Not if I want to leave, which I do. If Pete's friend comes through, my chemical shields will be up finally.

Once we're in his car, Matt points to a cooler. "Help yourself."

I open it, hoping for beer, but settle for two Gatorades he's got stored in the melted ice. And that makes me wonder, did his mom pack this for him? "Mom still making sure you're hydrated? So adorable."

"Ass."

I smirk, but still, I wish I could switch parents, switch situations, switch off my feelings. We stop at a light. Matt opens his Gatorade, drinks half of it, then burps incredibly loudly.

"Nice manners," I say.

He laughs. "So how's it been?"

I take another drink. "I assume you're not talking about the weather."

"How's Ryan?"

"Haven't spent that much time with him actually. He's sleeping by the time I get home, and I'm gone before he wakes up. But he's got quite the mouth on him, from what I've heard." I shake my head. Why does the fact that he curses make me a little proud of him? "Gotta be teenage angst, I guess."

Matt stops at a red light, waiting to turn into Pete's apartment complex. He drums on the wheel, then takes a sip of Gatorade. "I've heard he's given some of the teachers at that school he goes to a run for their money."

"He and I have always made the ladies crazy," I say.

"Not how I remember it but whatever."

The light turns green. We go but not before my mind slips into the past. Matt and I were inseparable before the accident. Another before. But after? Mom insisted I stay away from him.

But she was never there to enforce it. She was always with Ryan. He had therapy, an inclusion group. Always something. So I decided I'd hang with my neighborhood boys. And I got away with it until one Saturday, Matt and I were playing soccer with the guys on his street. I was goalie. A ball hit me smack in the face. I knew better than to cry. Not in front of the guys. It must have been pretty bad, because Matt went and got his mom.

"We gotta get you some ice," she said. She put a bunch of cubes in a bag and put it on my face. She grabbed her keys. "I'm gonna drive him home."

Even though it hurt like hell, even though there was a ton of blood, I knew Matt's mother coming over would be the worst idea ever. My hands flew up. "No. I'm fine."

She looked me in the eye.

"Really. I'm fine."

I could tell she knew why I didn't want her to come with me, but she shook her head. "Walk him home, Matt. Tell his father I think it's broken."

Tell his father. *No way did anyone think I should tell my mother, because everyone knew how she'd been about Matt and Pete after the accident.*

When Dad saw the blood, he got down on his knees and put his hands on both sides of my face. "Wow. You did a great job there, kiddo." He picked me up and sat me on the kitchen counter. Some of the blood dripped on the floor, and I was worried about that, but he said, "I'll get that later. You wait here." I heard the freezer door open. Close. The drawer open. Close. The new ice on my face and my father's concern made me believe everything would be OK. "Thanks for walking him home, Matt, but you should go. Before..."

Just like that, the garage door opened. It was old and loud and unmistakable how it lifted, stuttering over the rails as it went.

Matt's face went white. So did Dad's. I heard Ryan's wheelchair come into the hallway from the garage. Within seconds, they'd be in the kitchen.

Matt's eyes went to the back door, but he didn't move fast enough.

Mom stood in the kitchen. "What the hell is going on here?"

Dad's hand cupped the back of my head. "John was playing soccer and got hit pretty hard. Matt brought him home."

Mom's face went tight. I could see her trying to conceal her anger. Each word was a knife that I knew would soon be aimed at me. "Thank you, Matt. Maybe you should go home."

"His mother thinks his nose's broken. We've got to…" Dad tried.

Mom's hands flew up. "Well, if his mother thinks…"

Dad stepped in front of her. "That's enough, Lydia."

Mom threw her keys on the counter. "Hasn't his family done enough?"

I mouthed, Go, to Matt, and he took off running.

The yelling made my head throb, and I was already woozy.

"He's hurt, Lydia," Dad said.

Mom threw a glass. "He's always getting hurt. Always, always, always…" And another. And the sounds of the glass smashing reminded me of that day, the day Ryan was hit. It started just like this. With Mom smashing a glass. I wanted to yell at her to stop. I wanted Dad to tell her she should never do that again. With each crash, it seemed as if the world was going to open up and swallow me whole. "Why can't you follow simple rules, John? Simple." Smash. "Fucking." Smash. "Rules. You can't stay away from one person? For our family's sake?"

Her hair had fallen out of its clip, and she kicked the clip across the room. "No more Pete. No more Matt. No more." She was crying now. Banging her fists on the counter across from where I was sitting. I felt every blow as if she'd been hitting me.

Dad lifted me from the counter, and Livy came into the room crying. He scooped her up and set his hand on my shoulder, guiding us out to the garage.

Dad put Livy and I in the car and drove us around and around. I kept thinking he'd take me to the doctor or a hospital or something, like Pete's mom said, but he never did. He just bought us McDonald's burgers and fries and a shake. I couldn't eat, but no one noticed. When we came home, it was dark, and the house was too. Mom was sitting in the living room with some show on TV lighting her face. She looked up as we came in, her eyes red from crying, and she was hiccupping a little as if she'd just stopped. "Hope it was all worth it," was all she said.

I was never sure if she was talking to me. Or about me. The crazy thing is it wasn't Pete's fault that day, the day of that first accident. Our neighbor, the really grouchy one who used to live in Emily's house, said she saw Ryan skateboard into the street that day. She told the cops and anyone else who would listen that no one could have avoided Ryan. Not even the most experienced driver. But that didn't stop Mom from blaming Pete. Not that day. Not the next. Not even now. I couldn't take how mad she was all the time. How unforgiving.

"Dude, you with me?" Matt says as he puts the car in park. Here we are in front of the dank little apartment where I've visited Pete a bunch of times over the years.

"Yeah. Sorry. Zoned out."

"This shit never gets easier, does it?" Matt stares out the window. He's got no idea. First Ryan. Then Leah.

Matt smacks me in the chest. "Rehashing old history doesn't help. You got that? You do not get to brood with Pete."

I nod.

Matt swigs the rest of his Gatorade and points the bottle in the direction of Pete's doorway. "He's got to get a grip."

"Agreed." I put my empty bottle in the cup holder. "But it's hard. You know?"

Matt shakes his head. "You know what's hard? Growing up without a big brother because he's become a total lump."

I get out of the car before Matt can wrap his head around how awful what he said was. He's not the only one with a lump for a brother. Ryan may not have always been as nice as Pete, but he was still pretty cool.

Ryan loved to build with LEGOs. He never let me *play* with them. Ryan said playing was for little kids. We were going to be architects. I couldn't even say the word, I was such a little twerp, but I knew it was important.

Matt pushes ahead of me. Knocks loud and obnoxiously until Pete answers the door, dressed in sweats and a T-shirt that reads *Witness the Fitness*. We bump fists, and he pulls me in for one of those one-armed man hugs.

I laugh and point to his shirt. "Preach it, brother."

His laugh is small and almost grateful sounding. He rubs the back of his head as if he just woke up. Given the sleep in his eyes, that may be the case. "You know it."

Matt hands Pete what looks like crumpled money from his pocket. "Mom said to come home Sunday." Then he pushes into the apartment and beelines for the kitchen table.

Pete clears his throat like he's embarrassed, either because his mother sent money or because Matt's being an ass. He calls after him, "I got a pizza. Guess you found that already."

There are empty beer cans all over the kitchen table, but Matt picks up one that, by the sound of it, is half full and chugs it.

"Little brothers are such pains in the ass," Pete says. Then, "Sorry my guy hasn't called you back. He's just really careful."

"It's cool." My mouth waters at the smell of beer.

Pete reads my mood. "You thirsty? Please excuse Matt's complete lack of manners." Pete opens his refrigerator, pulls two cans, pops the tops on both, then hands one to me. He slurps the top of his beer, and I do the same.

Matt switches on the TV and cascades through the channels, which currently consist of two or three and a whole lot of static. "Dude, what happened to your TV? You don't even get ESPN?"

Pete ignores Matt, but I want to kick him. There's no need to be a jerk.

Pete takes another swig, then turns to me. "I've heard some things. Wondered if they were true."

I drink. "What things?"

"That your mom is looking to send Ryan to a group home."

I choke on my beer. "News to me." Wiping my mouth with the back of my hand, I try to recover. "Where'd you hear that?"

"My mom."

The source makes sense. Pete's mom is a nurse, so she's hooked up to a lot of those agencies that Mom would have had to go through if she really was looking for a group home or one of those assisted living places Dad used to try to talk to Mom about. Those conversations led to Dad being shown the door. But now? Is it even possible?

Pete shrugs. "Might be good for him, you know?"

I take another drink, let the foamy beer slide down my throat. The whole time, I'm telling myself not to play this horrible wishing game anymore. I try not to wish that Ryan would get to grow up and go off on his own. I try not to wish that Mom's changed her mind about keeping him at home. I try not to wish for things I can't have, but I'm already envisioning what I'd trade, working my way up Maslow's hierarchy of needs, like how I'd love to trade this beer for a bottle of Jack Daniel's. This pizza for some weed. My family after for my family before.

Pete stands up. "Be right back."

I sit there drinking beer and eating pizza while my mind is circling. Could the news about Ryan be true? Why do I care if it is? I'm out of here in a few months anyway.

"Maybe Ryan's doing better?" Matt comes over to the table. "I mean, maybe he wants to be with kids like him," he says, and it's the first indication Matt's an actual human being, not just an asshole.

"Maybe." I drink some more. "Can't picture my mom sending him anywhere though. I mean, her whole world centers around Ryan. What he eats. When. How." I take a swig of beer. Look directly at Matt. "You've got no idea."

"Sometimes, people surprise you." Matt's eyes cast toward the bedroom where Pete is still scavenging for pot for me. Matt's lost out almost as much as I have. Pete was a cool big brother, but after everything that happened, neither one of us has our brother in our lives the way we should.

Pete reemerges from the back room. "I'll call my guy again. This is all I have. It's yours." He hands me a baggie filled with a few small buds. I recognize this particular strand of pot. Purple Dreams. Excellent stuff.

Pete goes back into the little kitchen and opens a ratty cabinet, and the door practically falls off as he does. He takes out a fifth of Jack Daniel's. "Take this too. You might need a little extra help being back here."

Like I said, Pete's always been cool. "Why wait?" I twist the cap. The sound of the seal breaking making my heart race and mind and muscles relax. "Let's drink. To old friends." I take a swig, the amber liquid so smooth as it slides down my throat. I pass the bottle to Pete.

"To friends who don't forget you." He drinks and hands the bottle to Matt, who shrugs it off.

"I'm in training, dude. And so are you, man. Go easy on that shit. You're barely good enough to ride the bench as is."

"Jet fuel." I take another drink. "Besides, I took, like, two minutes off my times already. I'm pretty sure Coach was impressed."

Matt takes a small sip. "You're going to have to do a hell of a lot more than that to impress Coach Gibson."

"No doubt. But it's Friday night. I don't have to impress anyone tomorrow, do I?"

Someone bangs on the door. A bunch of someones by the sound of it. Matt opens it, and the juniors and seniors on the lacrosse team spill into the room.

"What's up?" Brandon smacks hands with Pete. "How've you been, Coach?"

"Not your coach anymore," Pete answers.

"You should be." Will's arm goes around Pete's shoulders. The two of them walk to the table. Will plunks a six-pack of Miller Lite on the table. "You were always the best."

"You like that I let you drink here." Pete points to the fridge. "Let's keep some of this cold, huh?"

Brandon adds the six-pack he's carrying to the fridge, and soon, everyone's drinking.

A dartboard on the side of the room gets tons of play. Matt aims carefully, hits bull's-eye, and his arms go up in the air.

Pete shakes his head. "My modest little brother."

Pete sticks his hand out, and I happily put the bottle of Jack in it. The whiskey is doing its job. My head is fuzzy and loose, and not one thing is wrong in this world. I look around the room and see a bunch of guys who I get to hang with. Not because I'm their supplier but just because we're teammates. I forgot how good that could feel. That everything is exactly as it's supposed to be.

Brandon and Will and Parker shove each other out of the way

for the chance to take Matt on in the next game. Someone blasts Spotify, and Avenged Sevenfold fills the room.

Pete leans on the table, his head lowered and his hands on the top of the bottle. "Momentary loss of muscular coordination…" He quotes *The Shining*. We both crack up, but I know underneath the laughter is how he actually feels, and I wonder for probably the hundredth time since the accident how it felt from Pete's perspective when he hit Ryan. The fear. The crushing realization of what he'd done.

"I keep thinking…" I know I'm slurring my words, and when I look at the bottle, I'm surprised it's more than half gone. Between the two of us. "If only…you know, but I guess what's done can't be undone. It is what it is. " I'm a metaphysical genius. Obviously.

Matt's head jerks in our direction. He bounds across the room and slams his hand down on the table in front of us. He points at me, a dart still in his hand. "We are not doing this."

Brandon puts his big mitts on Matt's shoulders. "What's the matter with you?"

"Sick of this shit," Matt says.

Brandon turns Matt toward the dartboard. "You're up, man."

"Yeah. I got that." Matt moves back to the other side of the room, straightens, focuses, and throws another bull's-eye, making the guys yell.

Pete doesn't look affected by the alcohol, which says something for the tolerance he's built. His gaze goes to Matt and then back to the bottle.

51

"I've replayed that moment a million times," Pete says. "I wish…"

"Stop. You can't."

Pete takes another drink. "I hope Ryan *is* doing better. I really do. Nothing would make me happier."

"*You* need to be getting better too, man. You need to figure out what you want to do now."

Pete's about to answer when there's another knock on the door. Only it's quieter and is followed by girl voices. "Open up. Let us in!"

"Finally, some life to this party," Matt says.

Pete says, "I never said you could have a party here…"

"You never said I couldn't." Matt opens the door, and five girls pile in, each one bouncier than the previous.

I search for Emily, but I know she won't be here. She's not like these girls. She wouldn't show up to some asshole's apartment, knowing everyone'd be drunk. But I am not surprised to see Dominique, who smiles at me across the room. She glides over like she's working the runway, acts like someone bumped into her, and falls into my lap. Convenient.

It's not that I don't want what she's offering. It's just that, these days, the happy ending in question is nothing I can't give myself. Grinning at my inside joke, I bounce Dominique off my lap, salute my boys, and bump fists with Pete. "Gotta go."

Dominique's face rearranges itself from surprise to fury. That convinces me I'm doing the right thing.

Matt's on the old recliner with Jessica. "Well, don't think I'm driving you home now. I'm a little busy."

Jessica laughs.

"No worries. I'll walk. Gotta work on my times anyway. I'll get my stuff from you tomorrow," I call over the chatter and head out into the night. It's just me and the stars, and at least, for once, I'm not hanging around to make another stupid mistake. I'm kinda proud of myself until I take out my phone to see that home is exactly five point two miles away. I shrug, then start to jog. I'm pissing people off left and right these days, which just proves I'm too enmeshed here. Time to leave all this behind and start California living for real.

As my feet pound on the dark streets, each step reminds me of who I am, what I've done, and why I need to escape the memories.

CHAPTER 7

It's one of those mornings after that I used to have a lot at Dad's house, so at first, I'm thinking I'm back there, but then a banging pushes through the fuzz, and I realize that Mom's voice is coupled with the pounding. And that can't be good. My hands press hard into my eye sockets, trying to push some sense into my foggy brain.

"John! Wake up!"

My mind searches for what I did last night. Pete's house. Right. That means it's Saturday. Mom has never made me get up early on a Saturday for no reason.

Bang! Bang! Bang! "John. We have to leave in half an hour."

I blink as I reach for my cell. Have I slept till four in the afternoon or some shit? Leave for where? My cell says it's eight thirty, so now I'm really confused. My head is not in any shape to try to figure out this real-world word problem.

"What's up?" I croak as Mom heads down the steps.

"You have an appointment this morning."

"Since when?"

She stops on the staircase and turns. "Since yesterday. And don't give me that look. I left you a note."

My head spins—and not from my hangover. I know better

than to ask the questions running through my mind. With Mom, the who-what-where-and-whens are always a trap, and I don't want to get caught.

"You have twenty-five minutes now. I'd hurry if I were you."

I don't waste any more time and jump in the shower, letting the cold water blast my face.

I turn it as hot as it can go. The combination of extremes gets my blood going. I'm out of the shower and back in my room in under ten minutes. That's when I see the note Mom left me last night.

> Made appointment with Steve for tomorrow
> at nine thirty. Sorry so early. He'll give you a
> later time from now on. I'll take you.

Great. It's not that I mind seeing Stevie-boy. It's a court order anyway.

But this early after a night of Jack Daniel's? Not my favorite plan. Also, why the rush? Steve's office is five minutes away even with Mom driving.

I throw on gym shorts and a new lacrosse T-shirt that somehow found its way into my drawer, my anger starting to stir. What gives Mom the right to go through my crap, even if it *is* to give me new clothes? I grab my stash from last night that is wedged under my pillow and a roll of duct tape from my desk. I lay on the floor, tape the bag to the underside of the desk drawer, and grab my cell.

I'm not even downstairs before I hear him. "Momomomom." Ryan's up.

I paste a smile on my face and enter the kitchen.

Livy waves at me from her seat, waffle bits still on her plate. "Morning," she says, her mouth full. My stomach growls. Loud.

"You've got five minutes." Mom takes a washcloth to Ryan's face, his wheelchair pushed up to the table. He closes his eyes and pushes one arm forward, the other arm swinging wildly. Mom ducks, then turns to Livy. "You staying here or coming with?"

"I'll stay."

I look at Ryan. Really look at him. I haven't seen him much since I got home. But here he is in the flesh. His hair is longer, and it actually looks cute like this, you know, if he was someone else's brother. My big brother Ryan, Old Ryan, went through a long hair phase too. He thought he was the shit, right before the accident. Pissed me off how he used to ruffle my hair and say, "Don't worry, some day you'll grow into it." Such a smart-ass. I smile, thinking about it now, but back then, it drove me crazy.

I look at this New Ryan. This New Ryan is not cocky or arrogant. He's not scheming about ways to disappear so I couldn't hang with him and his friends. This New Ryan probably has no idea who I am.

He swings his head toward me. "Jaaaahhhh."

OK, maybe I'm wrong about that. Maybe he does know me. My heart does a little jump, like it's trying to get in tune with my brother. I wave. "Hey, Ryan."

He smiles.

Ryan's upper body is normal sized, but his legs are skinny, and his head is a little oversized still. If I pushed back his hair, we'd see scars from the operations he'd had to release the pressure in his skull.

Ryan used to be a super jock. My big brother, kind of super at everything. Mom's perfect child. Everything she dreamed of in a son. Until I wrecked it for everyone. *Can't you follow simple rules? Simple fucking rules?*

Ryan's head lolls on his neck, and his eyes go to the ceiling like he's looking for a sniper or something. But then he looks back at me, smiles, and bangs on the table with one hand. He's got braces on his legs that keep his legs from locking, but he spends most of his time in his wheelchair.

I smile back and bang on the table, which he finds hysterical based on his goofy, smiley reaction. Which makes Mom laugh, which makes me feel like maybe I'm winning this round a little.

Rosie pops her head around the corner, offering me a plate of waffles and a cup of coffee, and all of a sudden, today feels like my birthday.

I reach for the plate, my stomach groaning.

"Hurry," she says, nodding at Mom, who's wheeling Ryan to the car.

"Three minutes, John." Mom's in full take-charge mode. Along with Mom's other triggers, she cannot stand being late.

I cram two huge bites of waffle in my mouth and swear I hear myself moan. I'm so not used to home-cooked food.

"John! Now!" Mom calls from the garage.

I kiss Rosie on the cheek. She pretends to be flustered. "Go."

I shovel the rest of the waffle in my mouth, swipe my face with my napkin, and head for the van. When I get there, Mom's already got Ryan's wheelchair in the back and him in his seat, where she is trying to fasten the clips that hold him in place.

Mom looks up from Ryan's seat, her face set at pissed. "Can you help?"

"You get in. I'll take care of Ryan."

Ryan turns at the sound of his name and smiles at me. It's kind of sweet, and it chokes me up a little. "Hey, buddy. What's up?"

"Stupid seat! Shit!" He yells. "Shit! Shit! Shit!" He slams his seat with stiff hands.

"Nice mouth." I reach forward for the buckle. "Settle down."

That must piss him off, because he starts swiping at me. I duck, but judging from how mad he is, if his punch connected with me, it would hurt. I put my finger in his face. "Don't." I buckle his seat belt and slide his door shut. I open the passenger door and jump in. I don't say anything, because at this point, my head pounding, my brother going nuclear, and my mom not dealing, I am over it.

"He hates his car seat. Doesn't mind the car, just the seat."

"No seat," Ryan chants. "No seat. No seat. No seat."

Mom flips the mirror so she can see him. "Settle down, Ryan. You're fine."

She flips the mirror back and pulls out of the driveway.

"So I'll drop you off and…"

"Momomomomom!"

The sound is unreal. So loud. Mom's face gets tight. I know that look. I hate that look.

Usually, I'm the one firing her up to blow. I want to do anything to keep that from happening. "So Ryan's therapy is…"

"Momomomom." Ryan screams some more. Then bangs his head against the side of the car, which Mom padded so he won't get hurt.

Mom rotates in her seat fast. "Stop that! Don't you dare do that!"

That just makes him bang his head more.

She tightens her grip on the steering wheel, shakes her head. My stomach goes from hangover sick to sickened. I unhook my seat belt.

"What are you doing?"

I climb into the captain's chair next to Ryan. "Just keeping my brother company. Hey, buddy, what's up? You've got to stop that. We *all* have to sit in our seats. All of us."

For whatever reason, my climbing back there stops his tantrum. I can see that he's made a red mark on the side of his head from hitting it despite the padding that Mom's attached to his seat. I can't reach that spot, but I rub his head anyway, and he looks at me. His eyes do this thing where his pupils get pin tight then really big and black. And I wonder for, like, the hundred millionth time if only things had been different that day. If he had. If I had. If only… He looks out the window, and one of his legs bounces up and down a little.

"Get your seat belt on, John," Mom says, her voice a little choked up.

Ryan turns toward me and reaches out. I take his hand. "She drive you crazy too?"

"Mom crazy." Ryan twirls his finger next to his ear like we used to do when we were little. Back then, we both called Mom loco, and I feel like I'm losing it. I can almost see Old Ryan calling Mom crazy behind her back, me laughing. Does he remember that?

We drive like this for a few minutes, Ryan holding my hand, me not hating that, and also wondering a lot about my brother, both Old and New Ryan. Mom peeks in the rearview a bunch of times until she stops the car in front of Steve's office. "You want me to walk you in?"

I laugh. "I'm not five."

"I could leave Ryan in the car for a few minutes…"

Even if I wanted that, no way would I let her based on what I just witnessed. My brother is out of control. Mom's on the edge. I can do this without them. I unbuckle my seat belt. "I'm fine."

"When you're done, text me. Ryan's therapy is just down the street in the Richmond building. You remember where that is?"

"I'll be fine."

"He'll be done right after you, so you could even wait here if you didn't want to walk."

"I'll walk. Don't worry." I look Ryan straight in the eye. "Don't you do that anymore." I point to where he hit his head.

I know my plea is no different than anything Mom's said to him a hundred times, but I do it anyway, because I don't know what else to do. I've become the big brother now, telling him what to do. He needs to listen.

Mom closes the van door, and Ryan starts up again. It's a wonder she can drive when he's like that. And once again, the beast shows up. *He's always been like this. He always wins.*

I try to close my mind to the dragon I know is just trying to protect me, but it's not going to change anything, being all mad. So I wave to Mom and brace myself for what comes next.

———o———

The office building is the same as it's always been. The memory of my first time here rushes to greet me as I walk down the hallway.

I go into the elevator, hold the door for a mom who is trying to hurry her son.

"Thanks." She smiles at me. He's on a video game and looks younger than Livy. "You want to push the button?" she asks.

He rolls his eyes. "I'm not five anymore."

I laugh. He's kind of a little asshole like I was. I appreciate that.

"Three, please," she says.

I push the button, and my mind goes back.

I remember walking into the building holding Uncle Dave's hand.

"We're going to go see someone," Uncle Dave explained. "His name is Steve."

I ran ahead. I wanted to push the button for the elevator.

In the office, there were huge tanks filled with the coolest fish I'd ever seen. I was trying to count how many there were when a door opened. A man in jeans and a T-shirt walked out.

"Think you can guess my favorite?" he asked from across the room.

"Um, this one." I pointed to a red fish with black spots on its tail.

He nodded. "She's a beauty. But not her."

I pointed to another one. He shook his head. I gave up after pointing to every fish in the tank. I didn't get it.

He smiled. "I sort of tricked you. My favorite is in my office. It's not a fish at all. It's called a Chinese water dragon, and it lives in its own tank. Wanna see him? He's amazing."

A dragon? He had to be kidding. *I ran into the office. A tank ran the entire length of the wall with branches and plants and a little pond. And inside it was the coolest lizard I'd ever seen.*

I open the door to Suite 213. The receptionist is new, but everything else is the same. I give her my name, and she tells me to take a seat, that Steve will just be a few minutes.

Instead of sitting, I make my way to the fish tank. It's filled with new fish, pretty gold ones, striped Nemo ones. A royal-blue one.

"That's Dory." Steve's voice startles me to the present. "She's my new favorite."

I turn to face him. "No more Chinese water dragon?"

"Lost him last year. If your mom had given me the heads-up, I'd have had a replacement here in time for your return."

"You think I'd fall for that shit?"

"I hoped you would."

I rub my hand over my razor stubble. "Don't you think I'm too old for that bullshit?"

He looks at his hands. "Maybe. But maybe the older we get, the more we need to believe in magic and dragons."

I smile. Steve. Always the same.

He puts his hand out, and we shake, then do the man hug thing. It's kind of comforting that Steve's the same mostly. A few more pounds in the gut, a little older looking, but still so easy and calm and lots of laugh marks around his eyes.

He gestures to his office. "Shall we go get our talk on?"

"You betcha."

Steve's laugh is easygoing, and when I get in the office, see the tank where the new Chinese water dragon is waiting, I say, "I thought you said…"

"I'd never let you down, John. This office wasn't the same without him anyway."

I lean against the glass that separates the lizard from the office. "Poor guy is trapped. Don't you feel sorry for him?"

"You never described the last one like that. Why the change?"

"I'm a different asshole now?"

"You've grown up. You had your freedom when you lived with your uncle. Now you're trapped with your mother, where you never wanted to be."

That was way too easy for Steve. And also very true. But that doesn't mean I want to get into it. I knew I had to see Steve, and the truth is, I didn't really mind, but I also didn't really think about what that would mean entirely.

"This guy's deeper green. You got any opinions on why I'd say that?" I flop onto the love seat, gray and soft, the pillows like a cloud cushioning my fall.

Steve's sitting in a brown leather chair directly across from me. He's got a table next to him and a bottle of smartwater on it.

"Smartwater? Really?"

He shrugs. "What can I say? I'm getting older and require more upkeep." He points to the mini fridge at the end of the room. "Need anything?"

"Some Jack would be perfect."

"Coke, Sprite, or bottled water."

"You gotta work on your menu. Sad really."

Steve weaves his fingers together. "So when do you want to get started on the real stuff?"

"Man, Steve, no foreplay? Wow."

Steve's voice is deep and warm and easy and makes me relax, even though I'd never tell him that. "How've you been since you moved away?"

I sit straight up, point to the massive file Steve has strewn across his lap. My file. "You mean sent away. Kicked out. Told to leave, or have you forgotten?"

Steve nods and runs his fingers through his goatee, tries to look all wise. "Yes. I remember."

"And if you don't, you could always look it up, right?" This is just how Steve and I are. We give each other shit. It's why I like him.

"Right. So you're saying you still have feelings of abandonment since your mother asked you to leave? Is that how you'd like me to write it?" He cocks his head like a son of a bitch and holds the pen in the air as if waiting for my order.

"And I have trust issues. Write that next." I get up and get a Coke out of the fridge. "I still think I'd open up easier if you plied me with Jack Daniel's."

"I'll take what I can get with the ten tablespoons of sugar you're downing."

"Man, you *have* gotten old. So what do you want to know?"

"How are things?"

"I'm back here, so how good could they be?"

He nods some more. "You want to talk about why you're here?"

"Come on, you've got the whole court-ordered bullshit."

Steve flips through the pages of the report. "You were a little busy in Chicago, huh?"

I want to rip those pages. The ones that mandated weekly sessions with Steve for anger management, probably random drug tests, a probations officer.

"Stupid kid stuff." I switch to a lower baritone, trying on my best grown-up voice. "But I'm pretty disappointed in myself anyway. Hey, why don't we take away my video games and kick me out of paradise? That sound about equal to some arrogant asshole's mailbox?"

"The mayor's mailbox, you mean?"

I smirk. "Yeah. What if I told you he started it?"

Steve leans back. Lets his leg drape over his other one,

knocking his foot up and down, up and down. "What if I said you sabotaged yourself?"

I laugh. "Now you've really flipped a lid or something. Why the hell would I do that?"

"You tell me."

Anger races through me. He's right—I killed my only chance of being with Uncle Dave. Dad's brother. The only one in the family who is like me in the least bit. I feel my beast stir. It focuses on Steve's bouncing foot. Watches it go up and down, up and down. Up and fucking down like Leah doing those bouncing little jumps. Over and over. Laughing. Her hair in its bun, but all I wanted to do was take it down and watch it fly.

"John?"

More bouncing. Until I can't take it anymore. "Stop it!" I stand. My hands go to my head. I'm acting crazy. I can't act crazy. Steve's cool and all, but there are limits. Even for him. I sit. "I'm sorry. I just…" My head goes into my hands again, but through my fingers, I can see Steve's adjusted his posture so that both feet are flat on the floor, which lets me breathe out. "I'm sorry. Yeah. I screwed up. It was stupid. I was stupid. I'm always stupid."

Why can't you follow the fucking rules, John? Simple. Fucking. Rules.

Steve waits for me to calm down, then asks, "How's your mom?"

"She should be in here. She's ready to snap. For reals." I take a slurp of Coke.

"Tell me about that."

I sink back into the couch. The feeling of sitting here when I was ten, nine, eight years old comes back to me. All those times. Trying not to let Steve get too close to opening the vault. My dragon of protection guarding it like mad. Now it seems stupid. After Leah, there are worse things than admitting how I really feel. "She's on edge all the time. Ryan's not sleeping. He's aggressive. She keeps trying to act like it doesn't bother her. Still doing the family dinner thing. Salad plates, for fuck's sake."

"Meaning?"

"Meaning, who cares about salad when your life is going down the toilet?"

"Some might say your mom is being courageously optimistic?"

"Yeah. I get that. But it's never that easy with Lydia Strickland, is it? Because the thing is she's lying to all of us. Deep down, she doesn't even believe this shit either."

"What makes you say that?"

I take a drink and let the syrupy taste roll around in my mouth. I pretend there's Jack mixed in. I think about smoking that weed Pete gave me. I try to calm the dragon, who has fully woken up and is pacing inside me. "She's fucking looking for a place to put him. After all this time, after all her bullshit. After everything, she's going to send *him* away. None of it mattered. It was always going to end like this. God, she's so stupid. I'm so stupid."

Steve puts the tips of his fingers together, making a *v* with them. He brings them to his face, leaves them in that space between his mouth and chin. This is my signal to keep talking, but all I want to do is shut up. The anger is churning through me now; all the stuff I've been shoving down is boiling out of control, climbing, climbing from my gut up my throat. If I don't let it out, I'll die.

"John? You with me?"

I stand. "I just can't take how angry I am around her."

"Go on."

I'm pacing. "Being in the same room with her makes me feel like I'm on fire. I'm faking it. Big-time. Of course I am. I have to. But I can't help how much I hate her sometimes."

"Why do you hate her?"

I shoot him a look that he's gone too far. So he clears his throat, motions for me to sit, and says, "Instead of faking it, maybe we could work on some strategies to calm the beast."

I sit. "I'm listening."

Steve lowers the file on his lap. My file. He takes off his glasses. Rubs his eyes. "You know the solution to all the anger?"

I hold up my hand to stop him. "No."

"If we could get to the bottom of—"

"Off-limits."

"It would help. I could maybe hypnotize you so remembering that day is easier."

The dragon roars. The fire licks my face like the coffee did that day. I get dizzy. I stand. Have to move. Have to. "No. No. No. I don't ever want to talk about that day again."

"OK. So let's talk about ways to stay calm when you face the dragon."

I should bristle that he's used that term, but it's like he uses it to show me he remembers. And that calms me down a little.

Steve's got me. He's going to keep pushing me and pushing me about that day, the day Old Ryan died, and I'm going to keep saying no. It's what we do. That will never change. There's no freaking point to any of this therapy bullshit, but it's the way things are and always will be.

The dragon stands down as we listen to Steve tell us how to deal. My hands are still shaking a little, but the heat leaves me, and a coldness replaces it. Like how I imagine swimming in the cold Pacific Ocean would feel. The dragon slinks back into his cave, his cold-blooded body the same temperature as a block of ice—and ice is way better than fire.

———— o ————

When I finally make it out of my appointment and pull out my cell, Emily has texted.

Ready when you are.

I have to adjust my brain so I can focus on her message, because at first, it makes no sense. Then I realize she's talking about coming to get me so I can work on her car. I text back.

I'm at the Riverbridge building. Pick me up and we can go from here.

On my way.

I breathe out, and my fingers wish for a joint to magically appear. I sit on the brick wall and text Mom.

Emily is picking me up.

Mom calls right away. "Hey." I hear Ryan screaming in the background. Screaming his head off. "Hey. It's fine if you go

69

with Emily, but can you two swing by here? Ryan, it's OK. Settle down." Thud. The call drops.

Suddenly, my beast is standing up, roaring. I call Mom back. "Are you OK?"

"Yeah." Pant. "Oh, someone from the therapy place is helping." To somebody else. "Thank you."

"Mom?" In the two seconds it takes her to answer me, my head is exploding. "Mom? Are you OK? Can you please answer me?"

She's breathless. "John?" As if she's forgotten we were actually talking. As if I'm not even a blip on her radar, while I am hanging on her every fucked-up syllable. "John?" A small laugh. "Yeah. I'm OK. Sorry. Go with Emily."

Ryan says "Go, go, go."

"We'll see you later. We're fine. I'm fine. Sorry."

"Are you sure?"

"Yeah. We're fine. We'll see you later."

I want to tell Mom she's repeating herself. I want to tell her to call someone else when she needs help. I want to scream at her until she sees that she doesn't have just one child. That I matter too. That I exist. Instead, I look up as Emily pulls over. I wave to her. "Em's here. Got to go."

"OK. Let me know when you're coming home."

"Will do." I hang up, not waiting for any more orders from her. I will myself to stop shaking. To let the fire go out. The thought of the ocean comes to me, and I let it bathe me until I'm cool enough to proceed.

Emily looks even cuter than I remember her. Her hair is

down, silky straight, and her eyes are this amazing hazel color with honey-gold specks thrown in. "Hey. Ready?"

I banish the dragon for real and jump in her car. "As I'll ever be."

"Well, all right then." She navigates her car toward downtown. I realize how uncomfortable I am as a passenger in a car. My fingers drum on my leg. Her eyes take in my "In-A-Gadda-Da-Vida" solo. "A mechanic *and* a musician. Wow." We pull into a parking space in front of an AutoZone.

"You have paper and pencil?"

She opens her purse, pulls out a small spiral notebook with the Yale emblem on it.

"You want to be a Yalie?"

"Or Princeton. Or Harvard. Or USC. Or pretty much whatever school takes me. And gives me a huge scholarship. You know Yale pays full tuition for anyone who gets in." She hands me the pad. "I want to be a journalist. I think."

"USC would get my vote."

"You want to go there?"

"California? Definitely. College probably isn't in my future."

"Why?"

I pull open the glove compartment and take out the owner's manual. Write down the model number. Writing things down is good, because when I'm writing, I'm not thinking of Leah. 1996 Camry LE. Silver. I know I don't need the color, but I wish I did. I wish I had a ton of things to write right now to drown out Leah's voice that reaches across time.

"You'd never go to college?" She asked, her voice soft. I'd taken her on a picnic, which was the cutest thing I'd ever done for a girl. She was eating grapes. Everything had been perfect. The day. The picnic. Us. Then that question. "You'd never go to college? You're so smart."

And the realization that for her, I would go to college. I started to work on my grades. It wasn't hard.

Dad never noticed. Neither did Mom. I'm not even sure they looked at my grades since I'd left Mom's. There never was any reason to. I got by doing as little as I could. Solid C work was the way to fly under the radar. Only last year, my guidance counselor, Mr. Hicks, did obviously. He called me into his office the fall after Leah killed herself. Last year. It was supposed to be my senior year until I just gave up and dropped out.

"We got your scores back on your SAT, John. These are college scores."

"I'm not a college kid." I walked out of the office, slamming the lockers on my way.

It was like Leah was still with me in that moment. And that should have made me happy, but it just made me madder than I'd ever been. Not the dragon that time. Me.

"John?" Emily's voice this time. Here. Now.

Here, there's no Leah. No stupid guidance counselor. Nothing. I am in the now. I swear I am. I grit my teeth. Force myself to settle the fuck down.

"John?"

"Yeah. Sorry. I was just remembering something I need to do."

"Do you want to do this some other time?"

"No. It's cool. I mean, there's something I have to do after this."

My hand shakes as I give her back her pen. We walk into the store. She points to the row of jingle bells that hang over the door, announcing visitors. "Welcome to last century."

I chuckle, but I've already cased the strip mall for the liquor store I need and am readying my excuse to her.

She's got this little green leather backpack purse thing slung over her shoulder. It bounces as she walks, and it's hysterical, because she's plunged straight ahead without knowing what we are looking for or where we are going. If I was trying to get her to be into me, I'd ride her about it, but since I've sworn off being anything but friends, I keep going.

"This way." I tug on her bag. "The stuff we need is down here."

We are in the right aisle, and I'm looking for the specific part I need.

"How do you know how to do this stuff?"

"My uncle Dave is huge into cars."

"He the one you were living with? Before here?"

And once again, this girl knows way more about me than she needs to. Thanks, Livy. "Yeah."

"That's cool. I guess I'll have to thank Uncle Dave too?"

"I still haven't done anything." I hand her the box with the part.

"Well, I'm gonna go buy this, and then I'll let you impress me."

"Sure. I've gotta run a quick errand. Be right back."

I don't wait for her to answer before I'm out the front door, the stupid jingle bells accusing me of being an asshole. I'm down the sidewalk in six steps. In front of the liquor store. About to go in when a police car pulls into the parking lot. I stop to fake tie my shoes. The cop goes inside. I freeze. Fuck my life. Even if I wait until he's gone, the guy in the store will be on high alert. I stuff my hands in my pockets and meet Emily as she's leaving the Auto Zone.

"Hey." Her eyes trace my last steps. They light up along with a wicked little smile. "Any luck?"

"No." I rub my hand across my face. Consider trying to lie. Then decide there's no point. "My good fake ID was confiscated. Didn't want to try this one with that cop around."

"Your lacrosse friends couldn't hook you up?" She rocks back on her heels, her hands tucked under her backpack straps, a knowing smile on her lips. She's giving me shit.

I rub my hand across my stubble. "Sure. But…"

"Maybe I can help." She dials her cell. "Hey, Maybeline? I need a favor."

I point to the driver's side, and she shrugs, hands me her keys. She puts her hand over the phone. "What's your pleasure?"

I almost choke. "What?"

"What do you want my friend to get you? Tequila? Rum?"

"Jack. Jack Daniel's."

She gives the directive into the phone. Before we even leave the parking lot, I'm feeling all kinds of interested in this good girl who just made my day.

———o———

I finish fixing the fan, and Emily turns on the car to try it out.

"All right! You are amazing!" She kisses me on the cheek and holds up her phone. "Let's go get your reward. It's two blocks away."

We walk down the street just as Mom rounds the corner, pushing Ryan's wheelchair past the curve that leads into our neighborhood, the S-turn that Mom always says is a death trap. Livy and I used to laugh at that, even though it wasn't so nice, I mean, in light of everything. Pete came from inside the neighborhood that day, so the curve had nothing to do with the accident.

"Hey." Mom coughs a couple of times. She looks a little winded, and I'm kind of surprised, because she's usually in such good shape, but Ryan's gotten pretty big, so he must be hard to push.

When he sees me, he starts kicking his feet and waving his hands. "Jaaahhhhhn!"

I jog to meet up with them. "Hey, Ryan." Then to Mom, "Isn't he supposed to walk some?"

She nods, still gasping for breath. "Some. Just not long distances. Where are you guys headed?"

"Just picking up a study guide from one of my friends," Emily says smoothly.

"*Great Expectations*," I add. "We're reading that in English, and I'm behind."

"I used to love that book." She coughs again. "Miss Havisham is one of my favorite characters."

I pat her on the back. "You OK, Mom?"

"Probably just a cold."

"Why don't you head in? We can take Ryan with us." I look at Emily to see if she's cool with that, and she nods.

Mom looks at me like she can't believe what I've offered. Like I've suddenly sprouted wings and a halo, and that pisses me the hell off. "Never mind."

"No, that's great. I'd love that." Her hand goes to her hair, smoothing it back under the baseball hat she's wearing, the one I have never seen her wear. She points at the levers on the side of Ryan's chair. "You've got to put the brakes on when you're on the hill."

"I know, Mom."

I slide my arms down the side of the chair and onto Ryan's arms. "Tell Mom to chill. We are just going for a little walk."

He answers me with a resounding chant. "Push! Push! Push!"

Which makes Mom smile. She puts her hand over her eyes to block the sun. "How far you going?"

"Just on Sycamore," Emily says.

That's a block and a half.

"OK. That would be great if you took him. He'd probably really like that."

I stand behind his chair and whisper in Ryan's ear. "You ready for liftoff?" I push hard and make a rocket sound. Ryan laughs and squeals.

Mom's face goes white. She shakes her head. If it wasn't my family, it would be funny. Hilarious even. But when Mom growls low and mean, my face heats, and my insides churn. "Honestly, John, what are you thinking? You could drop him."

As if I could do anything to hurt him now. A meteor couldn't hurt him.

Ryan, buying a hundred percent into Mom's crazy, starts screaming and kicking. He's got this high-pitched squeal that I did not miss while I was away, and just like that, another perfect Strickland family moment is in the crapper. Deep.

Emily gets in front of Ryan, holds his hands. "Sh, all's fine. Come on, Ryan. You want to go with us, right?"

Amazingly, Ryan starts to settle down. It's like Emily is the Ryan whisperer or something. Emily winks at me. "My mom says all moms are overprotective. They can't help it."

Mom's face softens. "You know, you're right. I'm sorry, John. Just try to be careful. He's not used to roughhousing."

Ryan starts to hit his wheelchair arms. "Go! Go! Go!"

Mom laughs. "Now you're taking his side too, huh? I'm going to go in and lie down. I'm very tired. Obviously, you've got this under control."

As Mom dabs her eyes and walks toward our house, I can't help but stare at Emily, who is nothing short of astonishing in her ability to surprise me in every way.

CHAPTER 8

We sit in the park, my back up against a tree. Livy, who joined us as soon as we got to the park, is running around, and Ryan is in his wheelchair, laughing. Emily sits next to me, and I feel so comfortable and happy that it's almost weird. Can I trust this feeling? The few shots of Jack Daniel's I took when we first got here have definitely softened the mood, and knowing there's the rest of the fifth waiting for me when I need it has made me less twitchy, but watching Livy hang with her friends hasn't hurt.

Emily picks up a branch and plays with the leaves and the small flowers on the end. "You always seem so chill. Aren't you worried about senior year at all? I'm just a junior, and it's getting to me."

I pick up a piece of bark off the ground, start to peel it. "Nah. What's the point?"

"I wish I was more like you. I'm a mess."

"You don't look like a mess."

"I hide it well. Like the good girl I am." She smiles. Starts drawing in the dirt with her stick. "But seriously, I'm freaked the frick out."

My eyes go to her backpack. "We've got the cure for that."

"Not sure that'll help me."

"Can't hurt."

"Alcohol doesn't actually solve problems."

"Maybe, but it makes you not care that you have them."

She laughs. "So tell me what I'm supposed to be doing with my life."

"Living?"

"I'm being serious. Everyone I know knows what they want to do. Who they want to be when they grow up."

"You want to be a journalist. You told me the first time I met you."

"Truth?" She aims her amazing green eyes at me, holds my stare for five seconds.

I nod. "Absolutely."

"I've got no idea if I'm good enough for that." She picks up another twig and starts attacking the leaves, peeling them off like she's scaling a fish. "I'm actually pretty sure I'm not."

"You're, like, the poster child for good enough."

"To be honest?"

"Yeah?"

"I'm not even sure I want to be a writer. I mean, I think I do, but I'm not completely sure. Like you…you know exactly what you want, don't you? Exactly where you're going."

"I'm just not that complicated."

"It's not complication. It's drive. I don't know if I have it."

"I bet you do. Come on, close your eyes."

She laughs. "What? Why?"

"Just do it." I tuck a stray piece of hair behind her ear. "Trust me, I'm going to be a complete gentleman. Promise."

"OK." She closes her eyes and leans back against my tree.

I put my hands over her eyes for effect. "Ask yourself, if you could do whatever you wanted in this world—money isn't a factor or logistics. If you had ten million dollars and wanted to fill your time and your spirit, what would you do?"

"I…"

My finger slips over her mouth. "Sh. Just think to yourself. Forget everything around you. Ask yourself."

I watch her face, how it turns from nervous, to puzzled, to serene.

"You've got it?"

"Yeah."

"You can keep it to yourself if you want."

She opens her eyes. "I'd write."

"That's your answer. You're good enough."

She stares into my eyes with wonder. "You're kind of amazing."

"You sound surprised."

She laughs. "I guess I'm usually pretty guarded with people. Always putting on a face for them. Never really talking. You're easy to talk to."

I want to tell her that's the Jack Daniel's. I want to tell her I'm usually a beast and to stay away from me and that she only sees the parts of me I'm showing her. I want to tell her all that, but instead, I surprise the shit out of myself by saying, "So are you."

CHAPTER 9

Monday morning comes way too soon. I drag myself out of bed, and I'm amazed at how I already have a routine here. How quickly I've remade my life and become this other person. One who works out every day. One who is nice to his mother. One who is nice to his brother. I've always been nice to my little sister. That part comes easy to me. But this other stuff? Knowing the Jack Daniel's is available—and that tiny bit of weed—I'm able to push all the anger down.

"You need to eat more." Mom's on her stool, bathrobe on, sipping her coffee as usual. "You're exercising a lot, and your body needs nutrition."

I can't help feeling happy she's noticed my eating patterns or anything at all about me for that matter, but I'm exhausted, like Monday snuck up on me, so I just nod.

"Will you try a shake?"

My stomach turns at the thought of her intervention, remembering some of the awful stuff she made Ryan eat and drink over the years, all in the name of good nutrition. But she pushes a glass of something at me, and I feel I've got no play, so I take a sip. It isn't awful, but it's also not good. "Mmm, thanks. What's in it?"

"Some protein powder, some frozen fruit, and almond milk."

"Thanks."

I can't help inspecting Mom. I wonder if that's how parents feel about their children and why all of a sudden I feel the need to do that to her. What I see is not good. She's thin as usual. Her eyes look sunken and dark. She coughs, even as I scrutinize her. "Tell you what, I'll drink this if you'll get that cough checked out."

This makes her chuckle. "Since when is it your job to take care of me?"

"Family takes care of each other." This slips out, and I'm sort of surprised by how much I actually mean it.

Her eyes wet. "OK. Deal. I'll get it checked out if it doesn't go away by next week."

Beep.

I chug the rest of the shake, grab my coffee cup and lunch that Mom has ready for me and my lacrosse bag that no matter what I say or do Rosie will not let me take care of myself, and head out the door. All the while noticing Mom's wistful smile and glad that for a change, I'm actually making her happy. God, I hope I can keep this up.

"Happy Monday." Emily greets me with a smile. She points to the vent, which is thankfully blowing cool air. "You're a genius." As if that huge-assed smile on her face wasn't enough thanks.

I tip my coffee at her.

When we're on our way, she says, "Seriously, thanks for everything this weekend."

"No prob. Hey, can I ask you something?"

"Sure."

"You seem to know a lot about Ryan."

"That's not a question." She nods as she turns onto the street that leads to our high school. Then she flashes me another smart-assed grin.

"Getting to it. Have you ever heard my mom talk about sending Ryan away?"

"She's never said anything to me about that, but when I was watching Livy the other night, I did hear something."

"What?"

Her hands come off the steering wheel. "I'm not a snoop. I want you to know that. It's not my thing. I just overheard…"

"It's OK. Tell me."

"On the answering machine, I heard someone calling about an appointment. From the Next Step. It's one of those group homes. My mom's a social worker, so I happen to know that place."

The intense rush of emotion surprises me. Not anger this time, but worry. For Ryan. And all of a sudden, I want more than anything for him to stay. Which is so stupid, because I don't actually know he's going anywhere, and I don't exactly get a say anyway.

"I'm sorry, should I not have said anything?"

"No. I'm glad you did."

We get to the parking lot. Early as usual. I decide I like being here before everyone else gets here. It helps me to get my legs under me.

We walk together to the front of the building. "It's a nice place," she says, reading my mood. "I used to volunteer there. He'd be fine there."

I face her, those unbelievable green eyes focused on me, like a kaleidoscope I want to keep looking at, but it's her concern that touches me. I'm used to being the one to worry. Like Mom said. "Thanks. You're a sweetheart."

She laughs like maybe I insulted her a little, like maybe she thinks I'm dismissing her. But she is a sweetheart. I mean, she can't be my sweetheart, but she is a really great girl. I take her hand. "I mean it. Thanks." I lean over and kiss her cheek.

Her hand goes to where my kiss was, and her eyes flit to the ground, then meet my stare. We stay like this for what is probably only a second but feels like forever. A voice from behind me makes me look away but not before noticing Emily covering her mouth with her hand, probably to cover her embarrassed smile.

"Mr. Strickland." A woman, probably in her twenties, in a tight black skirt and jacket approaches me. "I've been looking for you."

"You've found me."

"I'm Miss Quinlan." She extends her hand. "Your guidance counselor, and I'd love it if you would come to my office with me."

"Sure."

Emily gives me a nod like *good luck*. I smile in answer. A guidance counselor is not concerning to me.

Miss Quinlan's office is, thankfully, not over the top with that crappy stuff that's supposed to smell good but looks like a pile of artificially colored mulch. The guidance counselors who have that shit are passive-aggressive, militant women who have nothing but bad things to tell me. This guidance counselor has some family pictures, a couple of her running a marathon, and a plaque that reads *life, happiness, love.* So far, so good. She waves to the chair opposite her desk, wraps her hand around her coffee mug. Her French-tipped nails and straight blond hair remind me of Leah, but I try not to let that get to me.

"So how are you settling in so far, John?"

I shift into good-boy mode, thinking whatever she's got on her mind will be dealt with much easier if I pretend to be on board. "Good."

"I see you're on the lacrosse team, and I hear you are doing well in your classes so far."

The anger starts seeping in. Who is this woman to ask about me? To check in with my teachers?

"I've been told your probation officer will be here to see you sometime this week. I wanted you to be aware."

I nod. Chew on the knuckles on my middle and ring fingers. It's awesome to have this good-looking woman already know I'm a piece of shit.

"I hope you remember they will be doing drug tests." She says that while she types my student number into a computer screen. There's no judgment in her voice, like she's working hard not to piss me off, which makes me wonder why she cares. She prints a couple of pages as I shift in my seat, trying like mad to damp down the dragon that is circling, circling.

She slides the papers across the desk in front of me. With a red pen, she starts her own brand of circling. My GPA. My SAT scores. All these stupid numbers that say absolutely nothing about me. Even though adults always seem to think they do.

"I took the time to contact your guidance counselor at West Lake."

Fire ignites in my belly. Stupid fucking counselors.

"Mr. Hicks, wasn't it?"

I chew on my knuckles some more. "Uh-huh."

"He says you're a really great kid."

"That's good to hear."

"But…one who hasn't exactly given a lot of thought to his future."

That's one person's opinion. My plans for the future may not be what this woman or Mr. Hicks feels is reasonable or relevant or in line with what kids like me who come from households like mine should be doing. I've got news for her. She's got no idea what my house is really like. Dad may make a crap ton of money at the bank, and Mom may be this highly educated person, but never have they sat me down to have this talk. They know better.

I rub my hand across my stubble and slouch lower in my chair. Could be she'll decide I don't have the posture to carry off college.

She takes a sip of her coffee. The sound irritates the crap out of me, even though it's quiet. She stares at me. "Do you have any idea what you want to do after high school?"

I slink lower in the chair. Of course I do—I'm not an idiot—but it's not like she's going to be on board with my plan. Even if it's completely legal.

She shakes her head. "Your GPA is not great."

"Good enough to play sports," I say.

"Yes, but given your SAT scores and your grades last year… you could be doing more than that."

I sit quietly. Wondering how long this do-good speech is going to take. Hoping this is the end of it. I'm about to push my way out of this chair when she launches the biggest bomb in her armory.

"Mr. Hicks told me you had a hard year last year."

And there is what I was hoping I wouldn't have to talk about. Maia Cetus stands on two legs and roars. His fire breath climbs up my throat.

"He said you lost someone who was close to you."

I try to sit still and act like none of this is getting to me, but visions of sitting in Mr. Hicks's office flood me, and I have to close my eyes. His hands were folded in front of him. I remember thinking he looked so casual as he slayed me. *I've always liked you, John. You've always had a chivalrous attitude, an honor code, that most guys your age don't. I'm sure that was a quality Leah saw in you.*

Every word worse than the last.

"She told me about you. In case you were wondering how I knew."
With each word, my wall went higher and higher.

Sitting here in this Miss Quinlan's office, I have to shift in my seat to keep the heat from building.

She leans forward, just like Mr. Hicks. Her hands are folded in front of her, like it's something they teach you when you become a guidance counselor. Some bullshit lesson on looking interested in the idiots who sit across from your desk and plan to waste their future. "John, these SAT scores are excellent. You could get into any state school with these scores. Some private ones too."

I clear my throat. "Yeah. I'm not so sure about…"

"I'd like to have you do grade forgiveness for some of your classes last year. In retrospect, they should have maybe even withdrawn you, but that's no big deal. But what is a big deal are the classes you are in now. They are not college-bound classes. So we need to fix that."

I don't answer, because obviously, she's not listening to anything I have to say. I'm filling my mind with thoughts of the Pacific Ocean. The last snowfall of the year. Ice on my neck and shoulder after practice. How a Coke ICEE feels in my mouth. Anything to get that stupid dragon of mine to stand down, because losing it in front of this do-gooder isn't going to help anyone.

Miss Quinlan pauses like she wants me to answer but also gets that I'm not going to. "Do you have any interests at all?"

"I'm pretty sure my interests are not offered at most colleges."

She smiles. "I'm pretty sure you're mistaken." She laughs a little as she says it. Then she stops looking at her computer screen and lays her hands flat on the table. This shit's about to get serious. "The thing is, John, education is power. And power means choices. I don't know how many choices you see for your future. Maybe you haven't even considered that you could have one."

I pick at the hem of my jeans that is starting to unravel. She doesn't even know me.

Her eyes go back to her computer screen. "And that's a shame. Because with scores like these"—she points to the papers with the stupid numbers all over them that say exactly zero about who I really am—"and with you being an athlete and with the recommendation from your guidance counselor from the last school…" She clicks keys on her computer. "You could probably do more than you think you can."

I stay silent.

"Would you like sports management?" she asks.

I shake my head. Trying to deal with a bunch of arrogant jocks would in no way appeal to me.

"What about art? Are you good at drawing?"

"Not really."

"Cooking? We have an excellent culinary track."

"I like to eat," I offer. "You have classes in that?"

She laughs. Clicks more keys. "Are you interested in architecture?"

A little beam of light shines. I sit up. She must notice my

change in posture, because she keeps going. "We have an excellent architectural drawing and computer-aided drawing class. I think that will serve you so much better than that extra gym class you're in. No offense, but you need to fill your schedule with classes that the college admissions counselors would like to see. We might need to switch some of your other classes to make the schedule work, but if you're interested…"

I think about the buildings in Chicago. The ones I loved. "Yeah. I like that stuff."

I listen as she clicks and types and clicks some more. She's deciding my future with her clever, clever choices, and I should be grateful—I know I should—but all I can think of is that bottle of Jack and how Mr. Hicks looked right inside me when he said, "The best way to honor people we love is to be our best person."

Which of course made me want to do the opposite. But that's just who I am. Gotta work on that.

Miss Quinlan, for her part, is sitting taller in her seat, a really pretty smile on her face, like I'm making her day by letting her help me.

As she types and types, I keep pouring buckets of ice water on my beast. What I know from my experience with adults who want to save me is there's no point in arguing with Miss Quinlan. But maybe this class would be fun. Maybe I could make something awesome. Maybe, just maybe, I could start thinking about being the person I was supposed to be all along. If there's an Old Ryan, maybe there's an old me too.

————o————

My new teacher, Mr. Bonham, is sitting behind his desk when I walk into his class. He motions me forward.

"John?"

I nod, slide my paper in front of him—the one that says I'm supposed to be here—and all of a sudden, I'm hit with this wave of doubt. In my other classes, I don't care, but taking in this room with all the amazing pictures of bridges and buildings on the walls and actual models on the shelves, I worry I'm not good enough. It's weird—that never stopped me on the lacrosse field or the football field or the basketball court.

Mr. Bonham catches me staring at a picture of one of the buildings I recognize. "That's Chicago's Home Insurance Building. You know it?"

I rub my hand over my cheek. "Not the name, no. But I've seen it. It's kind of my favorite building." The moment the words come out, I want to beat the crap out of myself. How effing needy do I have to be right now?

"It's one of my favorites too. I can see we are going to get along. Have you had any CAD training?"

I shake my head. "No."

"If you like those buildings, you're going to love that. Sit at this computer, and I'll show you around."

I drop my gear by the desk. I can't stop staring at the models. Some are made from this thin wood I've seen in those crappy airplane models in the stores Dad used to take us to before Ryan's accident, when all Ryan and I did together was build things. Two liter bottles, Popsicle sticks, LEGOs, K'NEX—we built with whatever we could find. My hand wants to touch the models, especially the ones that are made from this white plastic-looking material I've never seen before.

"We have a 3-D printer." A guy I don't know who is sitting to my left, a total computer geek for sure and probably a lot smarter than I am, points to the cool models. "We get to make those next semester."

My mind spins. I try to focus on the computer screen in front of me, but I can't help thinking it's cool to want something that has nothing to do with Leah or my family, that's just about me—the me I used to be. Before I became the wreck of a person I am now.

———o———

Practice today ends with us crowding around the coaches, winded, ready to go, waiting for them to release us.

"Great work today." Coach Gibson looks at his clipboard for verification. "We're ready to test our team, so tomorrow will be a scrimmage with Parkland."

Grumbles and some excitement travel around our little circle.

"John." He taps me with the clipboard. "You'll start at midfield. And maybe take a face-off or two."

He keeps going, naming people and the part they will play in his little war game, but all I can hear is that I'm starting, that I'm taking some face-offs. I can't wait. I hit the showers, then meet Emily in the parking lot.

"You look happy with yourself," she says.

"I had a pretty good day."

"You never said what Quinlan wanted."

"Oh yeah." I hand her my new schedule. "She wanted me to up my academic game too."

Emily checks out my new schedule. English honors, computer-aided drafting, architectural drawing. And for the few seconds it takes her to review my new classes, I start to panic a little. I mean, is this crazy? Can I do it?

Her eyes go wide, and her lips turn upward, and then I feel proud and hopeful. Like a little kid. But then she high-fives me, and I stop being self-conscious as she beams. "Wow, Strickland! You the man."

I'm not sure if it's the post-exercise high or what, but I forget all the reasons I'm not supposed to do this next thing. "Does that mean you'll let me take you out this weekend? To celebrate?"

Emily's mouth drops open like she can't believe I just said that. "You're asking me out?" She lowers her voice as if she's afraid someone will overhear. "Is that even allowed?"

"What do you mean?"

She parks the car. "Livy gave you the talk, didn't she?" She uses air quotes to highlight the words *the talk*.

My little sister is something. "I'm pretty sure I can handle all four feet, five inches of her. But if you're scared…"

"I am. Totally. But…I'm also curious. I've seen lacrosse John. Mechanic John. Drunk John and big brother John. I wonder what on-a-date John looks like."

"You make me sound like some kind of Barbie doll."

She laughs. "Yeah. I still need to collect cowboy John and surgeon John to make the complete set."

"Didn't know good girls were into role play…"

She blushes and opens her car door. I do the same. My lacrosse gear on my shoulder, I meet her on her side of the car, drag her field hockey stuff out of the backseat.

"So?" I close the distance between us. "Is that a yes?"

"It's a no to the role play but a yes to the date."

"I can live with that."

"Good."

"For now." I push. I can't not.

I watch her walk to her door, wait for her to put the key in the lock. She looks back at me one more time, and I nod at her like a total dork, which makes her smile, and I no longer care if I look needy or stupid. I want to hold on to this incredible feeling that has followed me around all day. It's one I haven't been familiar with without chemical help—happiness.

CHAPTER 10

Ryan's screams kill my good mood as soon as I enter the house. Before I can wonder if this is another before-bed tantrum, I catch another sound—a softer one. Tearful hiccups that are swallowed almost as soon as they are shed. *Livy.*

An alarm sounds inside me. I drop my bags to the ground. Livy's in the kitchen, and Rosie is with her, putting ice on her lip, which is bleeding.

"What's going on?"

They turn in my direction, fear on both of their faces.

I take the ice out of Rosie's hand and look at the damage. "Liv…"

Tears spill down her cheeks, which are red from crying. "He didn't mean it…"

I give Rosie the ice. "I'll be right back."

"Please, John, please, don't!"

The dragon has taken over. My legs push me up the steps. I fling open the door. Ryan is in his bed, thrashing around, screaming. Mom's standing over him, her hands out to try to calm him. "Sh, darling. Sh."

"Stop it!"

Mom whirls to face me. "Not now, John."

I push by her. "Stop it!" I make the sign language sign for *stop* that we learned years ago from a therapist who was teaching Ryan to speak again. And I'm glad for that, because it keeps my hands from smacking him or strangling him or knocking him the hell out.

"Nonononononono!" Ryan screams.

I get in front of him. Right in front. My hands go on his shoulders, and I hold him tight so he has to look at me. "Stop it. Stop. You can't hit Livy. You can't hit my sister. Or my mother. You can't." I shake him once, hard.

Ryan's eyes go wide.

I let go of his shoulders. Back away. I'm shaking. My mind is screaming at me to get out of there. To run.

Ryan starts to cry—real tears, not fake tantrum ones. The sound is awful, and I know with those tears comes Mom's anger. Both are building. Both are because of me.

The dragon slinks away. I should leave the room, but for some reason, I'm stuck in place. I am frozen here. "You can't hit people. You can't just do whatever you want. You have to stop."

It's stupid to try to make my case. "Out." Mom points to the door. She's not screaming, but she doesn't have to—the word comes out in a snarl. Ryan hits her, hits Livy, and *I* am the animal in her eyes. I'm the one who always fucks up. I'm the one who never gets it right. "Get out!"

I know she means Ryan's room, but it reminds me of when I got kicked out that last time. Her face is exactly the same. Her eyes are staring at me like I'm a monster. Like I don't belong here.

I back away. She's so busy comforting him, she has no room for my misery.

I crash into my door, slam into the wall. My hands close around the bag of weed I stashed under my desk. Miss Quinlan's warning me about my probation officer and the drug tests are pushed out of my head with just these words: fuck, fuck, fuck, fuck. Need. My hands claw at my backpack, unzip the front compartment, and grab my lighter, then I'm down the stairs, out the door, into the street.

"John!" Rosie calls after me.

"Johnny, Johnny, Johnny!" I hear Livy too, but I can't help her. I'm not here anymore. I don't even exist. I am gone in a puff of smoke.

My legs propel me forward. I'm not even sure where I'm going until I stop at that tree in the park, the one where I sat with Emily the other day, watching Ryan and Livy. When things were fine. When I had Jack in my system and all was cool.

I slide down the tree, and the bark tries to dig through my sweatshirt, tries to claw its way into my skin, but I don't care. I light a joint and let the smoke seep into my lungs. I hold it inside me like the scream I should have held.

A sound comes back to me. *Crash. The sound of me throwing the china cabinet over. Smash. The crystal on the floor. Mom's face that day seven years ago.* I put my face in my hands. I don't want to remember. When my breath comes out, ragged and worn, I let the tears come, since no one's around. I rock on my heels and bring the joint back to my lips. Take another hit. Another hit. Another one. Finally, the pot settles me. My hands stop shaking. I sit on the dirt, my legs out in front of me.

A flashlight spears the night.

"John?" Emily's voice. Livy must have called her.

"Hey." I throw my hands in the air. "I give up."

The flashlight beam falls to the ground, but it's enough along with the nearby streetlights and the full moon and clear star-filled sky so I can see her face. And her face is not happy to see me. It's worried and relieved and maybe a little annoyed too. I'm pretty expert at reading women's moods.

"You OK?" She sits on the ground across from me.

I put my face in my hand. "Better now that you're here."

She shakes her head and takes out her cell. She types. All her movements are in fits and starts. "Livy was really worried."

That takes the buzz right out of me. "I know. I know. I just…"

"She told me what happened." Emily goes back to being concerned. "The part I heard sounded awful."

"You could hear it?" Perspiration beads on the back of my neck, and then I get a chill.

She puts her hand on my arms. "You're cold."

I give her my best pirate smile. "You could warm me up?"

"Nice try, Romeo. But if we are going to…do anything, I'd like it to be when you are sober enough to remember it."

"So you've never gotten high?"

"What's that got to do with anything?"

"It's not like being drunk. It's not like I don't know what I'm doing."

My hands frame her face. She doesn't pull away, but she stiffens. Her eyes look into mine, deep, like she wants to find some meaning there. I would tell her not to bother, but that's not going to help my game.

"This isn't helping anything. You know that, right?"

I stay quiet.

"You're angry all the time. I understand it. But…I just can't…"

"I'm not asking you to do anything."

"You scare me."

I stand up. Fine. I scare her.

"And it's not like you're sober either. Is it?"

"I guess not." I admit.

"I'll wait."

"So you *do* want to kiss me. I knew it!"

"Let's get you home."

I lean against Emily, milking this being high thing long enough to let her take some of the weight off.

———o———

The alarm is like a saw going through my head. I reach for my phone and knock a glass of water off the night table. Pain stabs my head from all sides as I pick up the glass and pull my T-shirt over my head to mop up the mess.

"That you, John?" Mom's voice is icy. "You need to get up and get ready. I'm not driving you."

"I'm going," I call back, not wanting to be a smart-ass but wanting her to know that she doesn't have to worry about me.

It's not until I pass Livy's room that the full weight of regret crushes me. Her door opens a crack. I turn to face her, crouch low, peer inside. "Hey, Livy, you wanna talk?"

She opens the door the tiniest bit more, her eyes so sad, I can't stand it. "I don't know."

"OK. I understand. I just want to say I'm really sorry about last night. I lost my cool, and I'm never going to do that again."

Her door opens more, but her little foot stops it or me from opening it any farther. "How do I know you mean it?"

My heart cramps. "I don't know. You'll just have to trust me, I guess." Her face gets all scrunched, and I know she's used to people saying one thing and doing something else. Which I never used to do. "I know it is going to be hard."

She closes the door almost all the way. I'm losing this battle. "You didn't even come talk to me last night. I kept waiting for you."

I sit in the hallway with my back against the wall. "It was late. I didn't want to wake you."

"I wasn't sleeping." She sniffs.

"You're right. I should have come to see you."

"You didn't want me to know you were stoned."

It feels like she's shot me with a cannon. "How…"

"I could smell it. I'm ten, not stupid."

"You shouldn't know anything about…"

"You can't keep me from knowing things my whole life."

"I can't help wanting to."

The door opens, and I turn to face my little sister, trying hard not to look at the cut above her lip or the red eyes I know I've made worse. "He doesn't know any better."

"He should. Someone should teach him."

"Not that way."

I swallow hard, look her straight in the eye so she'll know I mean it. "I won't. I promise."

"OK."

"Hug it out?"

She throws her little body against mine, and I try to choke back the tears. I never want to hurt this little girl again. "I'm sorry, Liv. I'll be better."

"Seven minutes, John," Mom bellows up the stairs.

"I gotta go fix things with Mom. You should get ready for school."

"Not going. Mom said I could stay home since it's Friday."

Rage fills me, but I damp it down. *No way Mom lets her stay home for her sake. Everything is to protect him,* my dragon tells me as if I couldn't figure it out myself. "You don't care about missing?"

"Nah. We're just having a Reading Counts party anyway."

I kiss the top of her head. "OK, I've gotta go." I make it almost all the way to the stairs when she calls me.

"John?"

"Yeah."

She points to her room. "I remember when you went away last time."

My heart falls into my stomach. She was only three, and

there's no way I can explain how I was trying to protect her then too.

"You won't leave like that again, right?"

"No. I won't leave like that again."

"You'll always tell me before you go?"

"Always."

"OK." I can't help but notice how saggy her shoulders are. "I'm going to binge-watch *Switched at Birth*."

"Good plan."

I go down the stairs, not wanting to face this next part. Mom's not on her stool. She's at the sink. She points to the coffeemaker. My to-go cup waiting. I pour the coffee and put the top on.

"Lunch is in the fridge."

"OK. Thanks."

I open the fridge, thinking she means I need to pack something for myself but am shocked to find that she's packed for me, and I have to bite the inside of my cheek to keep from crying like a baby. I turn to face her. "I'm really sorry about last night, Mom."

She doesn't face me. "I know, but he doesn't understand how strong he is. He doesn't mean…"

"He can't keep hitting people."

She turns holding a protein shake, maybe deciding if I deserve it. This milk shake is more than an olive branch she's extending. It's the core of how she loves. And her willingness to withhold it pisses me off more than anything in this wide world.

"I know he can't, John. But you can't…"

I don't even listen. I summon sounds of waves crashing inside my head. If I heard what she is saying, really heard, I'd go completely mental. I'd be ten-year-old me and smash every single thing in this house and leave for good this time. But that's not going to help Livy. Then she says something that snaps me out of my fade-out.

"He's not going to be here forever, you know that?" Her eyes fill, and tears run down her face. She swats at them, but my heart is all jacked up.

"What do you mean?"

She shakes her head. Wipes her face. "You remember what the doctors said."

More like I couldn't forget what one insurance adjuster actually had the balls to say in front of my parents right after Ryan's accident, before they settled the claim. All of a sudden, I feel like the worst person in the world.

"It's OK, Mom. He's going to outlive all of us." That's what my dad used to say to her when she got like this.

She nods. "I know. I just…I worry about you kids."

"I'm sorry about last night, but we have to help him learn boundaries."

"You're right. I'm bringing in a behavioral therapist. I've already called one." Mom moves closer to me now so I can see how bloodshot her eyes are. I try not to give her attitude, because bringing in a therapist is shit. Ryan needs discipline and drugs. Ha! My prescription for everything, I guess. But the memory of that man, the one who said Ryan would die sooner than most people, is too fresh to reason with her now.

"Good."

Beep. Emily's here. Mom and I stare at each other for a second, and then she hands me the shake. "Good luck with your new classes."

"What?"

"Your guidance counselor called. You're so smart, John. I want you to start acting that way."

I glom down the shake, leave the cup on the counter.

"I'm getting you a computer with that program you need for your drafting class. It'll be waiting for you when you get home."

I'm so completely floored by her comment that I almost run into the wall on my way out. "Thanks," I call back, and I don't even care that she's trying to buy my love with her expensive presents, because this one is about me doing something important and that I like. This one is because she noticed.

———o———

Emily smiles at me when I get in the car. "Hey," she says.

I'm so grateful she's not shaming me or taking the temperature of the stupid mistake I made last night. "Hey," I say back.

"How'd it go?" She motions with her head toward my house before looking in her rearview and backing out of the driveway.

"Livy's mad, but we made up. Mom's OK surprisingly."

Emily laughs. "Never can predict the parents, can you?"

"No. What about you? I'm sorry you had to come get me last night."

"I should actually thank you. Got me out of the house at a very opportune time. You saved me from getting into it with my mom."

"Happy to be of service. What could your mom take issue with you over? I mean, aren't you the quintessential good girl?"

Emily's face scrunches up. "They definitely don't see me that way."

"Well, if you can't convince your parents, there's no hope for me."

"Let's just say that you are not the only one planning for next year, when we can get away from all this crap."

It makes me feel sad that someone as great as Emily feels like she has to escape.

"College is going to be the best," she says, almost as if she's talking herself into it.

"That's what they say."

She arches an eyebrow. "But until then, we can just have some fun." Her voice sounds confident, but it hitches a little.

"Fun?"

She giggles a little too forcibly. Recovers. "Fun. You ever heard of it?"

"I think you know I know what fun is…" For a moment, I'm reminded of Leah, how she never wanted people to know about us. How I was her secret go-to guy. I don't want to be that person again, not for anyone. And I'm not even sure I know how to have fun anymore. But it's not like I'm going to admit that.

Emily plays with the dial on the radio. Switches off the idiots and onto a rock station I like. "You know what's going to be fun? Watching you play today. You ready for your big scrimmage?"

"Not even close."

"I'll be watching. No pressure." Then she punches me in the arm and laughs.

And I laugh too. "Thanks for the support."

"Radar Love" comes on the radio, and she turns it up and belts it out while I kill it on the imaginary drums. She bounces her head as she sings. And all I can think is this girl could be dangerous for me if I let her. Which I won't.

———o———

The fog I feel in my head travels to my body, and I make stupid mistakes the entire day. Seventh period finally comes, and I'm in my favorite class with Mr. Bonham.

"You had a conversation with my mother?" I ask as I sit at the computer and pull up a project I was working on. It's a photograph of a bunch of different arches.

He shrugs. "She called and asked what she could do to support you in this class."

"So you told her to buy me a laptop and a CAD program?"

He laughs. "Hardly. I just told her what we used in class. The rest was her idea. That program's not cheap. I told her to wait to see what you did with it, if you were even still interested by the end of the term."

I can just imagine that conversation. "Turns out she went completely the other way."

He chuckles. "Moms. What are you gonna do? Anyway, she said you were a child prodigy. Always building amazing structures with LEGOs or blocks or sticks and rocks in the backyard. She even mentioned a particular Cheerio creation."

I hold up my hand. "I get the picture. Wow."

He puts his hands in his pockets, then puts up a finger like he just remembered the secret to the universe or some shit. "Wait." That finger points emphatically. "She actually sent me pictures of some of them."

Heat fills me—and not my dragon's heat.

He puts a hand on my shoulder. "Don't be embarrassed. It's nice. Plus, she's right. You had an eye for design even back then. I have no idea what kept you away from architecture, but I'm glad you're back." He hands me printed copies of the pictures Mom emailed to him.

Looking at the photos, I see six-year-old me next to the structures I'd built. Stupid fucking smile on my face. But there they were. My bridges. Tunnels. Buildings. All made from whatever I had around me. I haven't thought about any of these pictures in the longest time. I flip to the last one. It's the igloo Ryan and I made, and a sickening feeling spreads through me. I screwed that up too.

If I close my eyes, I can hear Mom laughing. "My little architects."

Other kids start filing into the room. I don't listen to them talking to each other or the chairs squeaking as they are dragged across the room. I'm focused on the pictures Mom sent to Mr. Bonham. I can hardly believe that part of me ever lived. I file the pictures into my backpack and stare at my computer.

Mr. Bonham addresses the class. "Today, you are going to analyze the arches in the picture and then recreate them on the next page. Once you've done that, I'll come around and check your work for you."

I stare at the photograph I've chosen to work from, its beautiful form. I start to think about the numbers that make each one up. My clumsy fingers and foggy head make a mess of my drawing.

"Some of the data points are incorrect," Mr. Bonham says as he points to my screen. "Check them again."

I stare at my mistakes and think about corrupt data in my drawing and myself. I page back to the original drawing, allow myself a moment to enjoy the correct angles. I page back. Page forward. Page back. The wrong plot points don't show themselves to me, and I feel completely stupid. This class was a horrible idea.

Mr. Bonham's shadow falls on me. "This is motor memory for you. You were used to building with your hands. Not with a computer. Maybe you should go back to doing 3-D until you figure it out."

My thoughts slip. I'm not sure if it's the weed hangover making me dumb or the memories that are clawing their way into my mind.

I clench my teeth. The pictures Mom sent are just an embarrassing stunt and nothing more. But that igloo started everything, the destruction snowballing into our family's personal avalanche.

I force my attention back to the CAD screen. Try to see what's wrong, but I don't. And now I can't remember any of the commands that make the computer draw what I want to see. I can hardly remember how to do any of this. With or without a computer. I am still the stupid little kid who can't do anything right. Everything's a mess. And this is exactly what comes from trying to challenge myself. Better to stick to my plan. Don't get close to anyone. Finish my high school sentence and then go to California, where my skill for rolling a righteous blunt will be appreciated for what it is: my only talent.

Just then, my phone gets a text. I pull it out, hoping against all hope that Pete's dealer is finally going to do business with me. At first, I don't recognize the number, but I definitely know the name. It's Allie. Leah's little sister.

Hey. Hope it's OK I texted you. Just wanted to check in with you.

I text back. It's fine. I'm here if you need me. Always.

I know you are. It's just hard starting senior year without her, you know?

Yes it is.

I want to be happy about painting and applying to college but it feels wrong too.

You have to.

I guess.

You do. She'd want you to. Besides, you are supposed to make art.

OK. I will if you do too.

If I do what?

Make whatever art you are supposed to. Weld. Build things.

My body flushes. How could she know I'm looking into that now?

Or whatever makes your heart pump faster.

OK. *Build* was a placeholder for whatever she thinks I want to do. Something about being almost found out for wanting to be good at architecture shakes me to the core.

So will you?

Will I what?

Will you keep going? So I can too?

Yes.

Promise?

I said yes.

OK. So I promise too. And that means dating for you. I mean that.

OK. But even as I text that, I know I don't really mean it. Emily may be cute, but it's not like it was with Leah. It can't be. You can only be that stupid once in your life. Allie needs to go on. Leah would want that. Even though moving on without Leah is hard for both of us.

———◦———

I'm grabbing a drink from the water fountain, coasting through the end of seventh period, trying to damp down the feelings that Allie's texts have lit inside of me, when a guy in a suit pushes past me into student services. Something about his crew cut and straight-backed walk makes me nervous.

Miss Quinlan exits the office, Mr. Perfect in tow, when she notices me dawdling. I figure she's going to lecture me about not being in class, but instead, she beckons to me. "John, just the person we were looking for. Do you have a sec?"

I want to answer her all smart-ass, but the feeling of cement filling my stomach stops me. This must be my probation officer, and I smoked weed, like, last night. Not only not smart, I may be in for it this time. I frantically try to think of the length of time people get in prison for a probation violation in Connecticut. Sweat beads on the back of my neck. The judge told me I could choose to live clean with my mother or go to juvie. All of a sudden, that feels very real.

"I'm Mr. Wexler." His hand shoots out, straight and firm.

I shake his hand, meet his eyes, hoping like mad I'm passing all the obligatory tests. He doesn't have a briefcase or any kind of bag with him, so unless that suit is less tailored than it looks and he's got a pee cup in his pocket, I might be OK.

Miss Quinlan's hand to my arm. "Let's talk in the conference room."

The twenty steps it takes for us to land in this room, the one with the big fancy table and windows and plants and pictures, gives me enough time to hate myself completely. Why can't I ever do the right thing? Why do I always fuck up? Why can't I follow the rules? *Simple fucking rules.*

Mr. Wexler reaches into his jacket's inside pocket. I almost can't stand to look, but when he pulls out papers instead of a specimen cup, my heart stops racing and slows to a slightly elevated drumming. He slides the papers in front of me.

"We are supposed to meet once a week. Give or take. Some of the meetings, Miss Quinlan and I can do over the phone as long as everything continues to go well for you."

I nod. Try not to lick my lips.

"We do need to figure out when you'll come in for your first drug test." He flips through the papers again. "We are required to do nine of those, roughly once a month." He looks up at me. "They are pretty serious. Most of them will be random, but let's plan on doing our first one three weeks from Friday. Cool?"

"Extremely."

Mr. Wexler smiles at me, a thin smile. He's not Steve. And he's not Miss Quinlan. He knows he's just given me a break. It's up to me not to fuck with that. The question remains, can I follow these rules?

"All right then. I hear you play lacrosse?"

"Sort of."

He claps me on the arm. "I played myself. Starting goalie for Townsend four straight years."

He's letting me know about him. Telling me I can't put anything past him. Gotcha.

"Cool."

Mr. Wexler stands, removes his wallet, extracts a business card, and holds it out to me as he says, "I'll stop by to see about you next week. Keep straight, and this will all be painless."

"Count on it."

He smiles and lets go of the card, releasing it and me with one fell swoop.

CHAPTER 11

I don't expect to be nervous before the lacrosse game, but I am. At least I'm not the only one. Matt is jumping up and down in place, Brandon is unexpectedly silent, and even Parker is pacing. The good thing is I'm no longer tired or spacey. Even a weed hangover can't hold up to the adrenaline rush of pregame nerves.

Coach has us gathered on the sideline in a huddle.

"Here's what we need to focus on. Stay in your positions. Play smart. Win the ground balls. It's simple. We focus on mechanics, we win."

The smell of the grass makes my stomach cramp, and the breeze makes my skin feel super alive. A feeling comes over me like I'm less me and more my team.

"And don't let the term scrimmage fool you. Parkland has come to play. They are the biggest stuck-up, entitled, arrogant assholes who ever walked the face of the earth." He holds up one finger. "But they trained for this scrimmage. They want this scrimmage. They want to own us." His eyes go around the huddle, then stop on our goalie. "Luke, hold your position in the net. Play the angles. Don't give them any easy scores."

My beast paces inside me. He wants to go on that field and

make people pay for pissing me off. For reminding me that I'm nothing. For trying to get me to feel emotions I don't want to. For expecting anything from me.

"Everyone listens to their teammates. Keep your eye on numbers twenty-two and thirteen. They are big on making goalies look bad. Do not let them embarrass your teammates."

My anger launches me onto the field as Coach calls my name for the midfield position. I crouch, wait for the bell, then hurl myself at the first Parkland player I see: number twenty-two. He's got the ball, and he smokes me with a juke, and I'm, like, one second from catching him. I hear the crowd groan and know he scored. Because I let him. Fury seeps into my veins. I am not good enough. Maia Cetus punishes me with a powerful roar.

I get in my position and wait for the whistle. This time, I am on number twenty-two right away. We bang bodies and sticks, but he does a side pass to number thirteen, and then we are chasing him, and he's beating the crap out of our players on the way to the goal.

"Strickland, take the face-off," Coach Gibson bellows.

I crouch in front of a kid named Bonner, each of us ready to go to blows.

"Get him, Nate," one of the Parkland middies call.

I become acutely aware of every single sensation. My heart beats strong and hard, readying my muscles to fire. Sweat drips off my face and onto the ground. Nate's glare is trying to wear me down, but he's got nothing that scares me.

The whistle blows. I hit him. The ball is on the ground. I root around for it.

"Scoop, scoop, scoop," Brandon calls.

I hold Nate back with my body and scoop the ball, which I flip out toward Brandon, who takes it downfield. I race after them. No score. I take the next face-off. And the next. At the end of the game, Coach calls us in.

"Nice work, guys. Can't win 'em all. But you did good out there."

Good doesn't feel so good when you don't win. We walk to the locker room, heads hanging low, and that's when I see him. Dad. Standing next to his car in the parking lot. I'm not sure how I feel about Dad being here. I wish he'd brought my Jeep back for sure. I lift my hand to wave to him, and he returns my salute.

———o———

The ride home with Dad starts out decent. "I spoke with your coach. He says you're coming along faster than he thought you would."

"Good." I look out the window.

"More conditioning would help you win some of those ground ball battles though."

I close my eyes. I'm not exactly used to him coaching me. Ryan was supposed to be the jock. It's not like I wasn't good at sports; it's just that after Ryan's accident, there wasn't much time for me to play. And besides, I did not want to be the kid who had no one show for his games. Dad worked a lot. Mom had Ryan. I did the math pretty early and stuck to street ball and pick-up games where it was just you against the other guy. Simple. Perfect. Fun.

Dad continues, "The huddle with that Bonner guy especially, you take one fraction of a second off…"

I tune him out and think about Leah. I picture her standing on the sidelines, cheering me on in her dance team captain uniform. Or even just in shorts and a T-shirt. Leah loved her athletes. She never knew I could be one, and that makes me kind of sad. I think of Allie's texts and how she said I have to move on. I know that—of course I do—but it's like my head defaults right back to Leah all the time.

It starts to rain. Drizzles that fit the mood. I get a text.

Great game. It's from Emily.

I text back. Didn't see you there.

Wouldn't miss it. You looked sharp!

We lost.

You impressed me.

I smile. I impressed her. She's taking care of me like I used to take care of Leah. There's part of me that worries I should do what I said, stay far from her, for her sake, but that would be hard. She lives next door. She came to my game. Obviously, she's kind of already into me. And maybe, just maybe, Allie's right.

"John? Are you even listening to me?"

"I'm sorry. What?"

"I asked how it was going with Mom and Ryan."

I bang my knuckles against the window, try to knock one of

the raindrops off of it. It's stupid and pointless, but it amuses me. "It's fine."

"She said you're doing well in school."

"Yeah. So far, I haven't managed to blow that."

Dad looks like he swallowed something that tasted bad. "Give me a break, John. I'm not criticizing you. I'm trying to help."

I consider telling him to look up the word *criticize* in the dictionary, but that's the kind of smart-ass answer that will keep me from ever getting my Jeep back.

"So how long are you here for?"

"The whole weekend."

"Why?"

"Your mother and I have some things to discuss."

I let those words roll around in my head. "He's getting worse, Dad. He hit Livy."

"I know. We're talking about it."

My head fills with images of Ryan and Livy and Mom and Dad. All of them crying. I can't think of one single way to make things right for everyone. Ryan leaving will make him sad. Him not leaving puts everyone in jeopardy. How long will it be before he really hurts someone? The rain continues to fall. Maybe there's no cure for any of us. No wonder I want to head west.

———o———

Livy and I sit on the couch in the TV room, trying to listen in to Mom and Dad's conference in the dining room.

"It's been over an hour."

"I know." I hand her the bucket of Kentucky Fried Chicken, Dad's concession to Livy's whines for it earlier and, unbelievably, Mom's nod of approval despite how she feels about this stuff.

Livy takes a wing and nibbles on it. "What do you think they're saying?"

I pour gravy on top of one of those plastic bowls of mashed potatoes, dig my spoon in. "What they always talk about. Ryan."

"Ryan's not a what. He's a who."

"Yes. Thank you, my grammar princess."

She pretends to wave her spoon like a scepter. Then her face gets sad. "What about Ryan?"

"What to do about him."

She puts her wing down on her plate. "It's because of me, isn't it?" Her fingers go to the cut above her lip.

"It's because of *him*. He's too aggressive. It has to stop."

"I can't think about him leaving. He'll be so scared." Her eyes well.

"He isn't going anywhere yet. Maybe with the right medication…" Livy scoots over, and I sling my arm around her. "Let them figure it out. Meanwhile, you just have to face off with me for the last biscuit."

Livy picks up her plastic spork and play-stabs my hand. The two of us roll around on the couch, displacing books from the coffee table, but at least she's not crying anymore.

CHAPTER 12

D ad drives me to my appointment with Steve. Thankfully, it starts at a more reasonable eleven o'clock. When he arrives to pick me up, I almost ask Dad how things went with Mom, but I don't. One, because I'm not sure I want to know. Two, my talking about Ryan always gets me in trouble. And right now, I've got to start earning points with Dad. Points are how I get my Jeep back.

He pulls into a parking spot. "I know this whole Ryan thing has been tough on you."

I shift in my seat.

"I want you to know…"

"Dad…"

"Mom told me about that class you're taking. We're both really excited…"

And for some reason that makes no good sense, that pisses me right the fuck off. Like, where's he been this whole time? Like, if he knew I had this talent, why didn't he try to keep taking me to those museums? I'm disgusted with myself and with him. Mostly myself for wanting him to say things that don't even matter anymore. Things like I have a right to a life even if Ryan didn't have one. Like, he should have wanted dreams for me too, no matter what, just because I'm his son.

"John?"

I don't answer. I know I'm being an asshole, but I'm tired of replacing people with other people. Substitute Uncle Dave for Dad. Steve for Mom. Emily for Leah. Ryan for me. Me for anyone else. I put my hand on the handle of the door.

"I just wish you had told me…you know, that you were still interested in…"

Now I'm so done. I'm being nice to Mom, nice to Ryan. There's only so much nice I can do. That's the kind of jerk I am. I want to say Uncle Dave knew. That Dad would've known if he'd paid attention or asked. I want to remind him that dads are supposed to give a crap about their kids, even the ones who do unforgiveable things, like hurt their brothers, because he's got to know I didn't mean to. And I'm sorry.

"John?" Dad says in one last attempt to get on my reasonable side.

"Done in an hour," I call into the car as I close the door.

Dad stares out the window and nods.

I walk into the building, my beast already engaged. I jog up the stairs to avoid having to deal with that annoying mother and her son. I make it to Steve's, open the door, angry-salute the receptionist, and plunk myself down in a chair to wait.

Steve leans out of his office, beckons to me. "John, you're up."

"Awesome sauce."

He waits for me to pass by him before shutting the door. "You seem a little agitated today. You and Dad not getting along?"

I stare at him. "Is there anything you don't know?"

Steve shrugs. "He called. Said he'd be bringing you this morning."

I shake my head, try to bite back my anger. "I'm probably the worst human on the planet, but I just can't take another minute with either one of them."

Steve nods.

"And the thing is, I get it. I understand why they don't want to deal with Ryan, because that all sucks. And why they don't want to deal with me anymore…" I start to pull at the bottom of my jeans where the fabric is torn and ragged.

"You believe they don't want to deal with you?"

I stare him down. Sometimes, he can be so dense.

"Are you sure they're the ones you are angry with?"

"Yeah, pretty much. Unless you count Ryan, yeah. I'm pretty annoyed with him too. Both Old and New Ryan, in case you were wondering." I lean back, pretty impressed with myself and feeling lighter after unloading on Stevie-boy.

"We haven't talked about Old Ryan in a while. Maybe we should start there."

"Why? What's the point?"

Steve looks at his watch. "We've got an hour to fill?"

Smart-ass, but he still gets to me and sends me back to that day in the snow.

Dad was at work. Livy was sleeping. Mom had a deadline and chased us out of the house. "Give me an hour at least," she'd said, coffee mug in hand, her head already lost in the story she was going to write. "Hats and gloves, both. And Ryan, watch your little brother. You're in charge."

Ryan shoved me out the door, a small push but enough to remind me of Mom's last words. He was in charge of me. Just like always.

"Let's go see who's out," he suggested, and I knew that meant he'd find his friends to hang with and dump me, no matter what Mom had said.

Nobody was out yet. It was early, like nine o'clock, so it was still super cold. Ryan threw a snowball at me, so I nailed him back. But after a few minutes, we were both shivering. We sat on our stoop.

"How long?" I asked.

He looked at his phone. "Twenty minutes."

"We're going to freeze to death out here."

"Drama queen." He took a handful of snow and put it down my back. So I knocked him off the steps. Soon, we were both drenched, teeth chattering, but no way we could go in early. Mom would kill us.

"Let's build an igloo," Ryan said, and with that, I got so excited, I forgot how cold I was.

"How do we start?" I asked, already following him to the backyard. Like I knew he would know the right way.

Steve, completely oblivious about my walk down memory lane, looks at my file, nods, then takes off his glasses. He leans forward, hands flat on his legs. This is Stevie-boy body language that signals he's about to launch a doozy. What now? I almost tell him to keep it to himself, but the words, which are ready to spill, become permanently sealed inside me when he leans forward and says, "Tell me about Leah." And just like that, Steve slays me. "You seemed to have left her out when we last spoke."

It takes a second for me to catch my breath. I shake my head. Go from leaning back in the chair, relaxed and calm, to now sitting upright, muscles engaged, ready to rumble. "Really, man?"

"Yes. Really."

"Wow, Steve. Dad's paying the bills, so you've got to deliver for him?"

He waves off me and my bad attitude. "Tell me about Leah."

"How come all of a sudden my giving it up about Dad isn't enough? I thought this was what I'm supposed to do…vomit my feelings and you give me a gold star and everything is fucking perfect."

Steve puts his hands together. "You know you can say anything you want to in here, John. And it's not a question of it being enough. But I can't help you if you only talk about safe subjects."

"Since when are my feelings about my parents 'safe' for anyone?"

"Leah made you vulnerable. We don't have to talk about her now, but she's a sign of huge growth for you. You fell in love. But she's also someone who let you down."

The rage that's building in me is too much even for my dragon to take. He cowers as the flames rage. It's one of those ten-alarm fires that no one ever wants to face. "This would be a good time to stop talking, man. You know nothing about her. She never let *me* down. I let *her* down."

He stands. "I don't believe that."

I stand also. "She's off-limits." My eyes go to the door.

"Why is she off-limits? Because she got to you?"

I see red. I want to throw things. I want to destroy every-thing. I can almost hear the sounds the pictures on his desk would make if I swept them to the ground. Sharp shrill crashes, without the boom of the heavy china cabinet. More like Mom's lamps. Her vases.

"Tell me about Leah." Steve's voice is calm, but he's leaning forward, showing me he's ready to take whatever heat I throw at him.

And that makes me want to go the other way entirely, so I try to make the cold find me. I try to bathe in the ocean. Roll in the snow with my brother. I'm standing here, trying my best to put the fire out, but Steve's got other plans. "John?"

I walk over to the wall with the caged dragon. Lean against it. "Why are you doing this?" I know I sound weak, but I can't help it.

"Because I want to help you."

"Not like this." I'm almost pleading. "*This* is not helping."

"You need this, so even if you hate me, I have to do it."

He moves toward me, forcing me to close my eyes, try to bring back the calm, but I can't. All I can feel is the huge black pit that's followed me around since she killed herself. If only I could fall into that pit for real, let it swallow me up. I'd do it if it would stop the gnawing pain that's eating me up. I wasn't good enough for Leah. I wasn't enough. Just like I was never enough for Mom. Or Dad.

"John? You deserve to be loved."

I swipe at a stupid tear that slipped out. "Yeah. Right."

"You do."

I turn my gaze to the caged reptile, who's sitting there, not caring at all. I should be in that cage, not him. I'm the one who wants to light everyone on fire.

"I know she hurt you, John."

It's all I can do to not pound on the dragon's cage. Not to scream at him about how stupid he must have been to get caught like this. How he went from being the coolest beast in the world to a pathetic pet in a cage. Steve comes up behind me. His hands fall on my shoulders. I try to wrench free. He holds on. I bend my head. The tears come, and I'm ashamed. My throat burns with the words I won't say.

"She was important to you."

I lean on my arm. "Stop. Can't you stop?"

"I remember the first girl I loved. How it felt when she left me."

"She didn't leave me."

He squeezes my shoulders.

"She just couldn't stay." I breathe out. Remember what it felt like when I first heard. I was in the park, closing a deal, when a kid I barely knew, a total jerk, told me. "Did you hear about that cheerleader? Killed herself?" He made this sound when he'd said it, a small laugh, like he couldn't believe how stupid she was for doing it.

I remember thinking Leah wasn't a cheerleader—she was a

dancer. I remember hoping it was some other girl. Anyone but her. Even though I knew it was wrong to hope that someone else's family would be going through the pain. I knew what it was like to lose someone, and it sucked. But not Leah. It couldn't be. Only, I knew it was. The minute he'd said it, I knew. I wanted to beat the fuck out of that asshole, how he let the information slip out of his uncaring lips as if it was no big deal. I pretended he was talking about a speeding ticket so I wouldn't hit him. So I wouldn't kill the messenger. But I knew. Leah was dead. My life was over. I hit him in the face. His blood squirted out of him, and that made me happy. So I hit him again. And again. And again.

"I know," Steve says, bringing me back to the present.

But he doesn't know how it felt to lose Leah. No one does.

"This isn't your fault."

How could he possibly know that? I was supposed to protect her.

"You can't keep people in this world. You can't change the past. You can't go back in time and make it so Ryan never got hit. You're only human. But you're a damned good human."

No. I'm not. If I were...

"Tell me about her."

I shake my head.

"Was she pretty?"

A sob comes out. But not because she was pretty. Because she was beautiful. To me.

"Did you feel better just being with her?"

127

I nod. The muscles in my shoulders sag.

"I bet she felt that way about you. I bet she felt like you took care of her."

And just like that, the weight feels a little lighter, and I hate him for breaking me and then helping me. I hate him. I hate myself. Because she left me. Because I wasn't good enough.

He turns me to face him. Puts his hands on my shoulders. I lower my head.

"The thing is, John, you have to do all the work, not just deal with the stuff that's on the surface."

I wipe my eyes with my sleeve. "You said I didn't always have to tell you everything."

"I lied. You can't keep this stuff in."

"Why the hell not?"

"Because it'll kill you, man."

"Maybe I'm already dead."

"Nope. No way. Because if you were, none of this would hurt anymore."

He goes to the fridge and pulls out a Coke. He pops the top and hands it to me. I take a swig, let it cool me as I drink and drink and drink. I walk to the couch and sit, blindsided and numb and just too tired to talk.

"Tell me one thing about her."

"I could always make her laugh." The words come out even before I realize I'm talking. "She had the most beautiful smile. And I loved her hair. It was so shiny. So pretty. So…"

"Alive?" Steve asks.

"Yeah. She was so alive." It feels stupid to say when she's not now. "She was always so worried about what people thought of her, but she shouldn't have been. She was beautiful. In every way."

"I know this hurts, John, but I'm glad you did this."

"Did what?"

"I'm glad you let yourself be loved."

I sit with that for a minute. How it felt when Leah needed me. How she looked at me when it was just the two of us.

"All the anger inside you after the Ryan accident. All the pain you felt with your parents, and you still allowed yourself to be loved."

"I never said she loved me. I don't even know if she did."

"I don't believe that for a minute. I think she loved you just as much as you loved her."

I stare at a spot on the floor.

"The next time you fall in love, maybe it'll be with someone who does for you as much as you do for them. Maybe you'll decide you deserve to be taken care of too."

I want to scoff at Steve and his stupid-assed psychic predictions. I want to ask him if he's running one of those hotlines for lonely people they show on TV in the middle of the night. I want to be all smart-ass, but I just can't. Maybe because I'm tired from all this but maybe also because there's a tiny piece of me, a speck really, that kind of hopes he's right.

CHAPTER 13

I almost consider canceling my date with Emily, because my head is still so messed up from the emotional lobotomy Steve dished out, but sitting at a table for two at Joey's Pizza, my control is almost back, and my checkout plan is one doctored Coke away from getting started. Emily folds her slice in half, pulls pieces of the melted cheese off the end, takes tiny bites, sucking the sauce off her finger, and it's so cute, it almost makes me laugh.

"What?" she demands.

"Nothing."

"Sorry I don't eat salads like the girls you're used to."

"How do you know what kind of girls I'm used to?"

"I'm pretty sure I could guess."

I put my hand over hers. "Don't." My eyes are serious but not angry.

She goes back to picking at the cheese on her slice. She smiles. "Soooo, new conversation?"

"Probably best." I nod soberly but add a smile so she knows I'm still playing.

I drink my Coke, letting it cool me inside and out. Then I pull out a flask I've filled with Jack. She watches as I pour a small splash of my favorite drink into my soda. Much smaller than if I were going to be drinking this alone. "This is why you should have ordered a soda, but don't worry, I'll share."

"You're incorrigible," Emily says.

"That's just a big word for sexy, right?"

She laughs so much, she almost does a spit-take, and I realize I'm having a really good time with this girl.

"So tell me about you. Your family. What makes Emily tick?"

Her eyes go a little darker, and I'm sorry I pushed. She takes a sip of water. Puts it down on the table, plays with the condensation drip on the side of the glass. "Well, I have an older brother, Christian, who is prelaw. Soon to be at Harvard Law. My sister, Abby, is the oldest in the family, and she is an accountant in New York. I am the laid-back one in my family."

My turn to almost spit-take.

"What?"

"While you are very easy to be with, I wouldn't consider you exactly easygoing."

"Why not?"

I take a bite of pizza, chew, and swallow it down with a huge drink of my mildly doctored Coke. "Let's see, you get to school a half hour early. From what I hear, you're a beast on the field. You're taking a crap ton of AP classes, and—this is my favorite part—you are going into the super highly competitive world of journalism. Yeah. Not laid-back. Maybe in your family but not laid-back in terms of anyone else's family."

Emily lights up with my little dissertation about her, and that gives me a warm feeling.

"So what did your father think of your mad lacrosse skills?"

"I'm pretty sure he was hoping for better."

She shakes her head like she's pissed at Dad, which makes me feel good in a way. "You really went after the ball, and you did great on the face-offs."

"I need to do better. Be better."

She swallows a bite of pizza. Nods. Tilts her head. "You played really well for your first game in forever."

"Nah. It's like I've got to be a jock for myself and for Ryan. I don't know, that sounded way whinier than I meant it."

"No. I understand what you mean." She eyes my Coke. "May I?"

I slide it to her. She takes a sip. "Yum."

I drink again. "It's like they were made for each other."

"You are a booze romantic." She takes another swig, then slides the glass back. I take my turn, then push it her way. She drinks some more. "But I think you're right."

"More like I'm a booze genius," I say.

"You just might be, Jax Teller. I mean…"

"Man…" I pretend-slap the table. Turn my biggest smile on her. "You girls are all the same…want a bad boyfriend to hold on to as we drive away recklessly on our Harleys."

"Well, yeaaah." Her smile loosening with each passing moment.

By the time I pay the check and we are ready to go, I can tell Emily's relaxed, because she has to really concentrate to stand without knocking over her water glass and to find the keys in her purse, which she hands to me. "You mind?"

"Not at all." Another benefit of her drinking, I get to drive. One slightly Jacked-up Coke won't affect my driving skills. Mad or otherwise.

————o————

I take us back to the park where we took Ryan and Livy. It's deserted at night, too early even for people to park and do their thing. I take out my flask and hand it to her. She drinks, then closes her eyes. This girl's not only drank before, she's missed it.

"Take it easy, princess."

"Princess? I'm not sure I like that designation."

"Jeez, I was trying to compliment you."

"Then call me a queen. Queens have power."

I blink. The memory of Leah telling me she wanted to be king one day almost knocks the wind out of me. She'd said it almost exactly like Emily did. She'd said, "Kings have more power."

Emily's hand goes on mine. Her voice breaks through the fog. "What's the matter? John? Did I do something wrong?"

I blink. Shake my head. "No. I'm sorry. I'm fine. Just remembering something."

"Something or someone?"

I let the liquid slide down my throat like honey until I've emptied the flask. I screw the top back on.

"I'm sorry. I didn't mean…"

"You didn't do anything wrong. It was just…"

Her eyes are so soft and understanding, and after the whole Steve session today, Leah is front and center, and I feel like she's with me now as much as when she was alive. The alcohol has loosened my mind and, apparently, my tongue. "I had a girlfriend. Leah. Her name was Leah."

She nods.

"Leah. Um. She died last year." I fiddle with the knobs on the radio, even though it's not on. "She killed herself."

Emily's hand goes on my shoulder. It's a heavy weight, even though I can tell it's the kind of touch that is intended to be the opposite. "I'm so sorry."

I nod. I wish I'd kept my stupid mouth shut.

She opens the glove compartment. "I brought this." It's a pint of Jack and makes me feel better just looking at it. She hands it to me, and I crack it open and bring it to my lips. Before I'm even done drinking, her hand reaches out. "You're gonna be OK to drive me home, right?"

"Yeah. Not even close to being drunk."

"I've not exactly been truthful with you since we've met. But then again, I haven't been truthful with anyone." She drinks some more.

"What do you mean?"

"I'm kind of a problem girl."

I can't help laughing. "You are *not* a problem."

She's slurring her words now. "I am. I'm serious."

I stare at her perfectly innocent face. "What could you have done?"

She wipes a tear. "It's not me exactly. It's my cousin, Dylan." She leans back in her seat, her shoulders slumped. "He screws up a lot."

My face must ask the question, because she answers before my words come out. "He doesn't go to this school. He used to. Before."

I let the words she doesn't want to say fill in the gaps between us, and I wonder if those texts she's always getting are from him. Part of me hopes they are, not some other guy.

She takes another drink. "He got kicked out."

"I figured. It's OK, you don't have to…"

"I tried to help him. They…everyone sort of gave up on him."

"But not you?"

"I couldn't. He was everything to me." She puts her hand out. I put the bottle in her hand. "Go easy on this, OK?"

"Too late." She drinks some more. "I grew up with him. He was my best friend." She wipes her eyes.

"What happened to him?"

"He sort of went crazy, I guess."

"Why?"

She huffs. Shoots me a look. "People need a reason to go crazy?"

My turn to drink. "I guess not."

"Anyway, he got in a lot of trouble, and instead of turning him in, I helped him. And now, I've got to be the consummate good girl. To make it all up to my parents for, you know, going against the grain, ruining their perfect image in town."

"So isn't this"—I hold up the bottle—"kind of risky?"

"They don't need to know, do they?"

"No, not at all. Not from me anyway." I reach out and hold her hand.

135

"The thing is, I know you are biding your time here. I guess I'm kind of doing that too. And we both need to build cred with our parents…"

"So the good girl thing wasn't real?"

"It's just kind of new." She faces me. Her lips are so close to mine. "I mean, I never was that bad to begin with, even with Dylan and his friends."

My ears start to get jealous. "His friends?"

"Yeah. I sort of dated one of them for a while."

"And now?"

"He and I are just friends. It's better that way."

"His loss." I put my hand under her chin and bring her mouth toward mine. I kiss her softly. Her mouth is exactly like her: small, sweet, sincere.

I've been with tons of girls since Leah died, but none of them mattered, and now this one is here with me, a girl I can't help but like. We pull apart, and I put my hands in her hair. Her eyes look at me like I'm this person I'm not. And I feel myself want to push this, but I remember Livy telling me I can't hurt Emily. Emily, who's already been hurt enough. So I kiss her one more time, soft, then pull back. "I should take you home."

She puts her hand to her lips like they're chapped or something. "Yeah. Maybe that's best." She stares out the window and shakes her head. I've hurt her while trying to protect her.

"Em…"

"No." She holds up her hand. "Emily. No one calls me Em."

I put my hand under her chin. "I just want to be careful with you."

"Sure. No problem." She shakes loose of my grasp and stares out the window.

The ride back home is silent. That just reinforces my decision to keep things light. Before she gets out of the car, she reaches out, grabs my dragon necklace. "Tell me about this?" She's super close to me again. "It's very cool."

I feel each breath she releases as she speaks. Her breath steaming in the cool air. My face burning. My body heating. Because of her. So now I feel close to her and pissed at her at the same time. Didn't I just tell her we needed to keep our distance? I slip her fingers off the medallion. "It's nothing."

"It doesn't look like nothing."

"What does it look like?"

She stares into my eyes, gives me a smart-assed look. "It looks like you don't want me to get too close."

I shake my head. "You are dangerous."

"I get that." She thrusts the bottle of Jack into my hands. "Will you hold on to this for me?"

"You sure you trust me with it?"

"I just meant I wanted you to keep *me* from drinking it."

"Sure."

"Drinking doesn't help. Not really."

I want to argue with her—drinking helps me—but maybe we are looking for different things. I just want peace, and she wants to make things right. Making it right means keeping it as cool as possible with this girl. But I'm starting to feel like going completely the opposite way.

CHAPTER 14

I make my way to breakfast, hungover as shit but grateful that Mom isn't forcing us to do this breakfast at an actual restaurant like she used to. I grab a mug of coffee, sit in my seat, and note that Rosie isn't here, so that means we're going to have some sort of family meeting. That's cool with me. I'm all for putting our shit on the table.

Livy hasn't even gotten the plate of eggs to the table before Mom starts, "Your father and I have made a decision."

I want to tell her she's breaking decorum by speaking before we are all seated, but she looks so tired and tense, so the truth is, I feel bad for her.

"We were thinking…"

"We are going to try a place for Ryan," Dad finishes for her. His hand is super close to hers, and it's so weird to see them acting like they don't dislike each other or judge each other.

Mom nods, but I see she's working like crazy not to cry. She dabs her mouth with a napkin and puts her hands in her lap.

Ryan kicks his foot and flaps his hand around, but he's not close enough to anything to do any damage. He laughs, and it kills me, because even though he hears what we're saying, he has no idea what is going on. That Mom and Dad are talking about making him leave.

Mom breathes out, hard, and for some reason, that makes Ryan laugh. She smiles back at him, and I see how cute he can be. She spoons some pureed crap in his mouth, and he takes a small bite, if you can call it that. It takes hours to feed my brother like this, him slopping and munching with the food falling out of his mouth. Ryan's food has been one of the long-ranging battles between my parents. I remember the arguments. Then finally the decision.

It was, like, eight years ago. Mom was sitting in the living room, her hand on Ryan's chair. I remember she was crying back then too. "He should be able to eat real food."

"He still can. This is just to help with other things, like medication when he's sick."

"Or feeding him faster. Sure, it can take him two hours to eat a full meal. But honestly, Scott, I have the time."

"You have other children who need you, Lydia. You used to have a career too. Don't you want to take that back?"

"Not at Ryan's expense."

I remember thinking what about at our expense? Livy's and mine, but it had been made very clear by this time that she thought we should take care of ourselves, because we could.

Mom looks at Ryan now, still so long and skinny, still not able to eat well, even after they put the G-tube in, the one that was supposed to stop all the fights over his meals and meds. But that's not how things work in my family. Not with Ryan anyway. In the end, he had the operation—Dad won that one—but Mom still refused to feed him that way. And eventually, the G-tube war got Dad kicked out of the house. I remember the day he sat Livy and me down and told us he was moving.

"Just a half hour away. I'll still see you guys all the time."

I remember feeling that the world was falling away and that Mom was a dangerous person to get mad.

Mom stares at Ryan, knowing that his fighting eating a simple breakfast is not exactly making her case but speaking up anyway. "If he goes there…" Her eyes shine with the water-works I know will just piss off Dad.

My stomach clenches. I can hear Livy breathe in. Ryan says, "Shit! Shit! Shit!" But he's laughing. Then he fake-hits himself on the head to make everyone laugh.

"He's going to be fine." Dad actually takes her hand this time. "You can't act like this in front of him. He picks up on your reactions to things."

She nods, and I am rendered speechless about how the two of them have seemed to come to some sort of understanding all of a sudden. It's one of those small things that actually mean much bigger things. Mom starts to cry, maybe because she's like me and when people are nice, it makes it harder to hold in the tears. She puts her napkin on the table and disappears.

Dad points to us. "Eat up."

Ryan starts kicking his feet and complaining. "More! More! More!" His arms swing. Livy gets out of her chair and holds his hands. She starts to feed him.

"Where?" I'm surprised at how tight my throat is.

"There's a place about fifteen miles from here. A group home. I think it'll be good for him."

"We're just trying it out," Mom returns in time to say.

"When?" I ask, but there's no point. Dad's a man of action. So I'm not surprised at all when he answers.

"Monday." He clears his throat and starts eating his eggs, pushing them on his fork with his knife.

Mom, Livy, and I sit, silent, as he scrapes his plate with the knife and fork. Finally, he looks up.

"I know, but it's for the best." He motions to the food. "Eat. It's not going to help anyone to starve yourselves."

———o———

I'm sitting in my room, trying to load the software on my new laptop, when there's a knock on my door. Livy. I can tell by the smallness.

"Who is it?" I ask in a funny voice.

She opens the door. "Can I come in?"

"Of course."

She walks to my dresser, her eyes searching my pictures, making me instantly glad I put the one of Leah in the drawer for now. "I'm worried."

"About Ryan or Mom?"

"Both." She turns to face me.

"Me too."

"You're supposed to tell me not to worry."

"Can't. You're too smart for that."

"You think he'll be OK?"

"I hope so." I walk over to the bed and throw myself back on it.

"Have you thought about what things would have been like if…"

I throw my arm over my eyes. "It's all I used to think about before…"

"Before Leah?"

I close my eyes. "Who told you about her?"

"Dad said I had to be nice to you when you came home, and I asked why."

"You don't ever have to be nice to me." I sit up. Then I reach into my night table and take out my favorite picture of Leah. I hold it toward her, and Livy hurries to take it.

"She was so beautiful." She looks at me full on. "Do you miss her?"

I lie back on the bed and close my eyes. "Yes."

She jumps in bed next to me, her little body barely making the mattress bend. Her voice is a whisper. "Do you still love her?"

"Yes."

"Are you going to be all right?"

"Do I have a choice?" I cover my eyes with my hands.

Her fingers pry my hands, trying to make me look at her. "That's not what I asked."

"Yes, you little maniac, I'll be fine."

She lies back on the bed next to me. "Would she have liked me?"

"She would have loved you."

"How do you know?"

"Because she has a little sister. Had one."

"What's her name? The little sister, I mean."

"Allie."

"Do you think Allie would like me?"

"Yes."

"Can we go see her someday?"

"Yeah."

We keep doing this, the music of my little sister's endless questions lulling me like the waves on that beach I keep dreaming about.

CHAPTER 15

I'm not expecting much from Mom when I go downstairs in the morning. She's not sitting at her stool. Instead, she's standing at the sink, looking out the window. She's got her coffee in her hand, but I'd take bets that she hasn't had any yet.

"I'm sorry, John," she says as I look in the pantry, find the to-go cups, and pour myself some coffee. "I was going to do that. I lost track of time."

"It's fine, Mom. I'm fine. And Ryan's going to be fine too."

She sips her coffee and nods. "Mmm."

I'm sure there's no lunch packed, and I'm not even sure I could stomach it anyway, but she says, "Lunch is in the fridge."

I grab the bag and kiss her on the cheek just as Emily beeps.

"I'm serious. He's going to be fine. This might even be good for him."

She turns to face me, her eyes staring deep into mine. "I know. Harder for me than him, I'm sure. Boys are supposed to leave their mothers."

"We don't always want to."

This time, her smile is a little bigger. Emily beeps again. "See you later."

"Have a good day," Mom says, and I get goose bumps. No

matter what's happened, no matter how chaotic, Mom always calls that after me as I left for school. Most times, it annoyed me. Pissed me the hell off to be honest, but now it gets to me in an entirely different way. I wonder if I'd been different back then, if I'd not been so angry all the time, would life have been better? These thoughts circle my mind, loop around my heart as I let the regret settle into my bones, where it belongs. My dragon doesn't even lift its head. It's like it knows it wasn't all Mom's fault. The door clicks behind me, and I make myself a promise to try harder.

Emily waves to me as I get in the car, but I can tell she's elsewhere too.

"You OK?" My stomach actually clenches as I wait for her answer. Have I ruined things with her already?

She waves me away. "I'm so not ready for my AP psych test today, and I need to get an A to keep my grade in that class."

"What's your grade now?"

"A low A. Ninety. So I can't slip." She gnaws on her fingernail.

"So what if you get a B?"

Her eyes skate to me, open super wide. "If I get even one B… they take my car. They freeze my bank. I've got nothing."

"What? That's crazy."

She nods. "It's the symptoms that freak them out."

"The what?"

"Dylan used to get straight As. He was uber smart. I mean, he *is* uber smart. He was taking all the top classes. Was on swim team. Then…"

"Don't they think maybe all the pressure is what did him in?"

She shakes her head. "No. Genetics did."

"What does that mean?"

"Nothing. It just means if I slip up, they come at me like crazy. I have to keep good grades. Stay in shape. Play field hockey. I have to be this cyclone of production or…"

I can't help the fire that goes through me. This is like Leah's parents. Only worse.

"I want to go see Dylan in a few weeks. I told him I would visit. And I need my money and my car to get there."

All I can think about is getting my Jeep back. Giving this girl everything she needs.

"I'm doing fine in all my classes. It's just this one…"

"You want me to drive while you study?"

She shoots me a really sweet smile, but her eyes stay worried and glassy. "No thanks. Can't read when I'm in a car."

When we get to school, she parks and flies out of the car. "I gotta go meet with…"

I nod, but she rushes off ahead of me.

I'm actually grateful that we got here early so I can pull out my new laptop with the CAD software on it. I fire it up and start moving through designs I'd worked on last night. I'm sitting at one of the tables in the courtyard, studying, when Mr. Bonham stops by.

"Morning, John."

I look up.

"You're doing a great job in my class so far. I think you really have an eye for this, and that, paired with *decent* math skills"—he puts air quotes around the word decent—"could mean that architecture or CAD tech could be good career choices for you."

I want to ask him if Miss Quinlan put him up to this. Or Mr. Hicks, but I just sit here, listening to a teacher say good things about me, no matter the reason, which is so weird.

"Anyway, we have a district-wide contest in two weeks. I think the arch design you are coming up with might have a good chance for an award. The first round is simply looking at how you approach the project. You can hand-draw it, build it, or do it on the computer—totally up to you. If you go to semis, that's the interesting competition. You get to build an actual model out of anything you like." He laughs. "One guy used Rice Krispies treats. It was a judge favorite."

I think about the Coke-bottle igloo Ryan and I made after that winter one in the yard. The one I ruined. I'd researched how to make a Coke igloo on the computer and made Mom save tons of two-liter bottles so I could do it. Ryan said it was a baby project, especially compared to the one we'd almost built that winter, but I knew I could get the arch right if I had big blocks to build it with.

"Some kids build huge models, bridges, whatever floats your boat. One kid even welded a boat one time." He smiles, his arms crossed in front of him, resting on his protruding stomach. "OK if I submit it for you?"

"Yeah, sure. That would be great. I mean, if you think it's good enough."

"Stay after class today. I'll give you the info then."

"Great."

He walks away, and I wonder if this is a good idea, because all of a sudden, my stomach feels like it's dropping. It's a feeling I don't recognize. Nerves. Like pregame nerves but over school. So strange. But the word *welding* stays with me. I text Uncle Dave.

Going to do an architecture project for school. If I make it to semis, I can weld a 3-D model.

That's my boy! I'll send you that beginner's kit.

Apprentice kit you mean.

If that helps you sleep at night. Then, Proud of you.

That feels like a light inside of me. Dad probably won't get it why this is so cool, but Uncle Dave does. He may not be an architect, but he sure loves architecture. Like me.

CHAPTER 16

Ryan is only in the group home for two days and ten hours before Mom pulls him out. I come home from practice Wednesday to find Rosie making dinner, Mom yelling on the phone at Dad, and Livy sitting at the table, trying to do her homework while Ryan screams from his wheelchair.

"What did you want me to do, Scott? They were starving him."

I can only picture Dad's reaction on the other end of the phone.

Livy shoots me a look, then goes back to her homework as Rosie serves her homemade mac and cheese and steamed broccoli.

"Just in time, John," Rosie says. "Wash up."

My eyes go to the dining room, where Mom has retreated. I can see her slumped in one of the chairs. Her hair is a mess, and she's picking at it like a crazy person. Her cough interrupts her attempt to defend herself.

"She needs to go to the doctor," I say.

A plate is plunked down in front of me. "Wash up. I mean it," Rosie answers. "You can't help her right now. Just eat."

I go to the sink and do as I'm told—but quickly so I don't miss overhearing too much of Mom's conversation.

"I know that, but… Ensure? Are you kidding me? There's all sorts of stuff in there that will make him sick. He can't tolerate it. We have never fed him that." A pause. Then, "*I* never fed him that."

I take a bite.

"Come on, Ryan," Rosie says. "Bath time."

"Is it too much to ask that our son get to eat like a normal person?"

I give Livy a look, and she gives one right back. This fight is one they've fought over and over again. Why Ryan couldn't go to school. Why he couldn't go to camp. Why he couldn't...

"He got home, like, an hour ago," Livy says. "Dad must have paid someone from that place to rat Mom out, because he knew as soon as it happened."

I take a bite of Rosie's awesome cooking, but it doesn't taste right eating it during their fight.

"Just stop it. I did *not* want this to fail. You have no idea how hard any of this is." Mom starts to cry. Then coughs. Then cries some more.

Livy's face falls, and I wish like mad I had my car so I could take her out of the fallout zone. We'd go get pizza and Cokes. But because I screwed up, I've got no play. I think about texting Emily, but she's kind of wrapped up in her stuff, and I don't want to bother her, so instead, I say, "Finish up and I'll let you beat me in *Super Smash Bros.*"

She tries to smile.

"Or..." I grab her plate and mine. She grabs the cups and forks and napkins. "We can finish this in my room while we watch *Scream.*"

We're carrying everything we've got, making way for Rosie, who's gone down the hall to make up Ryan's bath. They converted Mom's office to Ryan's bedroom, because it was downstairs. "It's OK, babies." Rosie puts her hand on Livy's cheek. "Change is hard for everyone."

I want to believe Rosie. God knows she's been with us long enough to know how all this goes.

"This will happen. They will find a place for Ryan where he can be more functional and independent. Where he will have kids like him to hang out with and activities to do." She winks at me. "Trust me. It's all going to work out."

I want to trust Rosie—I do—but my beast is pacing now. Pacing and growling about how nothing ever changes and nothing ever will.

"Come on, Livy," I call over my shoulder.

Mom disappears into the shadows of the living room. I hear her coughing and crying, and I feel like my entire world is cracking.

———o———

I'm working on my arch project. Like Mr. Bonham said, I went 3-D so I can get the angles right. I've built a tiny model with pieces of gum, so the whole room smells minty fresh. Then I drew the damn thing. Now I'm trying to match what I've done on the computer screen. I do not want to enter this contest with sticks of gum or Rice Krispies treats or cell phones. I want to do this right.

Mom knocks. I don't even turn to face her. I've got stuff to do. "Come in."

She slides into my room, flattens the covers in place on my bed, and sits, her hands in her lap. She looks so small and thin, like a doll, so unreal. She smooths her hair down in the back. "I just wanted to tell you I'm really excited about your awards presentation next week."

"It's no big deal. I probably won't even win anything." I look at my drawing and hit a key on the computer but know that I've messed it up even before it draws the point. I hit undo. Undo. Undo. God, I wish life had an undo button.

"Dad's coming in for it. Rosie said she'd stay with Ryan so I can go too."

"So he's not going back?"

Mom covers her mouth while she coughs, her body hunching with each spasm. She puts a tissue to her nose. "No. Not to that place at least. I know your father…"

I put my hand up. "I've got work to do, Mom."

Mom comes closer. "What are you doing?"

I point to the gum model and then to the drawing and then to the computer. "It's screwed up, and if I don't fix it, it won't matter who shows it to what competition, because I won't even enter."

"No. You have to." She stares at the model. "You'll figure it out."

"I hope."

"Have you thought about sending a picture to Dad or Uncle Dave?"

Wow. Mom recommending Uncle Dave seems so unreal that I

153

almost balk, but I have to admit, it's not a bad idea. I snap a picture of the gum bridge and then the drawing and send it to him.

This is wrong. Can you help?

He texts back right away. What the hell is it?

It's supposed to be a bridge arch.

What's it made out of?

Trident gum.

That's your problem. I always use Wrigley's.

I laugh. Smart-ass.

Better than being a dumb-ass. Check the numbers on each side.

Like I wouldn't have thought of that?

Count again, but mark them as you count. Your eyes play tricks sometimes.

I grab a pen and put a dot on each one. Turns out I double counted on the right. Bingo. And then I'm back in time again in that igloo with Ryan.

He'd made me lay on the ground to make the snow angel that would be the guide for how big to make our igloo. Then I had to stamp down the snow into a sheet of ice. He got to use the saw, because he was older and he didn't want us to get in trouble. I was supposed to pack the snow between the bricks.

"Pass me the next one," Ryan said, his hand stretched out for the next block of snow. That's what little brothers do, right? Assist?

I held tight to my brick. Put it where it went on my side of the igloo. Ryan puffed out a cold breath, which I could tell was filled with all the annoyance of my little mutiny.

"Come on, we need another one there." He pointed to his side, but I'd counted. I knew where I put the brick was right, but he'd never listen.

We were both squeezed in so tight, it was hard to move. He was looking at the roof, but it was a little heavy, and the angle of the arch wasn't quite right. I counted the bricks we'd made out of one of Mom's empty planters, but it was hard to make the bricks line up in my head while I counted—it was like they jumped everywhere.

Our shoulders bumped, and his angry movements sent a cascade of ice and snow all over us, and I had to pull my scarf over my mouth. He was still filling in little cracks and making his side perfect. I just wanted to start building the fire he said we could. I sat up. My head hit part of the roof and opened a hole on my side, the lower side of the igloo. Within seconds, the whole wall collapsed, burying us under all that weight. I didn't know if it was the snow or him or both. I just knew I couldn't move. I couldn't breathe. Terror wedged itself inside my throat. Mom was in her study. Dad was at work. I'd read pirate stories where people fell into pits of quicksand and died.

We were going to die. I was going to die. I was dying.

Hands lifted me. Ryan's hands. He pulled me out of the wreckage I'd caused. I expected him to be angry, but instead, he brushed off my shoulders, pushed me back. *"You are such a little pain in the ass!"* But he was smiling. *"You scared the shit out of me."*

I wanted to yell back. I wanted to tell him he always made me feel like a little dipshit. I wanted to curse and scream, because I knew this was my fault. My stupid eyes. My stupid temper. I should *have listened to him. I knew it, and so did he. I stood staring at him, anger pouring off me, and he just laughed it away. Then he kicked at the remains of the igloo. "Hurry, before Mom finds out what we did."*

I joined him, smashing the rest of it. Glad my mistake would melt into the ground and no one else would know. Glad that my big brother saved me. Just then, Mom opened the door. She waved us in. "I've got hot chocolate ready. You must be freezing."

Ryan pushed me so he could go in first. And just like that, he became my jerky big brother again.

Mom cocks her head. "What?"

"Never mind. I think I fixed it."

"Good. Your ceremony is from six to eight. We're planning to go out to dinner afterward. Unless that's too late for you."

"It's fine," I say, but I'm still mixed up in the memory, cold and numb and so annoyed with myself. That igloo was when I started to get competitive with Ryan. I wanted to be better than he was. I didn't care what happened. I just had to be right, even if it killed us.

Mom turns to leave, then stops again. "I never told you how sorry I am about your girl." Her gaze skates over my pictures lined up on the dresser, and I'm annoyed that she's going there, but it's not like I didn't know she would.

My girl. Leah. I'm speechless.

"If we'd known…"

I shake my head. I don't tell Mom that Leah didn't exactly tell anyone about me either.

"John, I know I've made a terrible mess of our lives since Ryan…"

My hand goes out. "Mom, stop."

Like a steam engine plowing through me, the memories come. *The sound of glass shattering. Dad saying, "That's great, Lydia."*

"You like that?" Her voice mean and threatening.

Then the coffee burning me. Burning.

Livy crying. Mom saying, "Shush, baby, shush."

I shake my head to clear the memory. I can't keep doing this. This is why I don't want to be back here. The constant never-fucking-stopping train of memories that bury me.

Mom stands there, completely unaware of the war I'm going through. As usual. "I think you and I are too much alike sometimes."

She wants me to answer her, but I can't.

"I know you didn't want to come back here. I know I make you… I"—she gathers her hands in front of her, takes a breath—"I know I make you kind of crazy, but I'm glad you're here, John. This could be a second chance for us. You don't want that?"

I try to count to ten. Twenty. One hundred. Anything to stop this landslide of feelings. Not just about Mom but also about how unfair life is. How I could have been the one to die so many times. When I fell off my bike on that trail. The hundred or more times I ran into the street without looking, chasing some stupid ball. The igloo that collapsed and buried me. I could have died any of those times, but I didn't. But the Old Ryan did that day on the driveway. And it didn't make any fucking sense. None of it. How could one person make bad decision after bad decision without consequence, while, with Ryan, one second of stupid luck took everything from him? Why did Leah die when someone could have found her and saved her? When I should have. She gave me her phone for cripes' sake.

"John? I'm trying to talk to you. You can talk to me about this."

She just sliced me open seven different ways, and she wants me to talk while my guts are pouring out of me, slopping on the floor. We both know she blames me for Ryan's accident. She did then. She does now. Things like that don't change. People don't. We just grow up and move on. Like I'm going to do the minute I can. California, I remind myself. As soon as my probation is lifted.

Eventually, she gets the hint and shakes her head, her face sober, but at least there are no tears. Mom and I don't like to cry in front of people. Good thing. "Oh. I almost forgot." She points to my closet. "I bought you jeans and running shoes. The ones you had were so worn."

I'm not sure what pisses me off more: Mom looking through my things or using new things to buy my love. Or that I have to thank her for sneaking around my life, spying, instead of simply asking me what I want or need. Leaving little presents in this weird staying-on-the-periphery kind of parenting.

My eyes go back to my homework. "I've really got to get on this."

"Sure. Let me know what fits and what doesn't. I can take anything back you don't like."

As soon as Mom leaves, I close my books and take out my phone. It's been forever since I've talked to Pete. But instead of texting him, I see one from Emily.

Bad night. Could use someone to talk to.

I type back. I'm someone.

Can you meet me?

Where?

The park.

I don't ask her why she wants to meet two blocks away when we could just hang in each other's backyards. I simply send back Yes. Ten minutes.

Thank you.

I try to silence the voices in my head that tell me this is a bad idea. That I can't save her any more than I could save Leah. I hear Steve telling me to fall for someone who can take care of me for a change, but the thing is, I can't help Mom. I can't help Ryan. I can't change anything that's happened in the past. But I *can* meet Emily in the park. So I will.

CHAPTER 17

I expect to see Emily's car parked, but nothing. I look by the tree we sat near. Still nothing.

"Over here." She waves from one of the swings.

When I get closer, I can see she's been crying. I sit on the swing next to her. Pull her closer to me by the chain. "What's up?"

She wipes her eyes. "My cousin, the one I told you about?"

"Dylan?"

She sniffs, but I can tell by the way she looks at me that she's glad I remembered his name. "Yeah. He's in trouble again."

"What kind of trouble?"

"He stopped taking his meds. He ran away. Nobody knows where he is."

"Is there anything I can do?"

She laughs, looks at the moon, wipes her eyes again. "Not unless you can get your hands on a couple hundred dollars, you can't."

"That's all he needs? Money?"

"No. That's what I need to get on a train to go find him. Because once he ran, I was put on super-duper lockdown."

"Are you sure you could find him?"

She nods. "I know him better than anyone."

"Done."

"What?"

"I'll give you the money."

Her hands start flying around her face. "I didn't really mean I wanted you to give me money. You asked if you can help, and I said that because…"

"Because you need money. I've got that."

"No. I couldn't."

"Of course you could. If you take me to an ATM, I can get it for you right away."

"Are you sure? I mean, isn't it wrong to take money from your friends?"

"Nope. Not at all. Money is the least important thing in the world. But I gotta ask you. We're friends?"

She leans closer to me. "Maybe one day a little more than that."

"What day would that be?"

"The day when that haunted look leaves you."

She kisses me on the cheek. I let her. All the while I'm trying like mad not to let her get too attached to me, I wonder if maybe I missed the boat, because the thought of her leaving to go after this cousin I know nothing about terrifies me. I'll help her, of course. I just wish helping her didn't mean helping her leave. No matter for how long.

———o———

I almost forget about Emily asking me for help, because she doesn't mention it again for a few days, and when I offered the day after our park date, she'd just said, "The situation is stable at the moment."

So Friday morning on the way to school, I'm a little surprised when she brings it up. "You still OK with lending me money?"

"Sure, but I thought all was OK."

"It probably is, but I want to make sure. I'm thinking about leaving tomorrow."

"Your parents won't notice you're gone?"

"They think everything's settled, and they've got a big college reunion scheduled for this weekend. They won't cancel that to watch me. My good-girl routine has paid off."

"Apparently."

"If you don't want to give me the money…"

"That's not a problem. I told you. I'm just worried about you."

"I'll be fine. It's going to be an in-and-out kind of operation. And I'll pay you back, I swear."

"When will you leave?"

"My parents leave tonight after work. So after that."

"You can't go at night."

"Why not? You don't even know where I'm going."

"Wherever it is, it's safer during the day for sure."

"I'll go tomorrow morning then."

"How will you get there?"

"Train. Oh, can you take me? You can use my car for the weekend if you want."

My mind goes to all the different ways a car could help me. Then I imagine all the ways I could screw things up for her.

Getting a ticket. Getting into an accident. Having a flat. I picture having to tell Emily how I blew her cover. "Nah. I'll just take you there and back." Maybe I'm growing up? Actually putting someone else in front of my own needs?

"When do you want to leave?"

"First thing."

"I was afraid you'd say that. The money you can have, but my sleep? Wow."

She giggles. "Thanks."

"I haven't done anything yet."

She looks at me like I'm the best person in the world, and I can't really take that. Makes me want to be a total smart-ass.

"You always say that." Her voice is sort of sad, like she'd hoped she could have changed me already. "Maybe thanks should be given just for being willing to do something for someone else?"

"You ever heard of the road to hell being paved with good intentions?"

"Yeah. I've heard it. But I don't buy it. Not with you anyway."

And then I'm done. Somehow, some way, that girl's taken the ass right out of me. Weird.

———○———

I come downstairs at eight o'clock on Saturday morning. Open the drawer in the kitchen to leave Mom a note when she calls out from the hallway near Ryan's room. "John, that you? You OK?"

"Yeah. Just leaving you a note. Emily needs me to help her with her car this morning."

Mom blinks at me as she comes into the kitchen. Her hand goes over her eyes like the tiny bit of sun from the window is too bright for her. She leans against the wall. "Didn't you already fix the fan for her?"

"Yeah. This is something different."

"OK. You'll be back in time for your appointment with Steve?"

I look at how tired Mom looks and get annoyed with Dad, with Ryan, even with me. We take too much from her, and it's killing her.

"Yes. Did Dad say when I'm getting my Jeep back? You wouldn't have to take me anywhere if I could drive myself."

"I don't mind taking you. Besides, Ryan…"

"He can miss one Saturday. And so could I for that matter." She closes her eyes. "No."

"I'm serious, Mom. Go cancel our appointments, then go back to sleep. Rosie can watch Ryan, and I'll help when I get back from taking Emily."

"Taking Emily where?"

"I mean helping Emily."

"OK, maybe you're right. I am really tired." She puts her hand against the wall.

"You want me to help you upstairs?"

She smiles at me like a sick, weak bird. "I'm not such an invalid that I can't put myself to bed."

I walk out of the house, now super worried about Mom. Which is a really good appetizer for what comes next. Me being worried about Emily.

Emily is dressed in jeans, a long-sleeved T-shirt, and a jacket, her hair pulled back in a ponytail and a baseball hat on her head. She's got on a raincoat, and judging by the look of the dark skies, that's probably a good idea. It also makes me think maybe she's not going too far. For some reason, that makes me feel better, which is weird, because should it really matter? She's her own person. She's going to do as she pleases.

That doesn't keep me from saying this next thing. "You're really not going to tell me where you're going?"

"Can't. That way, in case my parents find out and torture you, you won't be able to reveal my secrets."

My smile turns to a smirk. "I'm pretty sure I could stand up to your father's stern lectures."

"It's my mother you have to watch out for. She is a mean woman with a blender."

"Shudder. But seriously, you'll keep your phone on? Check in?"

"Oh. Right. Here." She hands me her cell.

And just like that, the ground goes shaky underneath me. "Why are you giving this to me?"

"I'm pretty sure my parents are tracking my phone, so I can't take it with me."

I stare at it in my hand, will myself not to think about Leah, but how can I help it? She gave me her phone too, the night before she killed herself. I start to sweat. My vision turns into tunnels. I feel dizzy. I hold up my hand. "No. This isn't right."

Her face gets intense. "John, are you OK?"

"I can't. You can't do this."

"Do what? I'm just going to check on him. Then I'm coming back."

"You need to take your phone with you." My hands are on my head. I know I look like a lunatic, but I can't help it. I twist around. Look at the sky. "I can't. This isn't right."

"John, you're pale as a ghost. What's wrong?"

"I can't let you go without your phone. It means you're not coming back. No one leaves their phone."

She puts her hands on my arm. "No. I'm sorry. I didn't explain. I have another phone. I'll give you that number." She pulls out a different cell. "It's a burner phone. Dylan gave it to me. It's how he calls me."

She types in my number and sends me a text. Even as I feel my phone vibrate in my pocket, I also feel my stomach drop. "Let me come with you."

"He won't let me near him if I bring someone. Plus, you need to be here, protecting my cover. With this." She points to her cell in my hand. "If they text, just answer the best you can. You can scroll through and see my responses to them in the past if you want to be sure you sound like me."

I stare at her phone in her earnest hands. It's like the ties on the bracelets show how tight she's wound, and all I want to do is hold her hands and ask her to stay.

"I don't even think they'll text. You know, maybe once or twice. I'll be back by tomorrow morning. You can come get me at the station. OK?" She pulls the key to her house out of her pocket. "In case you need anything in there. Or to get away from your family." She smiles. "Please, John. I'll be back in no time. You can text me on this burner, and I promise I'll answer."

I see Leah hand me her phone. *She said, "Keep this for me so I won't answer Sean or Brittney. Be my strength for me."*

I feel her take my hand, her tiny hand around mine. "Please, John." Only it's here and now, and it's Emily this time. How many times have I wished I could go back and change the Ryan thing? How many times with Leah? Is this the second chance I asked for?

"Emily, I'm really worried…"

"I'll do it with or without your help. You know I will. Only with your help, it's a lot easier and safer for me."

I feel my insides crumbling. I swear I'm almost crying. But I can't change the past. I can't change Emily. I'm stuck here, not knowing what to do with all this. Wondering why the hell I'd be so stupid to let her do this to me. And then I remember that Steve said he was proud of me for opening myself up and letting myself be loved. I couldn't save Ryan. I couldn't save Leah. I'm not even sure I can save myself. But what I can do at this moment is help Emily the best way I can. She is not Leah. She is not Leah. She is Emily.

She touches my face. "I'm going to be fine. You'll see. I'll be back tomorrow. I'll check in every hour if that would make you feel better."

I nod. "Yeah."

"I'm coming back, John. I promise."

I think about how wrong I was about my first impression of Emily. She seemed safe and together and by the book. But I was right that she is also loyal and invested and brave.

I look straight in her eyes. "You better."

She laughs, soft and sweet.

"I don't want to have to face your mother and her blender," I say.

She makes her face look fake-serious. "I would never do that to you."

"Let's go get you money and send you on your way then."

We pull into the bank parking lot. I get out. Every step I take makes me feel like I'm doing the wrong thing. Alarms are blaring in my head, but I take out five hundred dollars. When I get back in the car, I give her all but a hundred.

"Whoa. This is more than I need. Way more."

"You don't know what you'll need, and most people underestimate how much things cost anyway."

"I'll pay you back."

"I don't care about the money." I can't even look at her. When did I get this needy? "I should come with you." I chew on my knuckle.

"Stop sounding so sad. I'll see you tomorrow. For reals."

She gets out at the train station, and I stare at the phone in my hand. Women and their stupid phones and their stupid need to leave me.

———o———

Saturday feels like the longest day on record. It pours most of the day, and that just adds to the chill. Dad calls, and I hear Mom speaking to him in soft whispers as Livy and I play our third game of backgammon. I text Pete three times. He's got to help me out here. I decide to text Allie, even though I know I'm being super needy.

So. Checking in. You doing OK?

The dots appear on my phone, letting me know she's texting me back. And then Livy notices. "Who ya texting?"

"No one special."

Her eyebrows arch. "If you say so."

"I do."

Finally, Allie's text comes in.

Do you ever wonder why you try? Guys suck.

We talking Nick still?

No. We broke up. I mean guys in general.

Not that Max guy, right?

No. Finally over him. For good.

Good. Guys suck anyway. All guys.

That doesn't sound too promising. Just sent my RISD application. Totally nervous.

Don't be. Let me know when you find out.

K

I look at my phone and consider telling Allie about drafting class. About the computer program I can't stop thinking about.

I want to ask her if she ever feels like she's stupid for trying something new or if she ever feels like she can't do art, but that would be ridiculous. She knows she's good. And I've got to stop being so damned pathetic.

Mom comes in the kitchen. She looks pale but definitely a little better. She's got the phone in her hand. "Your dad wants to talk to you guys."

Livy puts her hand out. Mom gives her the phone, then looks around the room. Ryan is in front of the television, watching one of his favorite videos, a bunch of kids having a party at Disney World. He laughs at the part where one of the kids jumps into a big swimming pool.

I look back at the game board but not before seeing Mom catch me smile at Ryan. She goes to the stove and puts on a kettle. I roll the dice, amazed at how natural this feels. If only I wasn't worried about Emily, I'd be pretty chill. And just like that, Emily's phone vibrates. I check Mom. She's reading the newspaper. I take out the phone. Her phone. It's a text from her parents. Hi, Sweetie. We're here. How are you?

I text back. I'm good.

They text. Good. Talk later. Have fun. Pizza in the freezer.

I text back. K.

Mom strides over to the table, mug of tea in her hands. I shove Emily's phone in my pocket. Livy hands me the house phone.

"Hi, Dad."

"Hi. Just wanted to let you know I'm coming in for your award ceremony on Tuesday night."

"OK. You guys know I may not even win anything. It's a huge long shot."

Livy rolls, knocks two of my guys off the board. Smiles at me. I smile back, even though I'm totally not feeling it.

"It's not about winning. This teacher sees something in you, and that makes us proud. Oh, and I'll be bringing your Jeep."

All of a sudden, I feel a little bit of happiness, like a warm glow inside me that spreads like the sun's rays.

"John? You there?"

I rub my face. "Yeah. Thanks."

"You've impressed your mother and me. You've earned this."

"Thanks, Dad."

"OK. See you Tuesday night."

I can't help it. Now I'm getting pretty excited about it myself.

My phone vibrates. Emily. Coming home. Can you get me at the station tonight?

I can't help smiling. When?

Ten thirty.

I'll be there.

You OK?

Fine. See you then.

Pete finally texts. Sorry, man. Was sleeping. I'll find some for you. Give me a little while.

I almost text back telling Pete not to bother, all is fine now, but maybe it would be good to have some ready just in case. So I text back OK.

———°———

It's easier than I think to get out of the house, since Mom had me drop Livy at a friend's house for a sleepover, and Mom and Ryan went to sleep at eight o'clock. That leaves the field clear for me to get Emily's car and go to the train station, which I get to at ten thirty, which just lends itself to a bunch of anxiety that lays in my belly and reproduces into fear, pebbles that pile on top of each other until they push up my throat. Where is she?

Throngs of passengers pass by me, and no Emily. My stomach is in a knot, and I can't help myself, I am leaning forward, searching. No Emily. I take out my phone. No messages. I take out hers. None. It's almost quarter to eleven, and still no Emily. I start to text her when I hear her voice.

"Hey."

I look up. She's there in front of me. She looks small and sad, but she's there. I want to grab her and shake her. I want to hold her close, but that would be so stupid and weak. That would be too much.

She puts her arms around me, and she leans into me. I feel her cry.

"Sh. It's OK."

She lets me hold her, and we stay like this for a few minutes. Then I say, "Let's get you home."

I hand her phone back. "Thanks."

I want to ask about her trip. See if it worked out, but if I were

172

her, I wouldn't want to be grilled the minute I step off the train, so instead, I say, "You hungry?"

"Starved."

"Pizza?" I ask.

"Perfect. Let's do take out. I kind of want to be home."

"Call it in. I'll drive."

"Our place? Joey's?"

"Yeah." Our place. Since when have I gotten so whipped? I drive through town, the storefronts flashing by me. I wait in the car while she runs in to get our pizza. Then I take her home.

"You're coming in, right?" she calls over her shoulder. "I really need the company."

I follow her like the pet I've become. She takes out plates and then gets glasses. She fills them with ice and opens the refrigerator. She takes out a two-liter bottle of Coke and splashes some into the glasses. She winks at me and pulls a small bottle of Jack out of her pocket. She adds some to each glass. "You're right. These two do belong together."

We eat in almost complete silence. We both drain our drinks, and she refills them.

"Mom and Dad won't be home till tomorrow." She checks her phone, the one that I'd held for her.

I drink some of my drink. Try not to let myself go where the bottom half of my body is screaming to go. I tell myself she's tired. I tell myself she's too hurt right now. That being with her under these circumstances would be wrong. She comes over to me and puts her hand on my cheek. I move my face, but she presses her palm so we're still connected. She stares in my eyes and kisses me.

I pull back. "No. We can't."

"Of course we can." She kisses me again.

"OK, grammar queen, we shouldn't."

She drinks some more of her Jack and Coke. Kisses me so I taste it on her tongue. "Why shouldn't we?"

"Because you have no idea when your parents could get home."

She throws her head back and laughs. "They aren't the only ones who know how to track people's whereabouts on their phone. This minute, my parents are at Penn State reliving their glory days." She rolls her eyes when she says this, and I can't help but laugh. Until she pushes her body against mine. Wraps her hands around my waist. Kisses me stronger this time. "Any other objections?" she asks.

It's hard to think. Seriously hard, but I do it anyway. "Yes. We have to wait until that haunted look leaves your face."

She laughs and does a little *tsk-tsk* thing that is super hot. "Yeah. No. I don't."

"OK, what about *my* haunted look?" I'm trying my best to be a gentleman here.

She pulls my head back by my hair. Which is also kind of hot. Stares at me. Gives me a good once-over. Still hot. Then she says, "I pronounce you unhaunted." Then she kisses me, and it's like all the worry that was bottled up inside me comes pouring out into that kiss. And then we're breathless, her hands on my neck and under my shirt, and I hear how I sound when I want her. My body can't get enough of her. We're glued together, and I don't want to let go. I don't want to stop, but I know I should.

Then she does. She pulls away, and I'm winded. Breathless. She puts her hands on my cheeks. "You want to go upstairs?"

"Emily…I think…"

"I know. Just fun. OK?" Her eyes hold mine. They're unsure and needy and so damn beautiful. I can see she's scared, but she wants to anyway.

I shake my head. "No. I don't think…"

She shakes her head. "It's OK. I know…how you are. I know what you want."

I take her hands. "What do I want?"

"You want to get away from here. You want to go to California. You don't want strings. That's OK. I just want you for as long…as long as you want me. That's it."

I kiss her hands. "I'm so messed up. You have no idea."

Her hand goes to my cheek again. "You are so beautiful."

I shake my head. "I helped you. You're just grateful…"

She pulls away from me. Blinks away angry tears. "This is *not* a mercy fuck…"

"Hey. I didn't say that."

"And I am not the good girl you think I am."

"You don't have to prove that to me."

She grabs me by the collar and pulls me to her. She kisses me hard. "Does this feel like gratitude?"

I shake my head.

She grabs my ass and pulls me against her. "If you don't want me…"

"I didn't say that…"

She walks away from me. Looks back. "Race you."

And we do. All the way up to her bedroom, where she falls backward on the bed, and I fall on top of her.

"You sure you're OK with this?" I ask one more time.

"Uh-huh." She runs her hand under my shirt. "Just for fun."

That almost stops me. Almost. But she's right—why don't we have a little fun? A little fun never hurt anyone. My eyes take in her beautiful face. Sad and perfect and on fire all at once, and I wonder if this girl is like me. Feeling too much all the time. My lips on hers, I try to take away the sadness. Eliminate the fear. Just bring the good kind of fire.

The sound of the door opening downstairs jolts me.

"Emily? You home?" Her mother's voice carries up the stairs.

Her hands grip my arms. Fear fills her face. She starts to laugh. She mouths, *What the fuck?*

I jump back, grab my shirt, which was luckily the only thing I'd taken off.

"Emily? What's going on?"

Steps pound upstairs. Emily points to her closet. Right. The closet. No one ever thinks to look there. I make my way to the window. I'm almost all the way out when Emily realizes she can lock her door. *Bang, bang, bang.*

"Emily…"

I scramble out the window, grab onto the tree that is out there.

"Open this door!"

Emily puts on her annoyed voice. "I'm getting dressed. Give me a minute."

"Open this door please."

I shimmy down the tree. Emily shuts the window. I feel like a total jerk for leaving her to deal with the fallout from our party downstairs. But her parents finding me in her room would have been much worse.

CHAPTER 18

I still haven't heard from Emily since last night, and that worries me. Just like Mom staying in bed does. So I'm downstairs early, trolling around, making my toast, making my own lunch. Wishing I had coffee. Waiting for the car honk. Finally, it comes.

Mom stumbles downstairs in her bathrobe. "I'm sorry, honey."

"It's fine, Mom. I gotta go."

I race by her, out the door, and into the car, where I find a really sad-looking Emily.

"Hey, are you OK?"

She's got tears in her eyes, and she shakes her head and closes them, working like mad to keep them from flowing. Her hands frame each word. "I'm sorry."

"Why are you sorry? I'm sorry you got in trouble for…"

She shakes her head. "They disabled their location notifications. Who does that?"

"I'm sorry. What did they say?"

"What didn't they say? They are disappointed in me."

"Because of…"

"They thought I was going to be make better decisions. They worry I'm going down a bad road. Alcohol. For God's sake, alcohol." She's imitating her mother's voice, but she's laughing. She turns to face me. "They don't know about you at all. They're so stupid."

"What? They are that mad because you had a little Jack?"

"Where did I get it from? How could I do that?" She gestures wildly, imitating her mother, I'm sure.

I laugh. But it kind of makes me mad. I mean, Emily is such a good kid, and her parents give her shit about a little drinking.

"I'm grounded. For life." She smiles like she can't believe her bad luck. She shakes her head, her hands still doing the flourish thing.

"They say grounded for life, but they don't actually *mean* for life."

"They probably do. But it doesn't matter. I want to go to your award ceremony. That's tomorrow night." Tears fill her eyes, and she blinks a couple of times. She slams the car into park.

I hold her hand. "Don't worry about it. I'm going to have a huge crowd anyway. It'll annoy the other kids."

Her eyes are all watery, and her face is blotchy. "I'm sorry, John, I really am. And about…you know…"

"I'm sure we'll figure something out."

She laughs. "Maybe."

It bugs me Emily won't be there, but underneath the entire thing, I'm worried that Mom and Dad will let me down somehow or be disappointed once they see my work or how I do in the competition. This entire thing stinks of stupid. Me being stupid for even letting Mr. Bonham talk me into it.

She laughs again.

"Are you sorry we almost…" God, I'm such a needy son of a bitch. Some Son of Anarchy.

She looks down. Blushes. Smiles. "No. Of course not."

"Hey." I point to the empty parking lot. "We better hurry to beat the crowd."

"Oh. Wait. I forgot. This is what I have left." She digs her hand in her pockets and pulls out a wad of cash. She hands it to me, all crinkled and clumped together, her hands so small, cradling mine. It's her hands that get to me. They are nothing like Leah's. Her nails are cut super short, and she's got these leather bracelets with knots that make me like her even more for some stupid reason. Leah would never wear anything like that. Emily wears almost no makeup. She has these incredibly urgent and intense little hands. I don't know why I'm making a not-like-Leah list in my head, but it feels like maybe it's the right thing. I straighten out the cash and put it in my wallet, chuckling as I do.

"What's so funny?"

"It's just cute the way you keep your money."

"Cute?" She smacks my arm. "Girls don't like being called cute anymore. It's insulting."

I put my hands up. "Sorry. Wow. Remind me not to make you mad anymore."

She puts a strand of hair behind her ear. Which I take as an invitation to lean in to kiss her.

Brandon and Will pull into the parking lot just as we are walking toward the courtyard. "Hey, Strickland. Wait up."

I stop.

"Guess I'll see you later."

"Guess so." She looks like she wants to say something to me. Or do something. I feel myself leaning toward her. Remind myself that this is OK. It's just fun. No one's getting hurt. I want to kiss her again. I almost do. But then someone throws a ball against the brick wall behind her, and her head whips in that direction.

"Asshole!" I yell to Matt, who has nothing better to do than mess with my love life.

"Bye, guys." Emily scoots off into school.

"Should we tell Dominique that you're officially off the market?" Brandon claps me on the back, then says, "Don't let that get in the way of your game, Strickland."

Matt jumps in. "I'm pretty sure Dominique's into *me* anyway."

Parker scowls at him. "You wish." Then to me, "Big scrimmage Thursday. We can't get beat again. You gotta leave it on the field, not in the bedroom."

Matt shakes his head. "You sound like a public service announcement." He lowers his voice like one of those TV announcers. "Boys, don't get caught with your dick outside your pants."

"Very funny. All of you. Seriously, I think you should do stand-up." My phone vibrates. I take it out. Pete. Got a quad for you.

I text back. Great. I get my Jeep back tomorrow. Will be in touch.

Pete texts. No prob. It'll keep for a few days.

I walk through the halls with Brandon and Parker and Matt and try to get ready for my day while trying like mad not to think of what's coming tomorrow night. Something tells me the universe thinks it's going to be bad if it's sending weed my way. But then I feel like I'm being an idiot and always trying to find the negative. Gotta work on that.

CHAPTER 19

D ad shows up at five with my Jeep, making me wonder
how the hell he'll get home, but then I dismiss that as not
my problem.

I meet him in the driveway, dressed in the new jeans Mom
got me and a new striped button-down shirt. No reason not
to make her happy tonight. Dad hands me the keys, a smirk
on his face—the one he gives me when he's proud of me—and
that makes me feel pretty good. "You go ahead, and Mom and
I will meet you there."

Livy comes out of the house and hugs Dad. "I want to go
early with John."

"You're coming with Mom and me."

Livy whines, but I yell to her as I get in the Jeep, "See you in
a few!"

I drive to the high school in two minutes flat. Mr. Bonham
was all excited about our school hosting the county event, but
I admit, it would have been cool to have this at the Windsor
Center downtown. That's where the kids who move to the next
round go. It's an amazingly cool building, all glass.

The auditorium is crowded, and tons of families stroll
through the exhibit, looking at different models and drawings.

I try to find my drawing and, for one truly terrifying minute, think I may have imagined the whole being-included-in-this-event thing, because it's nowhere to be found. But then Mr. Bonham finds me.

"Hey, John, big night. We all have our fingers crossed for you." He holds up crossed fingers as evidence of his last statement. "Where's your family? Look forward to meeting them."

"They're coming later." My eyes comb the display and still don't see it.

"Oh, your project's over here." He walks briskly to a group of drawings, and when we get there, I see there's a ribbon on my drawing. Third place. "Oh wow, I didn't think the judges had decided yet. Third place?" He claps me on the shoulder. "That sends you to semis. Way to go."

I'm feeling a cross between bewilderment and excitement and, in the back of all of that, a tiny nagging voice saying that they should have been here to see the ribbon with me when it was first put there. Not that Mr. Bonham and I did either. But I tell myself that's no big deal. They'll be here soon enough.

"I'm going to find Miss Quinlan. She's going to be so excited." He shakes my hand, pumping it up and down three times, hard. "Great job, John."

Now I realize the "we" he talked about was him and Miss Quinlan. I thread my way through the crowd, careful not to photobomb any of the other kids with their parents, taking pictures, smiling. There's a table up front where moms are pouring soda into tiny plastic cups. I grab one with Coke in it and shoot the mom a grateful smile. She says, "Enjoy." And for some stupid reason, I want to tell her about my ribbon, but when I look back at her, she's handing another soda to another kid, and I realize I'm being a total idiot about this. It's not like I won a medal at the Olympics or anything.

There's a small disturbance at the entrance to the gym. It's my lacrosse team. They're sweaty from practice, but all of them are heading my way. I meet them halfway across the room. "Hey, what's up, guys?"

"Coach let us out early so we could come see you get your award," Brandon says.

I can't help but smile. I had been worried about asking Coach for the night off, but Mr. Bonham and Miss Quinlan had already told him, and he told me he wanted a full report the next day. I guess he didn't feel like waiting, because before I know it, Coach Gibson strolls in. He stops to talk with Miss Quinlan, who points in the direction of my piece.

Parker claps me on the back and shoots forward to meet up with the coach in front of my drawing.

"Way to go, Strickland," Coach Gibson says. "We may have an architect on our team."

I try not to smile, try to act all strong and above all this, but I can't.

"Let's get a picture with you all together," Miss Quinlan suggests.

I take my phone out to give to her and see it's going on six thirty. Where are my parents?

"Squish together." She motions with her hands.

I smile, even though in the back of my mind, I'm wondering where the hell they are.

"John." Emily's voice makes me turn.

Livy is with her, both of them looking really upset but like they're trying to hide it. Livy hugs me. I talk over her head. "I thought you were grounded."

"I snuck out," Emily says. "I had to."

Livy unhooks from me and notices the ribbon. She points. "Awesome."

"Where are my parents?" I ask Emily.

She puts her hand on my arm. "Ryan fell. They had to take him to the hospital."

My beast rages. "What?"

"He pushed back in his chair. Fell backward. Dad wanted to come here, and Mom screamed at him. So I texted Emily. I wasn't going to miss this," Livy says.

Maia Cetus roars. I feel his rage feeding my own. "You'll get in trouble, Emily."

"I don't care, John. You needed someone with you."

Like her cousin needs her, so do I. I'm a fucking charity case. Miss Quinlan comes over. "So is this your…"

Emily speaks up, since I'm stunned silent. "Sister. Livy, this is Mr. Bonham. He's the one who…"

"Noticed your brother was extremely talented." Mr. Bonham looks around. "So your parents…"

"Couldn't be here," Emily says.

Mr. Bonham looks disappointed. Miss Quinlan's lips thin

like she's pissed as shit at Mom and Dad, but she says, "That's such a shame."

"Our other brother was in an accident," Livy says. "He had to go to the hospital."

"Oh no. Is he OK?"

I want to answer that. I want to tell them he's perfect. The perfect reason to never fucking show up for me. My hand itches to text Pete. I've got the money Emily handed me this morning, I've got my Jeep back, and Pete's got a quad for me. Seems like exactly what I need.

Coach Gibson is standing two exhibits away. I don't want him to hear, but he turns toward us. Makes eye contact with Mr. Bonham. Like this is some sort of feel-sorry-for-John team effort. Like I've become the new GoFundMe project for our faculty. Not into it. But Coach says, "OK, lacrosse players plus Livy and Emily, pizza on me."

And all of a sudden, the lights, the cameras, the talking and laughing is too much. The sounds morph in my head and remind me of crashing glass. I push past the crowd, bump into a bunch of people as I make my way out the door. I'm dizzy, and noise is pushing me forward, so I don't see the table with the woman serving the drinks. I bump into it, and little cups of sticky liquid spill everywhere. My hands go up like I'm surrendering, and I'm about to apologize, but the lady starts yelling at me. I feel like I'm in the ocean, being pulled under.

Mr. Bonham tries to step in front of me, and my eyes go all blurry. He puts his hands out. "John, why don't we…"

The anger that rages inside me consumes me from the inside out. Who the fuck is he to touch me? Who is he to care? If he hadn't made me do this stupid fucking contest to begin with…

I push him. Harder than I mean to. He moves back, his hands reaching out like he's in some high-wire act.

"John!" Livy calls after me, but when I look back, all I see are people staring at me like I'm some kind of wild animal.

Emily's face turns from scared to cold, and she grabs Livy by the shoulders and holds her back. "Let him go."

Maia Cetus roars, and we head out to my Jeep, then into the night, alone like we were meant to be.

CHAPTER 20

The sun comes up, and my teeth are chattering like mad while my bladder is screaming to be emptied. My head feels like it's been stuffed full of that polyester crap they put in toys for kids. I lean forward and inadvertently beep the horn, which makes me jump. My hands shake as I open the car door and step out to a parking lot in back of a liquor store.

Pieces of last night come back to me. Me leaving the school. Pushing Mr. Bonham. My coach there watching me act like an idiot. Livy's face. Emily's. Me not even caring, because ultimately, they'd be better off without me. I see myself paying for the handle of Jack I've almost finished. I go to the Dumpster and take a piss that lasts for fucking ever, and I realize once again how freaking cold I am.

When I get back to my car, I find my phone in the cup holder. It's lit up with texts and missed calls. I rub my hand down my face. I'm so not ready for this next part. The regret part.

I blow out a big breath and start scrolling through the texts.

Livy: Where are you? Are you OK?

Emily: Everyone's worried about you.

Emily: Where are you?

Emily: Call me, I'm srs.

Mom: Don't be stupid, John. We wanted to be there.

Dad: Please come home.

Emily: You're killing me with this. You know that? You looked just like Dylan.

Emily: I can't do this. He's sick. You're not.

The last one destroys me.

I text Emily first. I'm sorry.

Then Livy. I'm OK. Coming home.

Then Dad. On way home.

Dad's reply beats everyone else's. Are you OK?

Yes.

I'm sure he's going to be angry, but instead, he texts, I'm glad. I'll be waiting for you.

And suddenly, it feels like there's been a shift in the planets. I put my car in reverse, back it up, then head home.

———o———

When I pull into my driveway, I'm surprised to see another car there. It's only nine, so I've got no idea who could be here, but for some reason, the shiny blue Focus puts me on edge.

The front door opens, and Livy runs out, her face all red from crying. I let her wrap me up and then push me away, pounding me with her little fists. I'm always screwing up. All these years, I'm blaming Mom and Dad for forgetting about Livy, for upsetting her, for making her worry, and I'm home for two months, and I've done the same.

"I can't believe you. Selfish. Stupid." She hits me with her little fists. "You said you'd never leave without telling me."

"Sh. I'm sorry. I'm so sorry."

She lets go and points to the house. "Now he's here, and there's nothing you can do. They're going to take you away. Mom said so."

I hold her away from me so I can see her face. "Nobody's taking me away. Who's here?"

Before she answers, I realize whose car that must be. Just then, the front door opens again. Standing on the doorstep is none other than Mr. Mike Wexler.

"Who called him?" I ask, annoyed.

"So it's true?" Livy asks.

"Huh? What? Me going away? No, of course not."

Livy starts crying again. "You can't leave. You promised."

I put my hands on Livy's broken-hearted face, her tears making her hair stick to her hot cheeks. I brush her hair back behind her ears. "I promise. I'm staying the year."

"Mom said if you've done any"—she lowers her voice to a whisper—"drugs, they can take you away."

I look her straight in the eye. "I haven't. I'm good." I feel like a total heel lying to her, but in my head, I'm counting the days. It's Saturday, so he's probably not going to take me in now and demand a sample. Right? Next Friday will be four weeks. I just have to talk my way into waiting until then. Which is going to probably take a miracle based on how pissed Mr. Wexler looks right now.

I sling my arm around her as I make my way to the front door, wishing like mad for something to fix my hangover breath, knowing it won't make a difference. I'm underage. Drinking is illegal. It doesn't matter if I've smoked weed or not—this guy could tell the judge I've violated probation. If I violate, they could send me to jail.

I'm almost to the door to shake hands with Mr. Wexler when Livy twists to look next door. I turn also. Emily is there. Her arms crossed in front of her. She's pissed.

It's all about piling on here.

"Mr. Wexler." I put my hand out, trying to keep it from shaking.

"Mr. Strickland." Smart-ass and arrogant.

Mom stands behind him. She backs away to allow all of us inside and motions to the living room, where we all take a seat.

"Not you." Dad puts out a hand to stop Livy in her tracks.

Her face gets so desperate that I feel like an ass all over again. I call her over to me, bend down, whisper in her ear. "Text Emily." I hand her my phone. "Tell her it's you and that you need to stay with her."

Livy starts to protest but stops after another look at Dad.

When she's gone, I sit in the chair farthest from my parents. Mr. Wexler sits on the sofa in front of the window, and the light makes him look haloed, which under any other circumstances would make me laugh. I look at my hands. The knuckle I chew is red, and I want to gnaw away at it, but I can't look guilty.

"Well, John, you had half the town looking for you last night."

"Who called you?" I ask.

"For God's sake, John, of all the—"

Mr. Wexler cuts Mom's rant off with one solid palm facing her, something I've never seen before. "Miss Quinlan called to let me know you'd won an award, and I was on my way over to see for myself."

"Miss Quinlan do that a lot? Call you to tell you about her reject puppies who make good?"

"Nope, buddy boy. You happen to be special."

"Oh yeah, why is that?"

"Because you're such a punk you remind me of someone I used to know. And because for some reason, the adults in this town and the last two places you've lived seem to believe you are worth saving."

Once again, I'm some sort of community charity project. A slow boil starts inside me.

"Don't believe me?" He shuffles through his papers in a file he's got balanced on his knee, holds up pieces of paper. "These were written on your behalf by Coach Gibson, Miss Quinlan, and Mr. Bonham last night. All of them asking me not to violate your probation."

Mom starts sniffling. I sneak a peek at Dad, who is sitting next to her and pulls her head against his chest.

"Mr. Bonham said that?" I see his face, surprised and scared as he fell backward last night after I pushed him.

"Yes, he did. And these emails"—he shows me his phone—"from your uncle Dave and a"—he squints at the screen—"a Mr. Hicks, who was your…"

"My guidance counselor from my last school, yeah." I know I should be grateful, but all these people writing about me, even if it's to help me, kind of pisses me off. My old friend, anger, knocks at the door, but I hold him back. I need to be reasonable here. I need to postpone the inevitable drug test for as long as I can. I rub my hands together like I'm cold. Almost blow on them.

"Guess there's some kind of guidance counselor hotline, huh?" Mr. Wexler laughs, but I can tell he's not amused. He probably thinks these people are wasting their concern on the likes of me. Ungrateful. Rough. Stupid. Me. "So, I'm willing to listen to your side of the story. Where'd you go last night?"

I stare at the floor. "I just drove."

"All night?"

"No." I shake my head. "I pulled over by this field. Fell asleep there."

"So you weren't doing anything illegal?"

"No."

"No pot?"

"No, sir."

Mr. Wexler stares a hole into me, but I don't back down. Everyone stays silent. No one breathes. Finally, he says, in a voice that is completely neutral, "Well, let's see about that." He starts scrolling through a screen on his cell, flipping days of a calendar, I guess, until he lands on the spot he has open for me. "Twelve o'clock. Wednesday. My office."

I nod.

"He has school," Mom says, and it's like she still doesn't get the gravity of the situation. As usual.

Mr. Wexler smooths out the muscles of his face, becomes less pit bull and more patient adult. "He'll need to come in and give me a sample. We'll fill out some paperwork and talk. After the drug test results come back, we'll make decisions."

"What kind of decisions?"

Mr. Wexler smiles a thin smile. "Let's take this one step at a time. If John's clean, we'll set up a weekly schedule. All of it should take less than an hour, and he'll be back on campus before lunch is over."

"Can we take him?" Dad asks.

"I'm pretty sure he can find his way." He hands me a card, winks at Dad. "That is, if you haven't taken his Jeep away after last night's little stunt."

"No. It was our fault. One of us should have gone to his award ceremony." Mom looks at her skinny fingers.

"Your decision. See you Wednesday, John. A clean test would sure make this group happy. See what you can do."

Mom and Dad walk him to the door. Shake his hand. Thank him.

I'm already on my way up the stairs, doing mental math. How much weed can I dilute from my urine? How much can I sweat out of my system?

I hear the door click shut as I let my jeans fall to the ground and grab my running shorts out of my drawer. I pull my sweats over my shorts, bend to lace up my running shoes. Mom and I used to run together. I don't think about that much anymore, but I remember how great it felt when we did, the one thing we did together without fighting. Ryan came with us sometimes, but he never really liked it. Even jock Ryan couldn't match my speed.

I slip down the stairs, go into the kitchen, reach under the sink, and grab a garbage bag.

"What is he…wait," Dad says. Goes to the kitchen, fills a water bottle, caps it, and hands it to me. Our eyes meet for the briefest second before I am out the door. I can't help looking up at Emily's window as I jog down the street. She's not there anymore, but I swear I feel a chill from where she was standing. In addition to a clean test, I wouldn't mind a clean start.

CHAPTER 21

Monday morning riding in with Matt sucks worse than I think it will. Everything I swore I wouldn't do while I was here, I've done. I got involved with a team. A girl. I let some teachers talk me into trying to be more than I am. I am so busy cursing myself out in my head, I don't even respond when Matt says, "Ruh-roh."

There's Emily. And she's walking with someone else. A guy. "Who's that?"

"Marty. Track dude. Thought she was with you."

I look down, grab my lacrosse gear. "Not anymore."

"You knew?"

"About him? No. About me, yeah."

"Still sucks." He smacks me on the arm, then puts his arm around my shoulder. "Good thing you still got us."

Will and Parker step out of the crowd and join us almost on cue.

The bad news train keeps chugging along, this time dressed as Miss Quinlan. She's in her casual look today, and my smart-ass self wants to ask if it's dress-down Monday, but I'm pretty sure going on the offensive won't help ease the tension for the scene that's about to go down.

"Mr. Strickland," she says as I approach. "I'll need to see you in my office."

Matt and the boys peel away, leaving me to face another adult who is disappointed in me. I want to tell her it's her own damned fault, but I'm too tired from the twenty-five miles I ran this weekend, my legs like jelly. Weed sticks to your fat deposits. I need to get rid of those. Everyone wants a clean test, and I can't disappoint.

She ushers me into her office, and I can't help but remember the last time I was here, when she was actually hopeful that I'd do good things, make good choices, and all the other crap she laid on me. I plant myself in my chair and put my head in my hands, not because I don't want to hear her squawk at me but because I'm dizzy from the exercise and no food regimen I'm currently on.

She sits in her chair. I listen for her to gulp her Dunkin' Donuts iced coffee, but she doesn't even touch it this time. She clasps her hands in front of her. "I'm sorry, but we have to talk about your schedule again."

I nod.

"I can see that you feel bad…"

I put my hand up, look up at her. "No, I'm fine. Put me back in the dummy classes. I deserve that."

"It's not that easy. You can't be in Mr. Bonham's class, but I've looked at all the other options, and it would be impossible to fix your schedule without messing it all up."

"You can't just put me back in my other classes?"

"I'm afraid not. You're doing the work in all your classes." She clicks through my information on her computer. "You have solid grades in all of them. I hope you will continue to keep those grades up. I think we'll have to put you in as a teacher's aide or something, but I need to have a teacher agree to that."

"And no one wants to do that?"

"The media specialist said you can help her if you like."

"Sure."

"OK. Then we'll do that. I'm sorry it didn't work out, John."

"Huh?"

"The drafting class."

"It's not that it didn't work out. I didn't work out. I didn't belong there."

She cocks her head at me. "You made a mistake."

"Momentary loss of muscular coordination."

Her face brightens. "*The Shining*?"

"Yeah."

She hits the *P* button on her printer, and a paper spits out. She circles a bunch of things, stamps the sheet, then hands it to me. "Look, John, this doesn't have to be a make-or-break situation for you. You can still stay on track to graduate on time. Go to college. I'll help you apply."

"Thanks." I grab the new schedule.

"You have to have Mr. Bonham sign you out of his class, here." She points on the page. "Then you can have Mrs. Reilly sign you in as her aide, here."

My beast is tired, but he lifts his head. He tells me she could have made it easier on me. Could have gotten me signed out of Mr. Bonham's class so I wouldn't have to face him. But I grab the paper and nod at her instead of firing my rage at the one person who is still trying to be nice to me.

———o———

The gods of fucking up my life are working overtime right now, probably having a big-assed party, passing the chips and the beer, and toasting how freakin' awesome they are. That's how it feels when I—and I almost never run into Emily at school—see her at least six times today.

I try to catch her eye, but she makes sure that's not possible. I've never known a person to avoid eye contact that well.

So now I round the corner and see that Marty dude trying to lay his arm around her just before Mr. Bonham drums me out of his class. I'm going to have to give those gods an extra point for creativity there.

Emily steps away, a tired smile on her face, like maybe she's told him to not do that already and he's not listening. I storm into my old classroom. A wave of emotions hits me, but I make my dragon stand down. He can't help me here. Mr. Bonham sits next to one of those computer geeks, pointing at some drawing on the computer. That gives me time to examine all the 3-D models on the shelves, the ones I'll never get to make.

Mr. Bonham sees me waiting by the door, waves me in. "Let's get this over with." He sits at his desk, and I give him the paper, trying not to look at the half-eaten sub he's got in a wrapper on top of a brown paper bag. The pickles and peppers and dressing invade my nose, making my stomach growl like mad. I'm this complete freak of sensations now. Tired. Sore. Hungry. Angry. Wasting. My body is wasting. It's an actual term they use. Ketosis. I know this because one of Mom's big plays with New Ryan was to make him eat this ketogenic diet that was supposed to make him get better faster.

I remember how bad it smelled. Fat and protein mushed in a blender. She had me feed it to him so he'd know it wasn't disgusting, but even he knew better than to eat that crap. He swatted it away and pushed his lips together so it would just pour out. I remember thinking it was like a scene from a horror movie, and Mom yelled at all of us to stop acting that way. That's when she got the idea. Ryan would eat the food if we all did too.

I used to hide Oreos in my room for Livy so she wouldn't have to eat tuna salad for breakfast, steak with garlic oil for lunch. She was a little kid, for cripes' sake. She wanted chicken nuggets and french fries.

That's how I know what's happening to my body now. It is actually eating itself. Which is good for my tox screen, maybe, but not good for my state of mind. Because when your body is eating itself, you get kind of mean.

That's what was happening the first time Ryan hit Mom. I know that now, but I didn't then. Back then, I just knew he gave her a black eye, and she needed stitches inside her mouth, and then Dad threw out all the mayonnaise and said we could all eat what we wanted.

Mr. Bonham gets quiet. He rubs his hand over his face like he's trying to wake up from a deep sleep. Then he grabs a pen, signs my paper quickly, and then passes it back at me. I want to tell him I'm sorry, but I know it won't make a difference.

"Thanks," I say, because he actually was a human being to me, and I know I'm the one who screwed up.

"It wasn't my idea."

"Oh, OK." I start walking away but stop. I need to know the truth. My food-starved brain is screaming at me to stop this shit and get the fuck out of here before I ruin things even more. Too bad my need-to-know brain wins. "Excuse me, but do you mean the contest wasn't your idea?"

"No. That was my idea. Your drawing was good." He shakes his head. His hands lay flat on the desk. Hard man's hands. Unmoving. Unmoved.

I guess he means kicking me out of his class, but I'm not going to go all needy on him and ask. "Thanks again," I say, then I walk out to the bleachers on the field. I can go to the media center tomorrow.

For now, I stare at the grass, and the wind blows, and in my weird state, I feel like I'm actually watching the grass grow and change in front of my eyes. And I wonder if that's what happens to moms and their kids. That the wind changes them, and moms just have to sit and watch and love them just the same.

CHAPTER 22

Mom hears me throwing up Wednesday morning. "You're not going to school," she pronounces, and I don't fight her. I lie in my bed, staring at the ceiling, making as many bargains as I can make. If I pass this test, I'll never smoke dope again, at least until I'm on my own in California. If I pass this test, I'll be the model son. For once. If I pass this test…

I am weak from not eating. Dizzy. Nauseous. So I allow myself to open Leah's letter. The one she mailed to me the night she killed herself. I read it a hundred times when it came in the mail, but now I only let myself read it when I absolutely need it.

For John:

We are like the water. Salty. Stubborn. Frothy and rolling and scary all at once.

We are like the sea. Calm and still and alive. Changing all the time.

We have been alive forever. Long before our bodies were born. Long after our bodies will die.

We will live forever, our waters mixing with

the waters of others. All of us tossed together beneath the stars. Beneath that constellation you call your own. The sea monster one that looks down on us here on earth and knows all about us. Me and you and all the others, married and mixed in the ocean. Churned together.

Can I walk out into the water? If I say we are eternal, will you let me go? Let me slip into the sea, alone as I came into this world?

I am here, alone also, but still affecting everyone around me. I stare at the ceiling, my vision clouded, and I'm amazed I have any water left inside me to cry out. Mostly, I wonder if I've done enough to get the THC out of me. Or will this be the last time I'll be home, where I never wanted to be?

I sit on the brick ledge that surrounds a tree in front of the building. My brain knows I have to move, but my body isn't listening. That may be nerves, or it may be the effects of not eating for days and then puking up what little was in me.

I blow out a big breath and force myself to cross the threshold of the courthouse, go through security, and wait for Mr. Wexler to come get me, worrying the whole time this is not going to go well. The building isn't exactly helping. It feels dark and cramped. So cramped you can't breathe right. I try not to look as nervous as I feel. My hand goes to the silver dragon medallion.

Like I'm praying for his intervention or some shit. God, I'm still that dorky little kid.

Mr. Wexler comes forward, nods at me and gestures for me to follow him. "We'll make this as painless as possible," he says.

We walk by at least twenty cubicles. With each twist and turn, my nerves grow as large as my dragon. Some people look at me sympathetically. Others look away quickly. Maybe they think my bad luck is contagious. Like they know that I'm going down. They look back at their work when we pass, and I imagine them feeling like I deserve this. They wouldn't be wrong.

"Try to get you out of here as soon as possible," Mr. Wexler continues his running dialogue as he grabs some forms off a desk on our trip to his cave-like office, small and stuffy. Files are stacked neatly on his desk. How many of those had been started for me over the years? How many for my brother? And on the one corner, a urine specimen cup stares at me like a challenge.

Mr. Wexler sits back in his chair. "You look like shit, man."

I hold up my hand. "Save the flattery."

"Let me guess." Mr. Wexler's voice is controlled, calm, like he's talking to a wild animal. "You've spent the last few days trying to wring the pot out of you."

I feel my beast growl. He doesn't like people cornering me.

"Exercise, tons of water, maybe even a sweat suit. You know, one of those…" He motions across his body a pretty decent approximation of what I must have looked like putting on that stupid garbage bag. Then he laughs like an idiot. Shakes his head. "You've done everything in your power, but I can tell you from experience, it won't be enough."

I clear my throat. Look at my fingers.

"You do one of those clean kits?"

I stay silent.

"They're not worth it. Does the same thing. Gets rid of water weight. Fat—that's where the THC lives. Primarily."

I pick at a hole in my jeans.

"But for a regular user like you? There will still be traces."

My heart thuds in my chest, and it feels deep and thready at the same time, like it's rolling around inside an empty shell.

"Look," he says, changing his body language to tell me he's not a threat. My reaction? Anger as usual. Maia Cetus's got me. He likes confrontation. He is one sick dude.

Mr. Wexler continues, "I don't really want to give you a violation."

My head fills with all the possibilities and the probabilities that that statement is even the slightest bit true. But none of them compute.

"I can tell you care based on how crappy you look. That you care enough to not eat for days and work yourself to the point of obvious exhaustion. So here's what I want to do. I want you to tell me the truth."

"About what?"

He smiles like I've said the stupidest thing in the world. "About the weed, genius. When was the last time you smoked?"

"Three weeks ago."

He nods. "How much?"

"A couple of joints. Nothing much."

"Why did you do it?"

I consider telling him I smoked it because I needed a break from Mom hating me or that I needed a break from the constant fucking noise in my head or that when I smoke pot, I get to stop thinking about all the ways I've ruined my life, but that sounds too damned whiny. So instead, I simply say, "Tough day."

He nods, reaches forward, opens the top drawer on his desk, slides the specimen jar in, and closes the drawer again. I breathe out.

A knock on the door breaks the tension. He calls, "Come in."

The door opens, and a woman walks in carrying two boxes and two huge Cokes.

"Got us lunch. Hope that's OK." He motions. "Eat. I can wait."

I consider telling him I'm not hungry. I consider being a hard ass and refusing his help. I know this is a play, and he's winning this fucking war, but my stomach growls, and he laughs and says, "Come on, no strings attached."

So I bend my head and shovel the food in my mouth. Each bite tastes better than the last. My stomach groans, happy to be filled. Embarrassed by my savagery, I wipe my mouth with a napkin.

When I'm done with my sub, he pushes the second half of his toward me. My stomach tightens. Who is he to pity me? Still, I take the offer. I'm starving, you know? Plus, it'll make him feel that I trust him.

I chew slower this time. And drain the bottom of my drink.

"Sorry," I say between bites. "I guess I didn't realize how hungry I was." I shift in my chair. "Thanks." He should know that my mother taught me manners.

"So now we have to figure out what to do with you."

And just like that, all the food I consumed turns to cement in my stomach.

"I look around at your life, John, and I know you feel pushed in all the wrong directions. But you're not paying attention to the whole picture."

I'm annoyed at his dissection, like I'm some sort of lab rat, but I need to stay calm. I let my eyes drift to the pictures he's got on his shitty little shelves. One of him with what has to be his brother, younger than he is. The other, him in full navy uniform.

"So you're a squid? Should've figured."

He swivels around and picks up the picture. "Yeah. That's me. Top of my class at the Naval Academy." He picks up the navy picture, stares at it, and says, "I went to Pensacola. Was supposed to fly jets."

I nod. This is the part of the discussion where he shows me we are really alike. "What happened?" I ask, not because I care but because I know this is the part I've got to play in this little crap-fest production.

He looks at me. "I'm glad you asked." He gives me a

smart-assed smile. Then puts the picture back. "They give you all kinds of tests in Pensacola. You know?"

I nod. "You didn't study? Got wasted? *Tsk-tsk.*"

"These tests were not the kind you could study for."

"You puked in the oscillator? Embarrassing." I dig around with my straw, trying to find a last sip of Coke, slurping the bottom to see if the sound irritates him.

"No. Ocular afterimage."

Something about those words make me sit up. "What?"

"It's how my brain processes visual information. When I look at something and then look away, my brain still sees it. There's this afterimage, like a ghost. It happens, and there isn't anything I can do about it."

I'm floored by his confession. Not just because of the word he fed me: afterimage. But also how he can brush it off as not his fault. His face is serene, like it doesn't get to him. Afterimage. I think about that word.

"I want to see you in my office next week. Same time. And until then, you gotta promise me something."

"I know. Don't smoke."

"Yeah. That. But also, you can't let ghost images get to you. Getting the traces out of your system isn't just about the drugs. You get me?"

The tiny crack in his voice tells me the truth. No one gets over ghosts completely.

———o———

I'm sitting in Steve's office, and both of us are silent. He's waiting for me to say something he can build his session on. I'm just too damned beaten to feed him anything.

Finally, he says, "You had a rough week."

"Yup."

"You want to talk about it?"

"Nope."

He laughs good-heartedly. "We haven't had one of these sessions in a long time."

I think about all the things I don't want to say in here.

"Let's talk about the accident."

"My favorite subject."

Steve knows this isn't going to happen, but he's going to push it anyway. "You don't have to answer. I just want you to sit back and remember."

"Why the fuck would I want to do that?"

"Because you keep walking around, picking up rocks. At first, it's no big deal. You're a strong guy. It's just one rock. Besides, maybe you deserve it. You know?"

This is way too close for comfort. "You're crazy, man."

"But then, all of a sudden, you've got a handful of rocks, and they weigh a ton, and you're tired from carrying them, and someone offers you something you really want…"

"Like a Ferrari? Yeah. You know me." I am still trying to be all smart-ass, but I can tell my voice isn't selling it like I should.

"The thing is you have to let go of the rocks to get that thing you want."

"Whatever." I lean back in the couch, cover my eyes, and try to put on my armor.

"You have to decide—do you want the rocks or do you want love? Because you have to give up one to get the other. You have to let go."

The words stay with me, and he's right. As hard as I've tried to push these images out of my life, they've stayed. But I'm no way near ready to let go, so instead of seeing the day of the accident, I remember Leah when we ditched classes and went to Cape Cod.

The beach was deserted, but she led me out to the sand. She stripped off her boots, rolled up her pants, and stood at the edge of the rocks. Her hair was flying around her, and it was so cold. I wanted to call her back. I wanted to go home, but she was gorgeous and alive, standing there.

I wrapped her in a blanket and walked her back to my Jeep.

She was shivering. I held her to me, and she snuggled into my warmth. Like she needed that, and I needed it too. To be worth something to someone.

She said, "We're like the water, beating ourselves against the rocks, aren't we?"

I nodded. "I guess so."

"Why don't we stop?"

"I will if you will," I said.

She cried as I held her. I tried so hard not to let her throw herself against the rocks. I tried so hard to protect her.

Now, as Steve talks, her words come to me. *Can I walk out into the water? If I say we are eternal, will you let me go?*

211

Steve notices I'm gone. "You with me?"

"Yeah."

"Were you remembering Ryan?"

"No. Leah."

"You want to talk about it?"

"It felt good to be able to take care of her."

"Uh-huh." Steve leans forward, his posture telling me to keep going.

"That's it."

"You feel it's your job to take care of people. You want to take care of Livy."

"She's just a kid."

"You're very good to her."

"She didn't deserve any of this."

"Do you think you deserve any of this?"

I stare at the floor. Steve knows better than to ask that question. He takes in my silence and then comes at me again. "You take care of your Mom too."

"No, I don't."

"You do. You worry that she's sick. You've told me that."

"OK, so I'm not a total asshole."

"Not even a partial asshole."

"Don't take everything away from me."

"Seriously though. You don't have to save everyone."

"Ha! As if I could save anyone. You know my track record. It's, like, zero and…"

"It's OK to be mad at your mother. She didn't protect Ryan.

Then when he was hurt, she didn't protect you and Livy. You feel she left you behind."

She did leave me behind. Us. That day Ryan was hurt.

I try not to remember, but I can't help the image that comes to me. *There was blood on the street. All the neighbors were outside. Mom was screaming. Screaming. Mrs. Goldman, one of our old neighbors, bent next to her. Everyone else turned away, their eyes searching for the ambulance, I guess. It took forever to come. Someone put a blanket on Ryan. When the ambulance finally came and loaded Ryan in the back, Mom went with him. She never looked back to see if Livy and I were OK. She just went with him. And I knew that day that I was invisible to her, because I ruined my brother.*

"The trick is to know which rock to let go of and which one to keep," Steve says, but I'm not really listening anymore. Mostly, I'm thinking about what Mike Wexler said. Afterimages. Ghosts. It's hard to know which ones are real and which ones are tricks.

CHAPTER 23

When I get home, I find Mom sitting in the kitchen on her stool, reading the newspaper, Ryan in the TV room, watching one of his programs. She's probably the last person I want to see right now, my aggravation meter stuck at seriously pissed. The feeling of finally having food in my stomach has been replaced with a heavier one, caused by having to bear my soul to both Mike Wexler and Steve in one day. Not good.

"John," she starts. "Your guidance counselor called. I know you've switched your schedule, and I want to talk with you about that."

"Nothing to say." I grab a Coke out of the fridge.

"I know you're mad we missed your thing, but we *will* be at semis."

So I see their conversation included my medaling in the drawing round. The one she missed. My *thing*. Excellent. Some of my calm returns when she says that, because I'm about to burst her hopeful bubble. "I'm out of the competition."

Her face goes even paler. "John, you can't. This could be your future. Your teacher says…"

"Fuck my future. My future is going to be what it was always going to be. Me. As far away from you as possible."

Mom sits there, totally silent for one horrible moment. She brings her hand to her face, then clasps her hands. Her mouth looks like it's trying to talk, but her voice has left her. And I'm glad. I've finally stunned Lydia Strickland speechless. Then I go up to my room where I can be alone. Finally.

Eventually, Mom calls up the stairs that she's taking Ryan to therapy. "Can you get Livy at the bus?"

"Yeah," I call down.

My phone vibrates. Pete. I can deliver to you, man. When and where.

Now. At the park on Fourth Street?

See you in thirty minutes.

I think of Mike Wexler asking me not to smoke. To let my ghosts go. I reason with myself that buying the weed doesn't mean I'm going to smoke it. Besides, the timing is lining up perfectly. Like the universe is giving me this great big gift. Then there's this other thought buried underneath all of them. I've got my Jeep. I've got a ton of money. Now a little weed to send me on my way. Maybe California dreaming doesn't have to be just a dream.

———o———

I'm heading to the park when Mom calls. I hit ignore. She probably wants help getting Ryan in the van. I think about Steve saying I always want to take care of her. Like I tried to take care of Leah. Like I wanted to take care of Emily. Like I wanted Mom to take care of me. The image of her getting into the ambulance, without even looking back for Livy and me, comes screaming back to me.

Maia Cetus wakes up and growls, *Let her call someone else.*

Mom calls again. And again. Each time, I hit ignore, I feel better. Like how I know I'll feel better when I can finally smoke this weed. I meet with Pete, get my stuff, then wait for Livy's bus, which finally comes. My little sister bounds down the steps.

"Don't even ask about my day," she starts, her hands gesturing wildly. "For one thing, Gaby is the biggest jerk. I mean it. She told Dennis Hopkins I'm into him."

I laugh.

She puts her face in front of mine. "Into him, into him."

"Oh. That makes a huge difference."

"So I shut her up…"

It's such a warm day for the end of September, and I guess the ice cream truck feels like it wants to get one more route in before it's way too cold for anyone to consider.

"You want some?"

"Definitely."

I flag the guy down.

"Dove bar," Livy says.

The guy looks to me for confirmation. "Give her what she wants."

"And for you?"

"Drumstick."

A memory hits me. Mom buying Ryan and me ice cream from the ice cream truck. Livy was just a baby. A week before Ryan's accident. *He pushed forward. Ordered first. "Lemon ice."*

I got an ice cream sandwich.

He pushed ahead of me. Just a little and not so obvious, but it was how he was. He always wanted me to know the order of things in our house. He was first. I was second. It would never change. But now, I'm watching these two brothers battle it out in front of me, and it seems like a silly thing to be worked up about. I decide I'm going to try to chill a little. Remembering the bad all the time can't be good.

Livy eats her Dove bar, her cute mouth curved around the chocolate part, breaking bits of it off, then her lips closing around it like a treasure. "They're coming home." She points.

I see Mom's van round the curve.

"Here comes trouble," I mutter, the same thing Ryan used to say about me all the time in front of his friends. Then they'd laugh at me, and I'd feel so small, but then the next moment, he'd sling his arm around me and say, *Hey, be nice to my little brother. Only one who can give him shit is me.*

"Come on, Livy. Let's go."

We start walking toward our house. A screeching noise makes us turn around. Mom's van skids. I see it happen, and my hands go out as if I could help her. Livy shrieks. Both of us are running. Trying to get to them. Mom goes off the road and crashes into a tree.

———o———

Livy screams, and we run to the van, our ice creams hitting the ground as we charge forward.

Blood drips on the ground in front of me, and I know I must have imagined that, because we aren't close enough to have gotten hurt. Then I realize it's Livy's blood. She must have bit her lip.

I go to the van. The front of the van is buckled, and the air bags are deployed on both sides. There's blood. I can see blood, and I don't know what to do. The front door is bunched, and I can't get it open. Mom's knocked out, and she doesn't come to as I pull on the door. I hear sirens and footsteps. One of our neighbors, a guy I've seen drive to work and back, is pulling on my arm.

"Let me help you," he says.

Together, we pull and pull.

The sirens get closer. We pull and pull, and nothing happens.

"Is it just your mom in the van?" the guy asks.

"Oh my God, Ryan." I cup my hands and try to look inside the van, but it's just a wreck of stuff. Nothing makes sense. There are shopping bags and clothes and part of his wheelchair in the body of the van. But where's Ryan? I try to open the side door to find him, but a paramedic hits me on the shoulder.

"Back up."

I almost punch him. The adrenaline's got me so crazy. I try to speak, but my throat is closed. My neighbor says, "Disabled brother in the back," to another paramedic, who nods. The firemen push me back. They've got a tool to open the van.

I hear steps behind me. I don't turn to see who it is. Someone grabs my arm.

"John, it's me." Emily moves me away, and I've got no idea why when all I want to do is go to them. Help them. Save them. "Sh. Sh. It's OK." We stay on the edge, watching.

They unload Mom and put her on a stretcher. I work my way to her side.

"Are you OK, Mom?"

She's got an oxygen mask covering her face, and her eyes are searching, searching. I hold her hand. "You're going to be all right."

"Ryan?"

"Sh, Mom, it's OK. Sh."

She closes her eyes, and they load her on the ambulance.

"We're taking her to University Hospital."

I nod. Or I think I do. Nothing seems real. None of this feels real. My body is stuck in this quicksand that's around me, and I'm sinking, sinking.

The ambulance leaves, siren blaring. I want to reach my hand out to touch the lights. I need something to make this real.

A police officer asks me, "Are you her son?"

That's when I see the second stretcher. Ryan's stretcher.

I stumble forward. Another officer grabs my arm. "Let's go over here. Take a seat."

There's a blanket around me, which is good, because I feel so cold. The coldest I've ever felt.

They push my brother by me. His eyes are open, and his face is all cut up.

"Good thing he had this helmet on," one of the attendants says.

They put him in the ambulance and turn on the siren, and that feels wrong, like I don't want them to take my brother away from me.

The police officer tries to ask me questions, but Emily's mom waits. "We have to get in touch with their father. Get them to the hospital." She takes us in the house, me and Livy. The same house we went into when Ryan was hit in our driveway years ago. But this time, instead of the old woman who lived there, it's Emily's family who does.

"Do you have your dad's number?" she asks me.

I'm frozen. Numb. Emily points to my pocket where I have my cell. I give it to her mom. Livy comes and sits next to me at the kitchen table, and I lean on my arms. Livy puts her head against my shoulder. I hear Emily's mom speaking with my father, and I don't care. I just don't care.

———o———

Dad picks us up and takes us to the hospital. "I got her a private room," Dad says as if that is a huge accomplishment and makes him a great person. "They said she's going to be OK. Just a little banged up."

I put my arm around Livy. We find her room, number 224. Dad goes in first. Mom looks more than just a little banged up. She's hooked up to a ton of tubes and monitors. Her face is really red, and one side looks like it's been burned.

She puts her hand out. Livy goes to her. Dad and I stand back.

"She can't talk," a nurse who is writing on a clipboard says.

"The air bag hit her in the throat. She must have been turning around when she hit. She's got whiplash, and her face is burned from the air bag. That's normal."

Livy holds Mom's hand. "Are you OK, Mom?"

She nods. "Ryan?" she whispers.

I'm pissed no one told her.

"He's going to be fine. There's no stopping that kid, Lydia." Dad holds her hand. "Just a few scrapes. I'm taking him home today."

The nurse comes back a few minutes later with a needle. "She needs to rest. The results came back from the X-rays. You have pneumonia. Probably why you passed out."

Dad nods. The nurse puts the needle in her IV line and releases the fluid that makes Mom's eyes close.

Dad gives me the keys. "Take Livy home and get a pizza or something."

"I want to see Ryan," Livy says.

"We'll stop on our way out."

"I'm glad you're here," she says.

And for this moment, I actually am too.

———o———

There's no way to walk into this hospital room and not go back to the first accident. This time, he's in a room with four other kids, and he's not connected to tubes. He's sleeping, and I don't want to wake him, so we stop the nurse.

"They gave him something to help him sleep, but he's fine.

They just got all the tests back, and he just had a few scrapes. Very lucky considering he wasn't in his seat belt."

I nod. "He hated his car seat. Must have busted out."

She gives me a weird look but says, "Try not to wake him. We want him to sleep through the night."

"I thought he was going home today."

"They decided to keep him for a few days. Give him some good nutrition and IV meds. Antibiotics. Make sure he's good before we release him."

"Oh. That's probably good. Come on, Liv." I lead her out of the room. "We'll meet Dad downstairs."

Sitting in the chairs in the lobby, Livy sipping her Starbucks, mocha Frappuccino, I see Emily come in. I should probably be happy she's here, but I can't forget how a few days ago, she wouldn't even take my calls.

"Hey," she says, her eyes skating from my hands to my face, then back, like she's trying to decipher my body's code to figure out how I'm feeling. How I'm feeling is done. With everything here. With Ryan. And Mom. And me. And all of the stupid effing memories that don't change a thing. Like I'm a million pieces of me. Like if a wind blew into this room, I could be swept up in the dust of the pain I've caused, and that would be good.

Livy wraps her arms around Emily. I hear Livy's little sobs, and I know I'm being an ass. I know this, but I can't stop. "Sh. It's OK," Emily whispers into my little sister's head.

"I'm going to the bathroom," Livy says. "I'll be right back."

That gives Emily time to approach me. Though I wouldn't

recommend it now. She puts her hand on my arm, and I swear, it feels like it's burning me. "I wanted to be here for you. I hope it's OK."

I don't answer.

"I'm sorry I got so mad. I…I just got scared…you know?"

"Maybe you could take Livy home. I'm going to wait here for Dad."

Emily's quiet, which makes me a little glad. Like I am stronger than she is. Like this proves I don't need her. She's nothing to me.

Her face turns stony, and she gets up. I hear her whispering something about pizza to Livy, who looks at me.

"You go. I'll be home soon."

Emily puts her arm around Livy's shoulder, and I almost wish she'd look back, but I know by the fierceness of her stride that Emily is pretty pissed at me. Whatever. She's not the only one. Livy does turn to wave, and I smile so she'll know I'm all right. Then they slip away, and I'm alone again.

The sound of the automatic doors opening and closing kills me. It's all I can do to not lose it. Mom and Dad walked me into the lobby through those doors all those years ago, after Ryan's first accident. I remember how scared I was when we went into the elevator that took us to Ryan's floor.

The nurses knew Mom and Dad, but they didn't know me. They smiled at me, but that was just because they didn't know Ryan's accident was my fault. I didn't want to go in the room, but I had to.

Ryan was in the bed, tubes everywhere. Dad held my hand, but it was Mom I focused on. I could feel the breath she was holding, like she'd raised the drawbridge on one of those castles Ryan and I built together, trapping the breath inside her. Almost like she thought that not breathing would make the accident not true.

I held my breath right along with hers. My eyes closed, and I pretended we were in the backyard playing baseball or tag or whatever Ryan wanted to play. I wasn't even angry that he was winning or that he was better than I was. In my mind, I was just happy, and I believed for a second that that vision was real. That if I were good for the rest of my life, my brother would come back.

But then Dad spoke, and my eyes opened and so did Ryan's. Only his were different. They looked like big marbles more than eyes, and even though they were open, he didn't look like he was seeing anyone or anything.

Mom leaned over Ryan and squeezed his hand. "Ryan, baby. It's Mommy. Do you see Mommy?"

Ryan didn't move. He didn't blink. He didn't look at them. It was as if he didn't see. And I knew there was nothing I could ever do to fix this.

Tears ran down Mom's face, and I could practically taste the salt of her tears in my mouth. Like her pain was stronger, more deserved than my own. I didn't deserve my own pain. Just my guilt.

She backed away from Ryan, grabbed my shoulders. I thought she was going to yell at me, but she just pushed me in front of him. "Say hi to Ryan, John. Say hi to your brother."

I tried to stare at his eyes only. I tried to make him see me, but then I saw the big cut they'd sewn up on his forehead and his big unseeing eyes scared me, and I pulled away. I ran like the coward I was. I ran as fast as I could, as far as I could.

I come back to the here and now, only I wish I could disappear. I'm a body full of ache and pain and need. Only there's no word for what I need. There's no language. I am a wild beast. I put my head in my hands. My face is wet. My eyes close. I wait to die. I want to die. I pray to die so this will end. Finally. Leah's words come back to me. Truer than ever.

We're like the water, beating ourselves against the rocks. Why do we do that?

CHAPTER 24

It doesn't take long for the rumors to start flying around school. Brandon and Parker act like my bodyguards for most of the day. Even Matt takes point. At least that's what it feels like, because one of them is always next to me. It would be kind of touching if it wasn't all so surreal.

Their presence doesn't keep kids from staring at me. Or talking. I hear them whisper, and it puts my dragon on high alert, ready for a fight. Between me freaking out at the awards thing the other night and then Mom crashing the car, Ryan not being properly restrained, we are definitely feeding the news cycle. Me fighting is exactly the wrong kind of press my family needs right now, so I try to keep as calm as I can. I pretend I am on that beach. I pretend I am with Emily, and she's not mad at me, and I'm not acting like an asshole. I pretend I let her quiet concern wash over me like the waves of the Pacific Ocean. I make it all the way through the day, and finally, it's time for our scrimmage, and I feel almost too calm. Because on that lacrosse field, they expect me to be all beast, and I am happy to oblige.

The smell of the field and the crowd standing on the sidelines are all I need to get pumped. As soon as my cleats hit the grass, I start to feel normal again. I start to breathe. That's what I'm here for. Forty-eight minutes of regulation, where nobody has the time to ask me if I think Mom meant to hurt Ryan, the newest rumor to hit the mill today, served up by Dominique in the hallway, her faking concern the whole time, me trying hard not to strangle her.

Coach Gibson has everyone pulled in close to him. Pregame pep talk. "Parkland's a good team. We need to be sharp. Make no mistakes."

Mistakes. As if any of the mistakes we make on this field could compare to the ones I've made off the field. Why didn't I answer Mom's call yesterday? Why do I keep screwing everything up?

"John." Coach's eyes take me in. "Are you sure you want to be here?"

"Big game, Coach. Bragging rights, right?"

"OK, Parker, Brandon, Luke…" He rattles off names, none of which are mine. They take the field, leaving me and my problems behind.

"You don't think you should be home with your family?" Coach shakes his head, looks on, and checks his clipboard. I know he's worried about this game. And I know he wants me in. After what Parkland did to us last time and how I've become a monster player for the team, he's already doing the math, figuring how much I can contribute. We both need this.

"Ryan's fine. So is Mom. Both will be home tomorrow," I say. "They don't need me. Not like you do."

He looks me over, shakes his head, and finally nods. "OK, but you gotta play clean. I know these refs. They're like a bunch of forty-year-old ladies pissed 'cause they still have their periods."

I put on my helmet, showing him I'm ready for battle. "What the eff, Johnson," I call, campaigning to get my start. "Chase him down."

"Wake up, Walker. Don't let him by you. Slide, slide!" Then to me. "You go in next."

They score. Play is stopped. Coach waves Johnson in.

"You're in, John." He claps me on the back.

And just like that, the last three days of pain fade to black. I'm not Ryan's brother, the one who always screwed up. The one who Emily's pissed at. The one who lost Leah.

I'm just a machine. I run, I hit, I throw. I don't feel. Feeling's not part of the game.

"John!" Matt waves his stick at me as I take my position at midfield. I nod back.

We take the first face-off, the ball gets caught on the ground.

"Ball, ball, ball," Matt yells.

I'm already there, elbows and stick pushing people out of the way. With the ball cradled, I turn and crash into Wesley Turner from Parkland. He tries to stand up against me. Stupid today. I leave him on the ground, like the ball was a few minutes ago. Faces blur as I make my way down the field. I stand and shoot, side-armed. Wide right. Just. Matt races for the ball, stick out. We get it back.

Brandon takes it in.

Brandon passes it to Matt. Wesley's on my back, trying to

stay with me. I roll and leave him behind. The ball barely in my stick, I fire a bounce shot into the far-left corner. The goalie shifts but not in time. Score.

I run to my place on the right side of the field. Wesley lines up against me.

"Pretty good shot, Strickland," he says. "But you're not gonna get another chance."

"Whatever," I say. I'm not much for smack talk. Don't really see the point.

Waiting for Parker to take the face-off makes me nervous, gives me time to think.

Images invade my mind. Ryan in our driveway years ago after he got hit. I blink. See the blood spilling out of his head. I blink again. Sweat leaks into my eyes and forces them closed. I see Mom getting into the ambulance and leaving me and Livy. Not looking back.

We lose the face-off. I chase Wesley down after he takes the pass. My stick hits his, and he drops the ball. I push him off and root around on the ground. I'm surrounded by bodies and sticks. Everyone's digging for gold. Matt comes up with it, and we race downfield. The running helps me push everything out of my mind. I feel the animal inside me breathe fire.

Fourth quarter, we're down five to four. "Hey, Strickland, too bad about your brother, but since he's already a retard, can you even hurt him?" Nate, defenseman from Parkland, calls out to me.

Fire explodes in my head. When the ball's in play, I cross

the field and knock him to the ground. Don't even try to make it look clean. Ref calls a penalty. Two-minute personal foul. I look over at Nate as I walk to the sideline. He gets up smiling.

Coach shakes his head. "Settle down, John," he says.

As I kneel next to the scoring table to do my time, I see Mike Wexler on the sidelines and get a bad feeling. He and Coach are looking at me and talking. I push them out of my mind. My eyes on Nate. I count down till I can get back in and get back on him.

I jog onto the field. Matt comes up to me. "Take the face-off," he says.

I know what he's trying to do. He wants me away from Nate. Wesley comes forward.

I'll be facing off against him.

"I'm sorry, man. He's an asshole," Wesley says.

I agree, but I don't need his charity. I grit my teeth and get ready to battle. The whistle blows, and I'm up and away. Not even going after the ball. Nate wanted it to be personal, and I'm happy to oblige, even if that makes Mr. Wexler pissed off enough to give me a violation. Once you wake the dragon, there's no leashing him.

I turn, watch Wesley speed by me, and look for my prey. I'm three steps from him, can feel myself hurling into him, but stop as Matt lays out Nate. Ref calls a penalty. Another two minutes. Matt nods to me as he runs off the field. I hear the crowd groan as they score: six-four.

Next play, Brandon lines up against him. I lose him as the face-off becomes a huddle. When I make it past the traffic, I see Brandon take him down. They score. Nate is dizzy, and his coach pulls him out.

Ref comes on the field, whistle blowing. They have a conference, and both coaches go on the field. Brandon is ejected, and our team is given a warning. Next penalty will mean suspensions. We wanted this game. But *semper fi*.

Coach calls us off the field as the clock hits zero. He waves off the good sportsmanship handshake bullshit. The vein in his neck is bulging, and his face is beet red.

"Next time you guys pull shit like that, I'll sit you all down. I'll let the girls' field hockey team play for you, you ever get wild like that again."

"Coach, you should've heard…" Matt tries.

Coach's hand goes up. "Don't wanna hear it. John's a big boy. He doesn't need you guys to go vigilante for him. Do you, John?"

He's right. I should've left it alone. Nate got a cheap win. And a concussion probably. That thought makes me smile.

"OK, you guys, come to practice ready to run tomorrow, because nothing beats a bad attitude like running it out of you. Everyone hit the showers, except John. You stay here."

Matt claps me on the back. "Later, man."

"Thanks." I grab his hand, and we bump chests.

"All for one," Brandon says.

Coach shakes his head.

"Sorry, Coach," I start.

"Save it." Both of his hands go up like stop signs. "I didn't keep you back so we can get our love on."

"No?"

"This man says he's got business with you." Coach motions to Mr. Wexler, who's sitting on the bench, a stupid smile on his face.

"You came to watch me get all beast?"

"Not exactly. I did come to see how you are."

"I'm good. Great. You saw." I point to the field as proof, then walk back to the bench and start getting my gear.

"Look, John, we need to settle a few things."

"I'm good." I turn and start walking.

"I don't want…"

I stop and turn to face him. "I am *not* your little brother."

"What?"

"Whatever happened to him, saving me won't save him."

Direct hit. Mr. Wexler's face turns purple, but he keeps talking. "Right now, I'm asking. But at some point, this will stop being voluntary."

The animal inside me growls. He hates this shit. "Look, I'm not going to use. You happy?"

"I want to help you come up with a plan. Anyone who could get an entire team to give up a game against a big rival for you, that's pretty impressive."

"That?" I laugh. "That was stupid guy shit. And it was just a scrimmage. We'll tear their asses up during the regular season."

"I'd like to know what there is about you that inspires such loyalty."

"What can I say?" I spread my arms wide and start to walk backward toward the locker room. "I'm easy to love."

"So why don't you try loving yourself a little?"

I hike my gear bag higher up on my shoulder. "Can you cut the psychobabble act for two seconds? I have a therapist, and Steve is going to get super jealous if you don't back the fuck off me."

He speed-walks and gets in front of me, blocks my way. "You need to know something."

"I don't…"

"I'm trying to warn you."

"Warn me?"

"DCF is investigating the accident."

The words are so frightening, they can't be real. Department of Children and Families. Crap. DCF. DCF was the reason Mom kicked me out the first time. Not again. It can't be. The sounds of me smashing her furniture, her china, vases. Me doing all that so they would see *I* was the problem. So Livy could stay.

Mr. Wexler's eyes go to Livy standing with Emily and some of the girl lacrosse players who are hanging, talking with Brandon and Parker. "You want to protect her, right?"

I stand numb. Stupid.

"I'll do my best to keep her out of it, but I need you to come in. And now I need to test you for real. I can't get out of it. I can give you till Friday, but that's all I can do."

I nod.

"Your mom will be cleared, I'm sure, but they'll want to see that you're clean also. You understand?"

"Yeah."

He walks away, and I want to leave my body. Would Friday be long enough?

"John, wait." I soften at my little sister's voice. Livy.

"Who was that?" Emily asks, even though she knows she doesn't have the right anymore, and I answer her, though I don't know why.

"My probation officer." I reach down and hold Livy's hand.

"What's up?"

"No big. They want me to come in and talk. It's a good thing," I add.

"What if they want to talk to me too?"

"They won't. But if they do, just tell the truth. Mom would never hurt us." I put my arm around Livy's shoulder.

"I mean about Ryan."

"Oh, then just say that he's your second-favorite big brother." Livy laughs, but I can tell she's worried.

Emily unlocks her car. "Will you let me give you a ride home?"

"Yeah, thanks." I try not to sound too cold or let on that I'm planning to be out of here tonight.

CHAPTER 25

I'm in such a total fog when I walk in the door that I almost don't notice that Mom and Ryan are home. All I can think of is protecting Livy, but Dad's got this big family dinner laid out at the kitchen table, and there's really no way I'm going to get out of it.

Spaghetti in vodka sauce is the one thing he knows how to make, and it's usually so good that I can't get enough, but tonight, as he passes around the broccoli in garlic, I am trying to figure out how to chew the food that's already in my mouth, not to mention the rest that's on my plate.

"Sorry we missed the game. How'd it go?" Dad asks as he loads me up with garlic bread.

"Fine."

Mom laughs. "Serves you right for asking a high school boy a question."

Rosie wheels Ryan in from his bath. "Say good night, Ryan."

"Ni!" He waves and actually looks happy to be going to bed. He points to the hallway, and Rosie says, "I guess he's ready to hit the hay."

There's this really strong desire to reach out to him. To do one thing to let him know that I'm going to miss him, because the weird thing is, after all this, I am going to miss this New Ryan—the one I'm just getting to know.

Mom watches me. "He's fine, honey. Just a few scrapes. Good as new."

I nod.

"Kid is amazing," Dad says. "Nothing can stop him." He piles more food on his plate and then takes a big bite.

Livy twirling her spaghetti is so effing cute I almost can't stand it. *You OK?* she mouths in my direction.

I smile, take a big bite of spaghetti, and shine my good mood on her. Even if it's fake. Even if this time tomorrow, she'll hate me, my leaving is the only thing that will stop this whole stupid crazy train.

Mom coughs but eats.

I sit there with my family, sad because I'm about to walk away from something I said I didn't want. My parents are here, and they're together. And they're talking about me. Me. As if I matter. And that alone feels so good that it's almost unreal. I tell my mind to sit this one out and just listen with my heart. I don't worry about anything or anyone. I just exist. Like that constellation in the sky looking down at everyone on earth who is too small and insignificant to be relevant, except they are the most relevant thing in the world. And they know it. I know it. Livy smiles at me, and I'm healed and slayed at the same time, because by this time tomorrow, I'll break her heart like Leah broke mine.

———◦———

I wait until all the lights are out. Then I wait a half hour more. I'm all packed. The important stuff anyway. My pictures. My stuff. The weed I picked up from Pete. The rest of that Jack Daniel's Emily had. It's all in my lacrosse bag. My lacrosse stuff is stacked neatly in my closet. Mom can probably sell it on eBay. I could go out the front door. Mom's loaded up on cough medicine, I'm sure, and no way Ryan gets up and sees me, but I'm not taking that chance. 12:00 a.m. Leah used to call that the witching hour. I open my window as quietly as I can. I lean out and lower my bag with a rope, dropping it lightly on the ground. Then I climb out onto the tree outside my window. The tree Ryan used to always tell me was a ghost ready to come get me. I get it now. Brothers do stuff like that. It doesn't mean anything. I lower myself, branch by branch, until my feet hit the ground.

I am so stealthy, so quiet, that when I make it to my car, I don't even use the key fob to open the doors, knowing that'll make a sound. Key in the lock, I turn it, so quiet, throw my crap in the backseat. Start the Jeep, keeping the lights off. I'm about to pull out when there's a knock on my window that makes me jump out of my skin.

A light shines in on me, and I'm terrified it's the police or, just as bad, Mike Wexler, but it's Emily. I put my hand over my heart. "Holy crap, you scared the shit out of me."

"Good. Let me in. We need to talk."

I nod. Wait for her to climb in the passenger seat before pulling out, driving, slow, lights out, until we turn the corner and head for the park. Our park.

I barely get the car parked when she starts on me. "You think I don't know the signs of someone who's about to run?"

"I…"

She hits my arm. "It's so selfish. You have no idea…"

"I didn't have a choice."

"There's always a choice."

"Prison? You think that's a great choice?"

Her face goes white. "Why?"

"I used three weeks ago. You know this. I have to go in and give a sample now because of the accident."

"Wait. What?"

"Ryan wasn't in his car seat, so DCF was called. Now the whole family is under a microscope. It's not going to help anyone if I fail the drug test and get violated and go to prison."

"How is it going to help your family if you run away?"

"DCF always want a scapegoat. I'll be that."

"It won't help. Stay. Tell them she always belted him in. He must have gotten out. If you leave, no one will be left to stand up for her." Tears are running down her face now. "I know it's a risk. I know you don't want to go to jail, but it's almost four weeks. You'll pass."

"What if I don't?"

"I don't know. But if you leave, you'll definitely violate the court order, and you'll never be able to come back. Never." She starts to cry harder. "And when you leave, it kills everyone else. You have no idea what it feels like to be left behind. What you'll be doing to Livy."

I grab her face. "Sh. OK. You're right."

"And me. What about what it'll do to me if you leave?"

"You can be with Marty. He's better for you than I am."

She punches me in the arm. Again and again. "I get to decide that, or don't I?"

I start to laugh. "I give. Ow. Stop. I said I give." She's sobbing now, full out. I pull her into my chest. "I'm not going, OK? You're right. I thought it would be better for everyone if I did, but you're right."

"It would only be better for *you* if you did."

"There are things you don't know about me, Emily. Things that would change your mind about me."

"You don't know that."

I look at my hands. "What if I told you that it's my fault. All of this?"

"It can't be your fault."

"What if it is? What if my Mom has the right to hate me?"

"She doesn't hate you. Tell me. And I'll be objective, and if it is your fault, I promise you, I'll kiss you good-bye and send you on your way."

"So you want me to tell you?"

"I'm here, aren't I?"

The memories are lined up in my mind, pushing their way to the front. The accident that changed our lives shouldn't have even happened. It was stupid dumb luck. The worst kind. I'm sure everybody believes their version of the truth is the right one. The real one. I believe that the most important truth is that Ryan started it, but I finished it.

"It happened the summer I turned seven. Ryan was nine, and Livy was just a baby. It was supposed to be a great day. We were at the breakfast table. Ryan was eating Froot Loops. I was eating Frosted Flakes." I laugh. "It's funny the little things you remember."

"Yeah." Emily unzips my lacrosse bag, takes out the Jack Daniel's, offers it to me.

I wave her off. I don't want to stop talking, because I'm scared if I do, I won't be able to finish this. "Livy was in her high chair, and Mom was at the sink. The coffeemaker had just stopped percolating. I remember the sound that last drip being brewed made, because once it was gone, there was another sound: Mom crying."

I stop for a second. My mom crying used to be the worst sound I'd ever heard. It made me feel completely hopeless.

"Why was your mom crying?" Emily asks.

"She and Dad had been fighting all summer. About work mostly. And watching us. Dad came into the kitchen."

I was just about to ask him what was wrong with Mom when I saw he was wearing work clothes. Work clothes were wrong.

"We were supposed to be going to the museum of science to see the exhibition on Eskimos. Dad was supposed to have us out of the house all day so Mom could work on an article. And we were going to see real igloos."

Emily nods. She takes a drink of Jack, then points to me.

"Ryan and I were obsessed with them."

"I get that. Igloos are cool."

I can hear them arguing.

"Come on, Lydia," Dad said. "What did you want me to do? It's not like I had a choice."

Mom slammed some dishes into the dishwasher. "You could tell them you had plans with your family. With your sons. You could say no for a change. Which you have no problem saying to us. Just not to them."

Dad's eyes fell on us. "I'm sorry, guys. I have to go into work today. You understand, right?"

I nodded, but Ryan gave me an angry look.

"I'll take you next weekend."

"The exhibit is only here till Tuesday," Ryan said.

"Maybe Mom can take you?"

"Great. Promise something I can't possibly do. I've got a deadline tomorrow. A hard deadline."

"You could ask for more time."

"That's real professional."

Emily's hand falls on my arm. "You OK?"

I had no idea I just stopped talking. After keeping it all locked up inside for so long, I'm stunned how close the memories are still. How it feels as if I'm really there.

"Yeah. I"—I press the heel of my hand into my eye—"uh… they were going back and forth. Fighting over who would watch us. Who would take us to the museum. How would Mom write her article. Dad was being a dick."

Emily nods, so I keep going. I put my hand out and take a drink of Jack, not because I need it but because it'll buy me time to remember it myself first before interpreting it for her.

Dad stood up, banged into the table as he did. "Yeah, because it's the money you make from your little hobby*"—he used air quotes around that word—"that keeps this family afloat, right?"*

I didn't know what to do. I looked at Ryan. He looked down. I saw him on his phone.

"Finally, Mom got so pissed that she did the weirdest thing. She filled a glass of water and threw it at Dad."

"Are you serious?" Emily extends her hand, and I put the bottle in it. "Parents are so fucked up." She drinks a big swig.

"Yeah. It was kind of terrifying, you know? Seeing her act like that."

"Yeah. I guess your dad wasn't too happy about that."

"To say the least. He yelled back at her. So Mom said, 'You know what's perfect? Me serving you. Like the woman I am.' Then she stormed over to him and slammed a cup of coffee on the table. It spilled and burned his hand. He cried out and then swiped at it, sending it flying. The coffee sprayed everywhere."

Emily's eyes go to my face. Faint burn marks are still there. If she looked beneath my shirt, she'd find more burns on my neck and down my arm. I got it the worst of anyone that day. She puts her soft hand on my face, and I let her concern blanket me. I let her care for me, and it feels almost safe being with her now. But only because I haven't said the worst part yet. I wipe at my eyes. I need to finish this. Then I can decide if I stay or I go. And at least after all this, maybe I can stop seeing these flashes.

"Livy started wailing. I wasn't sure if it was because she got hit with the coffee or she was just scared by the shouting. Mom got a towel off the refrigerator door, put it under the ice maker. Some spilled out onto the floor—I could hear the cubes hit the floor like a bunch of rocks sliding down a mountain."

"Aw, John." Emily's hand goes on my face, but I brush it off. I've got to finish this.

"She…she caught the rest and put it on my neck where the burn was the reddest."

Emily nods.

"Mom screamed at Dad to leave, but he was already out the door. She picked up Livy and started rocking her."

Mom coos to her, but at least it was over. At least it was over, and Ryan and I could go upstairs, and it would be OK, because we'd be together. "Sh, baby. Sh."

"I was holding the ice to my chest and crying. Ryan was trying not to cry. I could tell. He left the room, and I followed him. I asked him where he was going."

"What do you mean? Where was Ryan going?"

"He was bailing on us, going to hang with his friends."

Mom was on the phone, Livy sleeping on her shoulder. "You wouldn't believe it…" She was talking to one of her friends, completely ignoring Ryan. She always let him get away with leaving to see his friends.

So I followed him. Got in front of him. "You didn't even ask Mom."

Ryan scoffed. "No way I'm taking you with me this time."

"You're a jerk." I grabbed his helmet.

He knew he wasn't allowed to go skating without it.

"Man. Whenever things got bad at home for either of us, Dylan would come over. We'd get through it together, you know?"

This time, I nod.

"Hold on a sec," Mom said into the phone, then slipped it into her pocket. She took Ryan's helmet from me. It swung from her hand. "Ryan, wait. I need you to watch your…"

Ryan got on his skateboard. Pointed to me. "I'm not babysitting him. Not after last time. You know how he is…"

"Ryan was pissed at me, because the last time he watched me, I fell down this hill, broke a couple of ribs, and he got blamed."

"Was it his fault?"

"Yes. But I lied for him. Told Mom and Dad I didn't listen to him, when really, he and his friends dared me to go down this big hill after I'd just learned to ride my bike."

"Wow. Nice big brother."

"You know, for years, I was pissed about that. But now I think maybe that's just the way brothers are. But that day, I was upset, and I didn't want him to leave us."

I was the one who was burned, and he didn't even care. He was going to bail. Leave me and Livy alone with Mom, crying and pissed. He was going to leave me because I embarrassed him. Got him in trouble. I couldn't hold it in anymore, no matter what we agreed to.

The feelings overcome me. The heat from the burn. Being left behind by Ryan. To know I embarrassed him. All of this feels fresh to me, as if it's happening right in front of me.

"And I did it. I told on him."

"So what happened?"

"Mom's face got white. She looked at him like he was Dad then. Like he was a horrible person. And for a second, I felt vindicated. Then…then he…he…"

"He what?"

"He called me a baby and he…turned away from me."

"And?"

"And I told him to go die in a hole."

"So? Everyone says stuff like that. It doesn't mean anything."

"Mom was so mad she turned to face me."

"So?"

"So that's when…"

That's when we heard Ryan get hit.

"And?"

"And I never saw my brother again."

"Oh, John…" And then her arms are around me. "That doesn't make it your fault."

"If I hadn't…if…"

"If he hadn't. If Pete hadn't…it just happened. It's not your fault."

I am crying like a baby, and I can't stop. I'm shaking, and I want to die. It's like I feel like Leah beating herself against the rocks. I can understand why she'd want that to stop. Why she couldn't keep beating herself bloody for things she couldn't change. I am like that too. I want the pain to stop more than I want to keep going. I hear myself howling, howling not like a dragon but a wolf. "Oh God, I want…I want…"

Emily rocks me and says, "Sh. It's OK. It's OK."

Her body is curled around mine, and I smell the Jack, and I feel my eyes leaking all over me, my nose running like a little kid, and I don't think I can stop. I forget how to breathe, and she's beating me on my back, and I'm not sure how long we sit there, her holding me and telling me it's OK. Rocking me. Shushing me. Her hands all over my head, holding it together, because it's about to explode with the feelings. When I'm finally done, she hands me the Jack, and I down a gulp of it. I'm not worried about getting drunk. I'm not worried about anything, because I'm numb now—just totally wrung the fuck out. I wipe my eyes with the back of my hand.

"It's a horrible story, John. It's terrible. But none of it was your fault."

I stare out the window. At the constellation I made my own years ago when I needed Uncle Dave to be my dad. When I would have traded anyone else to be my mom. Cetus. The sea monster. Me.

Emily stares at my dragon medallion. "You've been so strong for so long."

"Me? No. I'm not…"

She holds the pendant. "Sh. I'm not asking. I'm telling you that you have been." She wipes at my face. "You have to do this next part. You have to go be strong again. Go in. Get tested. Tell your parents to stand with you when you do it. They'll understand. I see how they look at you. They want you to be OK, but they're scared too."

I nod. "Maybe."

"Tell me about this." She holds on to my dragon necklace like she did that time in the park weeks ago.

Only this time, I tell her. She's earned it. "My uncle Dave, the one I lived with for a while in Chicago."

"The welder?"

"Yeah. When I was little, especially after the accident, he used to come and take Livy and me out. We'd go to the zoo sometimes or the museum. You know?"

"Sounds nice."

"He said Livy and I didn't get to have enough kid time. My favorite was the dinosaur exhibit."

"I thought it was igloos."

I reach out for the bottle of Jack. Then reach out for her to lean her head against my chest. "Nah. That was just with Ryan. That was our thing. So he took me to see this exhibit about the good mother dinosaur. The maiasaura named Sue. The name meant 'the good mother,' and she was called that because they found her babies all around her, proving for the first time that she took care of them. She was a good mother."

"I like that story."

"I like it too. Uncle Dave always took me to see her whenever he was in town. Then one time, he also bought me a telescope. And we sat outside and looked at the stars, and he bought me a book on constellations. My favorite was one called Cetus. The sea monster."

"I love that."

"The thing is, I was a really lonely kid. So—and this is the truly dorky part—I created my own dragon named Maia Cetus."

"A combination of the two of them."

I move her hand off the medallion. "Uh-huh. Pretty stupid, huh?"

"Pretty cool if you ask me. You made this?" She picks it up again.

"Yeah. With Uncle Dave."

She turns the piece over in her hand. In the streetlight, her face is so intensely beautiful as she examines my heart, dangling from the cord around my neck. She looks me in the eyes. "Maia Cetus." She kisses the dragon pendant. "Thank you for protecting John all these years until I could get to him."

That small kiss takes the wind out of me. I stare at this girl who feels like the softest place to land. She smiles up at me, and I have no choice but to kiss her, soft on the lips, like she kissed my dragon. "You're so beautiful, you know that?"

"So you won't leave?"

"No. I'd miss you too much. Would be caught sneaking back to see you."

She laughs, tears glistening in her eyelashes. I laugh too.

"How can you be pretty when you cry?"

She wipes her eyes with the back of her hand, and that gets to me, how strong she is trying to be all the time. Steve said I should find someone who took care of me as much as I did them. I lean forward, put my hand under her chin, and bring her lips to mine.

We kiss for what seems like hours and seconds at the same time. I stop, and her face looks confused. "Does this mean we're dating again?" I ask.

"Uh-huh," she says, pulling me toward her this time.

"No more Marty?"

This time, she laughs. "There never was."

We kiss some more, and then she pulls back. "The only question I have is how are you planning to sneak back in? That's got to be way harder than sneaking out."

And we both laugh, and that laugh makes everything feel a little better.

CHAPTER 26

D ad is here in the morning again, and I'm almost about to
ask what's up with that, but I've got bigger things to talk
about. When I make it to the kitchen, he hands me a cup of
coffee, and I say, "I'm not going to school today."

He takes a drink of his coffee. "Why?"

"We need to talk."

"Me and you?"

"Me, you, and Mom."

I have to give Dad credit. He doesn't balk, doesn't flinch. Just stirs
his coffee, places the spoon in the sink, and drinks. "I'll tell her."

I sit on the stool in the kitchen, drinking the coffee Dad poured
me, wishing I didn't have to do this next thing, but Emily's right—I
need to.

Mom and Livy enter the kitchen, Mom dressed in jeans and a
long-sleeved shirt, Livy still in her pajamas, which makes me ask,
"What's up?"

Mom slides her arm around Livy's shoulder. "We were thinking this would be a family day."

Suddenly, my skin feels like it's on fire. "Why?"

Mom says, "They're sending a DCF person to speak with
us today."

"I know. Mr. Wexler told me."

"So we thought we'd do it together," Dad says.

No wonder he was so calm about what I said—he already knew. The doorbell rings. We all sort of jump, then laugh. Rosie scoots ahead of us and opens the door. But instead of a person from DCF, there's Uncle Dave.

His arms are out before he even gets in the house. He goes from hugging Rosie, to Livy, who jumps in his arms, to me. I go for the one-armed man hug, but he pulls me close to him. Pats me on the back. "Good to see you, John."

Dad and Mom stand watching the lovefest. Dad and Uncle Dave haven't always gotten along. Uncle Dave told me that's because the oldest kid always feels the need to lord over the younger ones. Dad over Uncle Dave. Ryan over me. I used to tell him, by that logic, I should lord over Livy, but I don't want to. He always said it just wasn't in me. Middle child bullshit or something. Maybe.

"Thanks for coming, Dave," Mom says and offers him her cheek.

"You asked him to come? Why?" All of a sudden, it's hard to breathe.

"I wanted to." Uncle Dave moves into the kitchen. Dad holds up a mug, and Uncle Dave says, "Hell yes."

"Black?" Dad asks.

"Nah." Uncle Dave smiles. "A little cream."

Dad hands him the mug and smacks him on the back. "It's hell getting old, huh?"

Uncle Dave smiles, takes a drink of the coffee. "Sure is. Cream for you also?"

Mom scoots past him to open the fridge. "Anyone feel like eggs?"

I stand on the edges of this weird little interaction, stunned and stupid and worried as fuck. Do they even get what's going to happen? Does Mom remember the last time?

Dad grabs the potatoes, and Uncle Dave starts slicing and dicing an onion. I watch his impressive knife skills, the ones he tried to teach me that he's now trying to teach Livy, when he notices my stare. "Hey, Johnny, why don't you go out to the truck? I might have brought you something."

I stare at him, wanting him to be the adult who will decipher this situation for me, but he's patiently showing Livy how to do the onions while Dad gets the pan ready. I take Uncle Dave's keys and open the cab to his truck. Sitting there, waiting, among other things, are boxes filled with welding tools. A mask, clamps, a welding cable, a kit with the machine, and a tricked-out workbench.

I'm carrying my load full of crap into the house, and Uncle Dave nods. Dad asks, "What's that all about?"

"I heard Johnny's got an architectural project to finish. Wasn't sure what he was thinking of doing but thought welding might give him an edge for his 3-D model."

I expect Mom to freak out and Dad to get all stupid about it, but instead, Mom shocks the shit out of me by saying, "That's so sweet of you, Dave."

Livy steps forward. "Hey. What about me?"

Dad puts his hand on her shoulder.

"There may be something for you in the truck also."

"Wheee!" Livy screams and runs outside.

Mom sips her coffee. "You spoil them."

"My pleasure. They're good kids. Oh, I also got Ryan an iPad. Had it loaded with some of those communication programs they say are working miracles with kids."

"He's so hard on…"

"It's got a box that's guaranteed to keep it from breaking, no matter what he does."

Mom pats him on the shoulder and gives him one of her most approving looks.

I stare at my loot. "I'm not sure…"

"What you're going to do?" Uncle Dave finishes. "It'll come to you."

"I'm not in that class anymore."

Uncle Dave drinks his coffee and thinks. "Then I guess you'll have to do your own research, huh?" He claps me on the back and says, "Let's eat before the legal system descends on us."

"Dad, I wanted to talk to you…"

"I know, son. Let's eat. Then we'll talk. Whatever it is, we'll figure it out."

We sit at the dining room but eat off casual plates. Sausage, eggs, and potatoes and onions.

As Rosie clears the table, Uncle Dave pushes Ryan into the sunroom. Livy throws on her new Beat headphones and downloads songs from the iTunes store thanks to her new gift card.

"You wanted to talk?" Dad asks.

"Yeah. I knew we were going to be questioned."

"It's just a formality." Mom waves a butter knife in the air. "Because Ryan got out of his car seat."

"But I'm not sure it'll go as smoothly as you think. Remember before?"

I can't help but look around at all the things I threw that day. China. Furniture. Pictures. Vases. I smashed it all. To avoid this next part. I was the problem child. To make them see that Mom wasn't neglecting Livy and me. That everyone was doing the best they could.

Mom sighs but goes back to eating her eggs. "Yeah. Not forgetting that day any time soon. But things are better now, aren't they?" She puts her knife down, looks at me. "We are better. Right?"

"Mom…you don't understand…"

My mind goes back to the places I don't want to remember. After the accident. Versions of me all different ages and sizes. All doing the same thing. Breaking things. Pictures. Vases. Anything I thought Mom loved more than me. I didn't want her to push me away and hate me, so I hated her first. I started fires. I took an ax and tried to cut myself with it. I wanted to die. Until the dragon came to me. Maia Cetus. He was everything I wanted to be. Strong. Protected. Untouchable. He was the one who helped me that day.

I'd come home from school with another detention. I knew that would cause a fuss. Knew Dad would come back from the house that Mom exiled him to after he forced her to let the doctors put a G-tube in Ryan.

Mom was in the dining room, looking at papers. There was a woman at the table with her. Mom was shaking her head. I could tell she'd been crying.

"You must be John," the woman said as I walked into the dining room. She had one of those adult put-on smiles, the ones that are supposed to make you feel like everything's OK when things are really, really bad. "I'm Mrs. Gordon. I just need to ask you a few questions."

My eyes zeroed in on those pictures on the table. All of me after my accidents. Then onto her badge. DCF. I knew DCF. There was a kid at school who was taken from his parents by them. His brother and he were split up and sent to different places. DCF was bad.

Mom's face was tight. Livy was at school. Ryan was in the other room, screaming his head off.

"You really do seem to have your hands full, Mrs. Strickland."

Mom put her hand on one of the pictures. "No, it's not like that. I mean, it isn't easy, but…"

"John," Mrs. Gordon said, "I just have to ask you about some of these accidents."

"He's an active boy."

I froze. If they investigated Mom, they could take me and Livy. They could take my little sister. All because my stupid teacher noticed some bruises on me. Some accidents.

My body felt like it melted into hot lava. Like I could pour right out of that room. I couldn't let them take Livy. They couldn't take her. I had to do something. I picked up the poker by the fireplace and started hitting the walls. The furniture. The china. I let my beast out like he'd wanted this whole time. When I was finished, I looked at Mom, whose face was blotchy, and her voice was strained from screaming. "John, stop. What are you doing?"

Mrs. Gordon was on her phone.

I ran out the front door and kept running. Running. Running. I couldn't let them take Livy. I had to go. Find a way to live on my own. I was ten, but I knew I couldn't go back to that house. Dad found me. Took me in his car. He cried the entire way to his house. So did I.

"I don't know what happened, John. But you can't live with your mom anymore."

And now we were right back there.

"They were going to take Livy," I say.

"What?"

"They had all those pictures of my accidents, and they…"

Dad's face bleached a ghastly shade of white. "What made you think…"

"That's why you…acted like that? You thought they were going to take Livy?" Mom asks.

I nod.

"Jesus Christ," Dad whispers.

Mom stares at the ceiling and starts to cry. "I wouldn't have let that happen. I would have protected her. You."

The truth sits between us now. Do I open up this can of crap? Do I lay it on the table? My hand goes to my dragon medallion. "You…you weren't doing so well, Mom."

"John…"

"Let him talk, Lydia."

"You'd kicked Dad out. You were pissed at me all the time. I mean, all the freaking time. You even lost it with Livy sometimes, and who could lose it with her? The only person in this world you were nice to was him. Ryan."

"That's not true…I didn't mean… Don't look at me like that, Scott. It was hard raising these kids by myself."

"You didn't have to."

"And I came home from school, and this woman was there, giving you grief, and I saw where she was from, and I knew. I knew it was my fault she was there. If I hadn't gotten into so much trouble or gotten hurt all those times. If I'd just followed your rules…"

Simple fucking rules.

Mom's head bends. "I wish I'd known…I didn't… Oh my God. I've messed this all up." She stands and walks to the living room. Then back to us. Just moves and moves. To the chair. To the window. Like it's too much to stay still.

Dad tries to follow her trajectory, but he just lags behind her like a puppy. "The point is, things are different now," Dad says. "We all made mistakes."

"I'm sorry about Ryan, Mom. I really am."

"What?"

257

"It was my fault that day…I took his helmet. I distracted him and you. I know I can never make up for…"

She holds up her hand. "No. No. This is too much."

My body fills with this horrible sinking feeling. Like someone is feeding me river rocks that keep piling up in my stomach. "OK. I get it." The feeling of swallowing boulders weighs me down, but I have to keep moving. She can't deal with me. I'm too much. And I've got no right to ask her. All I know is I've got to get out of here. The air is hot and stuffy, and I can't breathe. I can't. Somehow, I slide to the floor. And I've got this second of thinking that it's crazy how Mom keeps moving and I'm just stuck.

Then Mom crouches down next to me. Her face is close to mine, severe, thin, her eyes bright and pinpoint like she's a vampire or something. She reaches out to touch my face, her fingers so thin. So incredibly thin. I try not to flinch, but I'm scared of her thin hands and not used to her touching me. She grabs my face. "Look at me, John."

"Mom…I…"

"Look at me." I can barely stand to lift my eyes to her, not because I'm scared but because I'm scared that we are actually talking about this. I'll know how she feels. How she'll never forgive me. "Look." I force my eyes to meet hers. I don't see anger or hate. And the relief of that washes over me like sitting under a waterfall. She touches my forehead like she's checking me for a fever, and that makes me feel like melting.

"John. My son. I never blamed you for the accident."

I shake my head. She's lying. It's what moms do at times like this, but I just can't do it. I can't. I need the truth today. "You left me and Livy. Then when you took me to see him…" I have to stop, chew on my knuckle. "You…"

She nods. One skinny tear runs down her cheek. "I was grieving for my son. It didn't make me a good mother, I get that, but that doesn't mean…" She shakes her head. "I never…I just wanted my son back. That's all."

"I was your son too. I needed you too."

She puts her hands back on my cheeks. "I know. I'm sorry. If I could take it back, I would. But you always managed. You took care of Livy. And I took care of Ryan. And I thought if I could just bring Ryan back…"

"We'd all be OK." I finish for her.

She nods.

"I was always making a mess of things. And I thought maybe you wished it was me who got hurt instead of him."

She shakes her head back and forth. "No. I never wished that. I wished a lot of things. But never that. I love you, John Michael Strickland. You are such an incredible person. You always have been. So brave and strong." She runs her hand through my hair, and normally, that would freak me the frick out, but now, it makes me feel so loved.

She puts her hand up. "As I lay in that hospital bed for the last few days, all I thought about was you."

A small warmth spreads over me.

Now I'm crying too. She can't be serious. Of course she

blamed me. I blamed myself. She grabs my arms with a strength that amazes me.

"I blamed so many people. Pete. Your father. But I never blamed you. Never. For a really long time, I blamed myself. And you know what, that's not right either. It was an accident. And afterward when you were so angry, and you had a right to be, I couldn't see it. I was mad that you were squandering your life when Ryan didn't have one anymore."

"He did have a life, Mom. It was just a different one."

She nods. "You're right. You're right. You're so smart."

"Someone has to be." Old family joke.

She laughs. "There are so many things I'd do differently if I could."

"Me too," I choke out.

"It's not too late for us. For any of us. We are looking into another place for Ryan."

"Really?"

"Yeah. Your father has been wanting this for years. This accident has made me see we need to consider the possibilities. That maybe he should…maybe it would be better if…"

I smile back. "Are you OK with that?"

"Yes. No. I'm scared, but it's the right thing for him and for everyone. Dad said that he's talked to one place, like, two hours away. Says the staff is amazing. That he'd learn to do things for himself. That he'd share a room and have friends. I kept wanting to bring him back. To fix him. This whole time. Ryan is who he is. I need to accept that."

I nod.

"Boys always leave their mothers. It's brutal."

"We don't always want to."

There's a knock on the door, and I know we've got to answer it. Get this next part over with.

"Wait. I want to tell you guys something. Because of this investigation, I've got to go and get drug-tested."

"I thought you did and you passed?"

"He didn't test me. Gave me a break. Now he has to. No choice."

"If you fail?"

"I go back to Chicago and face charges."

Dad puts his arm around my shoulders. "Let's see what happens. But we'd like to go with you if you let us."

"OK."

Uncle Dave goes to the front door and gives Dad a look. "OK?"

"Yeah. We're ready." Dad squeezes my shoulder. "This time, no drama."

I can't help laughing. "No drama."

CHAPTER 27

I lie in my bed, an old football in my hand. I toss it in the air. Catch it. Throw it again. It feels good to do it. Again and again and again. My head is filled with too much. It's hard to believe all that happed today. DCF came and went, and we made it through. I took my drug test in Steve's office with everyone but Emily there, and I passed.

When I got home, I had a message from Miss Quinlan reminding me that I can make up all the work I missed and telling me that Mr. Bonham said he'd consult with me on my project if I wanted that. If anyone had told me it would all go this way, I would've told them they were nuts. Or high. That's the other thing. I'm still sitting on that lid of pot I don't intend to smoke or sell. Weird.

A knock on my door makes me jump. Uncle Dave comes in, holding my new welding mask. "We gonna lay here all moony, or we gonna get to work, nephew?" Then he cocks his eyebrow at me like the sarcastic mofo he is. "Hmm?"

"Get to work, I guess."

"Nothing else to do."

"So what are you thinking?"

"Not sure."

"The thing about building is you should do something you love, because you're going to work on it for a long time."

My eyes shoot to my closet. The K'NEX boxes. The LEGOs. Uncle Dave's eyes follow mine.

"You and Ryan used to build a lot together, huh?"

I nod.

"I remember. You can't give up because he can't do it anymore. That would be even worse. Double the trouble."

And suddenly, I decide two things. One, I'm going to build an igloo for my project. Two, I need to go see Pete.

"Thanks, Uncle Dave. I gotta take care of something first."

"OK, but remember, an igloo waits for no man."

And once again, Uncle Dave gets me more than I get myself.

I grab my phone and text Pete. Hey can we meet up? Talk? Maybe watch The Shining?

Definitely. Not working tonight. Come over. I'll get pizza.

That's his standard joke. He always brings a pie home from work, so he'll just heat up what he's got.

Dad's in the kitchen with Livy. Uncle Dave pulls out a deck of cards. "Who's for gin rummy?"

"Me!" Livy laughs.

"You getting hungry?" Dad asks me. "We were going to run to the store and pick up steaks and potatoes."

I point to the door. "I've got go see a friend."

"Sure. Everything OK?" Dad's brow furrows.

"Yeah, Dad. Everything's good."

He smiles at me, and it feels like there's emotion behind it. I think about how he was trying to look out for me back then. How he took me in when he knew it would be hard to raise me. How he never really lost his cool with me. Ever. I smile back, kiss Livy on the cheek, and point to the game. "Keep an eye on this one…" I say to Uncle Dave. "She's a card shark."

He winks at me. "I'll try not to lose my shirt."

"Ew!" Livy says, and I let the music of her laughter act as my armor for this next part.

———o———

As I pull into Pete's apartment complex, I try not to get too emotional about what I'm going to do. It's been a long hard road for all of us. Ryan, Mom, me, and Pete. Pete had been the coolest kid in the neighborhood before the accident. Nice to everyone. Good head on his shoulders. Jock. Student. Pete was on track to go to Princeton. His mother told me that one of the times I went to see her.

I did that when I was old enough to drive and see Pete. I'd stop to see her first. She'd sort of lost a son too. But this time, this visit is just me and Pete. I wonder if he'll want to listen to what I have to say.

He gives me a man hug, and then I walk inside. His apartment is cleaner than the last time I came over but not much. It smells like pizza, and I realize how hungry I really am. He goes to the fridge and grabs two Miller Lites, twists the caps off, and hands me one. He's got a spliff smoking on the table, and he stops to take a hit off of it and holds it out to me. I wave it away, and his eyebrows raise. "What's up? Got a drug test coming up?"

"No." I say. "I've had one hell of a weird week, man."

"Weed helps everything."

"I used to think that."

His eyes are red, but he's not gone yet. I need to talk to him before he checks out. I point to the joint, motion to the ashtray. "Do you mind?" I ask. "Just for a few minutes."

"Sure. You're kinda scaring me though. Is everything OK?"

"Like I said, it's been a hell of a week."

He nods. Takes a sip of beer.

"Do you know that I used to pretend you were my brother?"

He takes a long, slow drink from his beer.

"You were always nice to me and to all of us little kids."

"I liked you. You were really smart."

My turn to drink. I was smart. Pete liked me. I remember I followed him around. We used to talk about rocks and stars and dinosaurs. He was always so patient with me. Never got mad like Ryan did. Before the accident, I was smart and so was Pete. I remember our talks.

"Didn't you want to go to Princeton once?" I ask.

Pete gets up, goes to the cupboard, and grabs a glass. "That was a lifetime ago. What's this all about, John?" He puts ice in his glass and pulls a bottle of vodka out of the freezer. "My mom said that Ryan's going to be OK. Said it was a miracle or some shit."

He pours the vodka over his ice, and I wait until he sits at the table before I start again. "Yeah, Ryan saves his miracle for this one."

We both laugh at that. Just two friends getting stoned and drunk together. Only I can't be that person right now. "My mom decided today of all days to talk to me about the accident."

"Oh. Yeah, not my favorite topic, man." He starts to get up, but I motion for him to sit. "You know the rules, John. We don't talk about that."

"It wasn't your fault."

He lifts his head long enough to take a drink. His eyes are pleading with me, and the thing is, I want to give in—I do—but I have to do this. He needs to hear this from me. He drinks some more vodka, shakes his head like a bull, then looks at me, fake smile plastered on his face. "How about we watch that movie?"

"I'm serious, man. Mom sat me down and told me she doesn't blame me for any of it. She doesn't blame you either."

"Great. Awesome. That is juuust the best news." He stands to take the pizza out of the oven. He's a little drunk. Not so drunk I worry he'll fall in the oven or anything but drunk enough to be worried that he won't hear me. I get up and follow him to the kitchen counter.

"I was amazed at the things she said. And I feel better for the first time since it happened."

Pete starts opening the drawers. "Where's that stupid pizza cutter?"

He pulls each drawer open so hard that the silverware inside clangs and jumps. The next drawer lands on the floor with a huge sound. I know he wants me to stop talking, but I can't.

"The thing is, when something like that happens, everything gets all screwed up. People get sad, and they can't deal with that feeling, so they get mad at other people. Mom got mad at me. At you. It wasn't fair, but it's over now."

Pete shakes his head. "You're kidding me with this, right?"

"With what?"

"With all of this. I am glad you and your mom made up. Great. But it has nothing to do with me!"

"But..."

He points to himself. "I blame me. *I* do. So fuck you and your charity and your 'everyone is all fine now' bullshit, because I am not fine, and I will never be fine. Ryan and I will forever be fucked up. So just leave it the fuck alone or just leave."

The blast of his anger hits me hard, but I know he needs to do this. I know he needs to hear what I'm saying.

"It was an accident. You have to let it go. You have to live your life. Move on."

"Move on? Are you kidding me? Are you out of your fucking mind? Move on? I paralyzed a person." He points to me. "Your brother. Why are you here anyway? Why give a shit about me when I ruined your life?"

"Because you didn't ruin my life. I did. Or nobody did, because it's not ruined. It's just getting started. Like yours can."

"We being honest here? That's what we're doing?"

I stand tall. "Yes."

"Honestly, I still see the whole fucking thing. Years of therapy bullshit and drugs to make me forget, and I still see him flying in front of my car, me trying to brake in time. I still hear all the sounds. The disgusting, crushing, horrible sound of my car hitting him."

"You have to let it go."

"Every time I think it's getting better, every time the noose loosens, I sober up, and it's bad again. So I drink more, and it goes away." He walks to the table, gets the joint, and lights it back up again. He takes two hits. Three. I watch the muscles in his face go from tight to soft. He blows out smoke. "The way things are."

I lower my voice, try to keep calm. "Five seconds of our life should not dictate the rest. You wanted to go to Princeton. You were going to be an astrophysicist. You were going to be something other than—"

"Great, now you're my mom."

"I'm not kidding, man. You've put your whole life on hold. You're punishing yourself, and there's no reason."

Pete's face screws up. He takes another hit. Holds it. Blows the smoke out. "Are you kidding me?"

"No. I mean it. When Mom talked to me, it's like the whole world opened up and made sense for once. And I saw that she and I have been so fucking stupid about this whole thing. Each of us was trying to forgive the other one, when it turns out we should have just forgiven ourselves. I've lost ten years being angry and alone. And that's so fucking mental."

Pete's eyes get moist. "I'm glad you two talked."

"Me too. But the whole time, I kept thinking about you. About how crappy this whole thing has been for you. I know nothing will change what happened, but you should know it wasn't your fault. You couldn't have stopped in time."

"Look, I think you better go. I've got to work tomorrow." He stands up. "Come by next week or something."

I don't get up. "I'm not leaving."

Pete looks at the ceiling. Then back at the floor. Then back at me. "There's not one thing you can say to me that will make me feel better about that day."

"I think I've got one thing that will."

"What?"

"It wasn't your fault."

He shakes his head. "You can't say that."

"Let me finish. It wasn't your fault…because it was mine."

"What?"

"You hit Ryan because he skated into the street, right?"

"Right."

"Well, he didn't exactly skate there."

"You're not making sense."

"He didn't skate there. Because I pushed him."

Pete stares at me. I start to sweat. I've never said those words to anyone. I pushed him. And now Pete's just staring at me, his face blank, and I've got no idea if he's hating me or if he doesn't even care. I don't know if he wants to beat my face in. He stands up, goes over to the couch. Looks back. "You coming?"

"What?" I say.

"I've got *The Shining* all tracked up."

"Aren't we going to talk about what I said?"

Pete drains the rest of his drink. "Nope." He pushes the remote button, and the TV comes to life.

"Why?"

"Because it doesn't matter how Ryan got in the street. It just matters that's where he was."

"I don't understand you, man. I've never admitted that to anyone. Not to one person. And you act like that's nothing."

"It's not nothing. But it's not everything either."

"Then what is it? What's got you stuck in that two seconds of lost muscular control?"

Pete smiles. Then his face gets dark. "I was texting my girlfriend."

"What?"

"I never told anyone that. I'd just sent her a text. She was pissed at me. So I didn't want to wait to get home to text her. It was so fucking important. That one text. Right?"

"I didn't know…"

"Well, now you do. I fucking texted my stupid-assed girl-friend who dumped me the second I got in trouble. You know what was so important? What I had to send so bad that I ended up hitting your brother?"

"What?"

"Three fucking letters. BRT. And if she'd been a little more patient or I'd been smart enough to figure she'll know I'll be there when I actually get there, maybe…" He's crying now, and it's horrible. "BRT. I can't stand myself. You say I should live my life? Why? Why do I fucking get to live when your brother…"

I sit next to him on the couch. "Because my mother was right about one thing. No matter how guilty we all feel, if he can't live the life he was supposed to, we shouldn't waste ours. We owe him that. Don't you think we owe him that?"

Pete nods, but I'm not sure he even knows what I'm saying—that's how wasted he is. How miserable too. "Maybe. BRT. What the fuck?"

He sobs for the first ten minutes of the movie, then we both just stare at it, numb and stupid and raw and done. What the fuck is right.

————o————

I wake up in the middle of the night and have no idea where I am. The darkness is only cut by the television that's now showing an infomercial on daily skin care for women. My neck is cricked, and I pull my cell out of my pocket. 2:03. Crap. As soon as I slide my phone on, it lights up with texts from Dad.

Are you OK? Sent at twelve. Then, Where are you? At one fifteen. A final plea, Please check in, at one thirty. Crap. I never had a curfew with Dad. He worked all the time, traveled all the time. Never really noticed before. But I feel guilty and pissed. And that's what's so fucked up about me. I'm always feeling two things at once or three or four, and all I want, all

I need, is the distinct pleasure of feeling one absolute, true feeling. Separate and perfect, whatever that feeling is.

Should I text Dad now? Would it wake him? I'm, like, ten minutes from home. Would it be better to just drive there and save everyone the trouble? Doubt. Regret. Annoyance. A stupid package deal strapped to the back of my dragon, who looks as drugged as I feel. He slinks in the corner of my mind, hoping I'll unchain him, let him loose on all this shit and on everyone who upsets me. But I don't want to do that now. Now I want to unchain *myself*. Now *I* want to be free.

I text Dad. Sorry. At a friend's. Fell asleep. Coming home now. Part of me thinks it's none of his business where I am or what I'm doing, but only a small part. An ember. One that is extinguished by what he texts back.

OK son. As long as you're safe. Drive carefully.

And it's like this latest accident has done what nothing else over the years could do—shocked my entire family to our senses. Shown us what we needed to know. That we still care we're alive.

CHAPTER 28

I don't call Emily when I get home. Because even though I know I can finally start living my life, I'm still angry that I've wasted all this time. The headache comes on strong, and I think about reaching for my weed or my bottle of Jack, but ultimately, I text Emily. Very hard day. Going to sleep. Will talk later.

She writes back. OK. Im here.

To which I don't answer. I just stare at the words. Is it OK that she's here? Is it OK for me to go on with my life? After Ryan? After Leah? Why do I keep getting more chances?

I text Allie.

Hey.

She doesn't answer right away, and at first, I'm a little relieved, because I'm sort of scared to have this conversation.

I lie in my bed and consider my choices. I could smoke some weed. God knows I deserve it. I could numb my head and calm my soul. All this getting real shit is hard. I could use a little break. But just as I'm about to get the bag out from under my desk, my phone vibrates. Allie.

Hey yourself. How are you?

I stare at the ceiling. I'm OK. Everything is fine here but I have something I want to tell you.

OK…

I'm dating someone.

That's good!

It feels kind of serious.

Oh.

My insides turn liquid, and I feel horrible for disappointing Allie. For cheating on her big sister. But then she texts back.

I have to vet her. That's my right. As your pseudo little sister.

OK.

She better be good enough for you.

She is.

Up to me to decide. Set up a meeting.

How come all the women in my life are unrelenting?

Then: I have a lacrosse game this week.

OK. I did a spit-take. U r a jock now?

Sort of. That OK?

It depends what you do on the field. No pressure.

And for the first time in a long time, I feel the pressure is releasing itself. Bit by bit. I don't tell Allie that. I just say that I'm going to rest up so I can be all beast. She says good night, and it feels kind of OK to have these people in my life—not as rocks but as anchors.

Now it's Monday morning all fast and furious. I not only have to go to school, but I kind of want to. As I make my way downstairs, part of me is scared that all that stuff that's happened lately was just a dream and nothing will have changed. When I get downstairs, I see that can't be farther from the truth.

Dad is leaning against the counter as if it's the most natural thing in the world. I almost do a double take. In the six years I lived alone with Dad, I almost never saw him in the morning before school.

"Morning," he says, holding the coffee mug he'd gotten to replace the one I broke after that day.

"Morning."

"You feel OK?" he asks as if I'm getting over a cold.

I expect him to hand me money but am surprised to find Mom's morning prescription ready for me as if they'd discussed it beforehand. There's my bagged lunch, a to-go cup with coffee, and my protein shake.

"Thanks," I say, even though I'm sure that my look is something between incredulous and worried.

Uncle Dave comes out of what used to be Ryan's room, which makes me wonder where the hell Dad stayed last night. "Glad to see you're eating better, John."

Dad reaches into his wallet to supplement the already-made lunch, and I wave him off. He refuses to put the money away, slides it toward me on the counter. "Just in case."

I scoop it up. No reason to fight him on this, especially since I know he's only doing what he knows. Plus, what's the real harm in giving me money? I'd have to be a total asshole to be pissed at something like that, and I'd like to believe I'm past being that guy now.

"You have a scrimmage today?" Uncle Dave's eyes go to my lacrosse bag on the floor.

And I realize I've got no idea what my lax schedule is or who got my gear ready for me. The feeling of having walked into someone else's life surrounds me, feels like a noose around my neck.

"Practice today. Game tomorrow." Dad drinks from his mug, the one he used all the time when he lived here. "I called the coach. Just to make sure you weren't going to miss anything important."

"Season opener." Uncle Dave nods as if remembering some of his glory days.

"Those were the days?" I can't help but be smart-ass.

"Definitely," Uncle Dave says. "Good thing I've got you to live vicariously through."

I smile. Drink my coffee. Uncle Dave's way of saying he'll be there.

Beep.

"OK, see you after practice." Dad walks me to the door.

"Sure."

"By the way, John, Coach said you'd be starting tomorrow. Said you're one hell of a warrior."

"Thanks," I say, even though there's no reason to thank Dad.

"No surprise to me," Dad says. "You've always been one helluva kid."

———o———

Emily smiles at me as I get in the car.

"You know, I could drive you every once in a while," I say.

"Nah. I like my power position in this relationship."

"I like powerful women."

"Well, all right then." She pulls out into the street, and we ride like this for the five minutes it takes to get to school. The car goes into park, and she swivels to face me. "Want to tell me about it?"

"Nope." I drink my coffee but don't move to get out of the car. "I think we should keep it light."

Her face falls. She misunderstood. But still she says, "You're probably right."

I take her hand. "I just mean the conversation."

"Oh. OK. I mean, we should probably keep it *all* light, right?"

"Only if you're planning to break my heart."

She puts her hand out, and I hold it. "Not a chance."

CHAPTER 29

I run off the field at halftime, look into the stands, and see my girls, Livy and Emily, watching me. And one more. My heart stops. Allie. She came. Nerves build in my stomach, and more than anything, I want to know that Emily and Allie are cool with each other. That Allie is cool with me moving on.

Allie smiles at me and pumps her fist.

I scan the stands until I find them. Mom, Dad, and Uncle Dave all raise their hands as I run back on the field. This is what it feels like to win. No matter what the score is on the field. Man, I'm getting way too in touch with my feelings. Good thing it's time to dish out some punishment. On the field anyway.

The game goes better than any of our scrimmages—we actually win this one 5–1—but this isn't Parkland, and I still want to make that Nate kid feel me get my hate on. I might be a better human being at this point, but I'm still no saint.

The locker room is filled with guys who have too much energy. Funny what a win will do for you. Parker stands on one of the benches.

"We are kings of the world!" He holds his hands over his

head, and everyone cheers as if he's said the most incredible thing. Then he points to our goalie, Luke. "So close to a shutout, man."

And everyone starts chanting, "Luke, Luke, Luke, Luke."

Even me.

The locker room door opens, and everyone gets quiet as Coach Gibson walks in, his arm resting around Pete's shoulders. It takes me a second to register that Pete is here, actually here, and also that he's with our coach. "Great game tonight, boys!" Coach Gibson says. "You played well. You stuck to the game plan and executed. It's that simple."

Matt moves closer to Pete, who is looking at the ground but smiling. Curiosity grips me, but there's this good feeling that pushes everything out of the way.

"I've tried to talk to you boys about patience. Patience makes you a better lacrosse player. A better student. A better person. Patience will get you this." He shakes Pete's shoulder. "This kid, Pete, was on the first team I coached here. He's had some tough breaks, but he's decided he wants to move forward. Pete is going to be our junior varsity coach and strength coach for you varsity animals."

Cheers erupt.

Pete sort of waves to the locker room. Awkward. Matt snakes his way through the crowd, hugs his brother, and, I swear, if a group of stupid-assed jocks don't get all teared up. Now the room starts chanting, "Pete, Pete, Pete!"

Especially me.

———o———

By the time I make it out onto the field, I'm a little worried I've made Emily and Allie and Livy wait too long for me and they'll be pissed, but they're standing by the soda stand.

"Hey," I say and break up their conversation.

Allie shoots forward, hugs me. "You played great."

"I'm so glad you came." She's got her hair cut short and sort of cool looking with sharp angles. Even with her navy beanie on, you can see her dark-brown hair is painted with blue-and-purple streaks in the front. She looks like the artist girl she wants to be, and that makes me glad.

"Me too."

Allie pulls my arm, and I follow her so we can have an off to the side conversation. "How are you? Really?"

"I'm good. Now. I think." My eyes skate over to Livy and Emily.

Allie notices. "Livy is so cute. Oh my God, I can't believe how cute she is. We've been talking about my adopting her. So to speak." Allie laughs, and it's good to see her happy.

"She's something. How are you? Really?"

"I'm good. Waiting to hear from Rhode Island School of Design. So I'm actually very nervous."

"You'll get in. You know it."

"Hope so." Her eyes brighten, and she says, "Livy told me there's some talk of you going to college."

"I'm just starting to think about…"

"You should. Leah would be so proud of you. She really would." Allie's eyes fill with tears but don't spill over.

"She'd be proud of you too."

Allie looks at the ground. "Yeah, I think she would." She elbows me and says, "Soooo…Emily seems very, very cool."

"I like her."

Allie links her arm in mine. "Good. It's time you settle down, don't you think?"

"You're really OK with it?"

"I don't know… Is she good to you?"

I nod.

"Does she take care of you?"

I nod.

"Good. You need someone to take care of you. You deserve it. Leah would want you happy." Allie reaches up and kisses me on the cheek. "I'm going to let you two talk."

Allie jogs ahead, wraps her arm around Livy, and pulls her toward the pretzel guy.

Emily waits for me. "Hey."

"Hey yourself."

"I was thinking, I'm feeling a little like getting serious about things in my life."

She pivots away, faces the field. "Things or people?"

I come up from behind her, wrap my arms around her shoulders. "Maybe both."

"Well, let me know when you figure it out." Her voice is

playful, and she pulls away from me, but I can tell she really wants me to pull her back.

"What if I told you I'm getting very serious about maybe going to college?"

"I would say awesome sauce."

"And what if I said I might actually be serious about a girl I met?"

"Hmmm. I'd say good luck. To her." She laughs, and I pull her so close, I can feel every part of her against every part of me.

I pull the hair away from her neck and whisper in her ear, "What if I said that girl was you?"

"I guess I'd say cool."

I turn her around to face me. "Cool? Cool? That's all I get?"

"You want a big parade?"

I wave her away, still playing. "OK, forget it."

That makes her run after me, crash into me, climb onto my back piggyback-style. "I mean, I'd say that makes me very happy."

I lower her to the ground, turn around, and take her hands in mine. I bring them to my lips. "I really am."

Her smile starts small but spreads all the way to her eyes. "I'm glad."

"So...does the lacrosse warrior get a kiss when he wins?"

She pulls away from me, gathers her hair into a ponytail. She's got this crooked smile, and she pulls at a corded necklace that has a heart and three small circles on it. "You're setting a dangerous precedent."

"What?" I move closer to her. Close enough to move the stray hair behind her ears, but I leave a few to blow in her face as the wind picks up, because I like how wild it makes her look.

"You only want me to kiss you when you win?"

"I didn't say that." I lean in and kiss her. "I want to kiss you when I win." I kiss her again. "And when you win." Another kiss. "And when either one of us loses."

"Because we'll need to be consoled." She leans in and kisses me this time.

"Obviously."

"Ew. You guys are disgusting!" Livy pushes between us. "Allie wants to go for pizza."

"Joey's!" Emily and I say at the same time. Then, "Our place."

Allie throws her arm around Livy's shoulder. "Let's give them their space, girlfriend."

I watch the two of them walk ahead. Allie bends to listen to something Livy is telling her. My fingers interlock with Emily's. I walk off the field feeling as happy as I have in a really long time.

When I get to the parking lot, I'm surprised to see Matt and Pete and Parker and Brandon waiting. "Where you guys heading?"

"Joey's," Livy answers.

I click my Jeep open.

"We'll meet you there." Parker winds his finger in the air, motioning to the rest of the lacrosse team, who, inexplicitly, have also been waiting for me. And this super weird feeling settles over me. Like maybe this is me actually moving on. Living my life. Because I can. Because I should.

CHAPTER 30

I'm not sure how many things can change in your life in a short time and it still *be* your life. When do you stop being the person you used to be and become a new one entirely?

I sit in Steve's office. Talk to him. Smart-ass comments for sure but with none of the anger to heat them. I eat meals with my family. I speak to my mother like a son who doesn't need armor. Or a dragon. I feel good. Bad. Tired. Sad. Each individual emotion presents itself in front of me, each one taking a turn. I feel clear.

But there are still things that keep me from feeling free. Number one is a conversation I need to have with my brother. A conversation that can't ever happen. That doesn't stop me from trying.

I sit across from Ryan at his new group home. He's at a table with a group of his new friends: Dylan, Eric, JJ, and Christian. They're playing Sorry, and Ryan keeps saying "Sorry, sorry, sorry." Then waits and says, "Not sorry." Then they all crack the hell up like they are comic geniuses. It's pretty cute.

I take that as my cue. "I'm sorry, Ryan," I say. Even though he couldn't care less that I'm talking, not when there's this group of kids who are all having fun with him. "I really am. I wish I'd been a better brother. I wish I hadn't pushed you away that day... I wish..."

He looks at me for a second, and it's almost like he gets what I'm saying. But then he breaks into a chant of "Sorry, sorry, sorry."

"Hey, Ryan?" I put my hand on the table in front of him. "Can I show you something?"

He nods, and I get out my phone and show him the picture of the metal igloo I built for my project. It did OK in the contest, but that wasn't really the point. I enlarge the picture and show him the door. I pull up the cross-section photo. "This is where we were going to have the fire pit. Like we always wanted to."

Ryan looks at me and smiles, then looks at the picture. "Mom?" he asks.

"Yeah. Mom's fine."

He laughs. Does the sign for Mom and then the sign for crazy. All his friends crack up.

One of the workers, a woman who is about Mom's age, with very curly blond hair and a badge with the name Barbara written on it, comes over and stands next to us. "Ryan, your brother wants you to see the igloo he made."

"It's OK," I say. "He doesn't have to look. He's kind of over igloos anyway, I guess."

"It would make more sense to him if it were here in person," she suggests.

"Maybe I'll bring it in."

"That would be great. It's about dinnertime. You going to stay?"

"Nah. I've got to get home." I reach over and kiss Ryan on the top of his head. "I love you, brother."

He swats at me in a friendly way, like maybe he's too cool for that.

"OK, guys, time to wrap this up." Barbara points to the board game. "Put everything away where it belongs."

I walk away, looking back over my shoulder as Ryan's hands, even as stiff as they are, even with the splints he'd never wear at home and has on here, no problem, close around the dice as he helps put the game back in its box, and I realize Ryan is exactly where he belongs.

"Bring that igloo in. I'm sure the kids would love it," Barbara calls to me.

I hold my hand up. "I will. Definitely."

Emily is waiting for me in the hallway. "How'd it go?"

"Fine."

We walk out to the car. "He like the igloo?"

"Sure. He just didn't remember it. The aide said I should bring in the big one for him to see the real thing. It would mean more to him that way."

"That's a great idea." And then she's got her phone out, and she's googling. She shows me her phone. "You could make it into a beehive. I've been reading about the effect of beekeeping with kids with schizophrenia and autism and head trauma."

I smile at Emily as I hold the door to my Jeep open for her.

"You OK?" she asks.

"I'm good," I say, and I guess I really am. The Old Ryan is

gone. He doesn't care about the befores anymore. Maybe I have to be more like he is. New Ryan is living in the now. As it turns out, I really can still learn a lot from my big brother.

ACKNOWLEDGMENTS

Each book is a world in and of its own. I'm lucky to have so many people helping me build each one.

My children have been lucky enough to have had Vicky and Bill Hassel in their lives for most if not their entire lives, and it all started with my boys. In short, Vicky helped me raise them. She used to tell me that boys couldn't be tamed. Not in a take-over-the-world or hurt-anyone way but in an adventurous, take-on-life way. When my boys caught flies and lizards and released them on me so that I fake screamed and ran, she'd always call them stinky boys and I sort of loved that. This book started with my love for those kind of boys. Big brothers. Teammates. Complicated. Messy. Angry. Loving. Boys.

The first boy I ever met after my dad was my brother, Mark, who has always been an incredible support to me. As of course, has been my sister, Bonnie. I always knew I won the family lottery, but it's never been truer than at this point in my life. My family now includes wonderful sisters-in-law and one of the most entertaining larger-than-life brothers-in-law ever. So to my entire family, including wild and wonderful nieces and nephews from Boston to San Diego and back, this book is filled with their spirit and my thanks. I wish my parents were in this world to celebrate all of this, but much thanks has to go to Kathy Ramey, who, in their stead, is filling in as parent-in-residence. And Mom and Dad are cheering from their heavenly perch, I know.

I of course also have to thank Nicole Resciniti. This writing business is a nerve wracking and wonderous thing, and without her faith in me and her constant and vigilant shepherding of my career, this book wouldn't have been born. Annette Pollert-Morgan has this uncanny way of finding the heart of a book and clearing away the rest. I will never be able to thank her enough. I've been lucky enough to meet some of the other Sourcebooks team but am hesitant to thank any specific members because they all have been so incredibly supportive and patient and I realize now that for as many as I have met there are so many unsung heroes within the Sourcebooks family. So a huuuge thanks goes to everyone at Sourcebooks.

As for the writing of *The Homecoming* itself, I need to thank the specific people who have heard and worked on this novel in its many, many forms along the way. First was Terri Farley, who fell in love with the character of John Strickland almost immediately. David Case and Laen Ghiloni were early readers for this book.

Steven Dos Santos and Jonathan Rosen receive thanks as always for their constant support and loyal friendship. To my betas, Steven Dos Santos and Tori Kelley, thanks so much. Thanks to Marjetta Geerling, who read the beginning of this one and offered her wonderful feedback, support, and friendship. To Jill Nadler with her Kombucha and write-ins.

To Joyce Sweeney who is always instrumental in all aspects of the process, biggest thanks. The PGA's, Palm Springers, Wellington SCBWI critique group, and finally, to the ever present Tuesdays. Thanks for graciously listening, critiquing, focusing, and keeping me and this book going.

Finally, to JKR, and my beautiful children (you know who you are—ha!), thank you for enduring another book baby. And to my pups, Fetch and Ashley, all my love. Woof.

Who holds your secrets?

Don't miss Stacie Ramey's

THE SISTER PACT

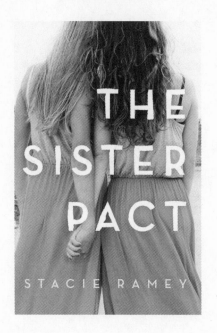

CHAPTER 1

The last thing we did as a family was bury my sister. That makes this meeting even harder to face.

I don't have to be a psychic to know what everyone thinks when they look at me. Why did she do it? Why didn't I? And the thing is, after all that happened, I'm not sure I know the answer to either.

Mom walks behind me, her hand gently curled around my bicep. Dad motions to show us where to sit, even though the guidance office is new ground for him.

I force myself to look into the faces of my judges and feel immediate relief. The principal, Mrs. Pendrick, smiles, warm and sweet, and the wrinkly skin around her eyes and lips lifts as she does. Mr. Hicks, my guidance counselor, the one the girls think is sort of cute, stands next to her. Where Mrs. Pendrick is all soft creases, he's wide shoulders, built for dealing with bad kids or bad parents, but he winks at me like he wants me to know he's on my side.

Mrs. Pendrick places a hand on mine. "It's nice to see you, Allie. We're so glad you're back."

Her hand is like an island of safe in a sea of danger. I smile at her so she thinks I'm okay. I smile so it looks like I'm not breaking. Like everything that happened was a mistake and I'm ready for a do-over.

Mr. Kispert, my art teacher, comes barreling into the room, carrying his iced coffee and my portfolio. "Sorry I'm late," he says. He nods at me and I try to nod back, but my body's kind of frozen. I had no idea he'd be here too.

"We were just getting started." Mrs. Pendrick opens a file, my name written on the tab. "I pulled Allie's records. She's on track for graduation next year, of course."

I tell myself to pay attention. I try to focus on Mrs. Pendrick, whose Southern accent makes her sound as misplaced as "the wrong Alice" in the new version of *Alice in Wonderland*, but it's hard.

"We may want to take a look at the courses she's chosen for this year." Mrs. Pendrick adjusts her reading glasses and flips through the pages.

My eyes hurt, the start of a migraine. I blink.

"We want to make certain we're not asking too much of her." Mr. Hicks shifts forward, his hands loosely steepled on the fake mahogany table in front of him.

The surface of the table is so shiny, I see my face in it, distorted and strange. I blink again. Caught somewhere between the blink and the reflection, I see her, Leah, in her black leotard and pink tights, like she's waiting in the wings for her cue.

Even though I realize it's just a trick of the light, I can't help staring at not-real-Leah, waiting to see if she's going to dance. I'm staring so hard, I must have stopped paying attention to what's going on around me because Dad's voice is stern. "Sit up, Allie. These people are here for you."

I square myself in my seat, horrified by the look of pity that crosses Mr. Hicks's face.

Mrs. Pendrick reaches across the table and takes my hand again, her touch soft as butter. "Are you okay, dear?"

"I'm fine. I just have a headache."

Dad shoots me a look like he wants me to behave, to make up for Leah. As if I could.

"Mr. Blackmore, we have to be patient with Allie," Mrs. Pendrick insists.

I should probably warn Mrs. Pendrick that Dad doesn't believe in being patient. It's all about domination and war games with him. He's the general. I'm the soldier he commands, and he will not lose this hill. No matter what. When I look at him, I see dried blood caked on his hands. Mom's. Leah's. Mine.

I shake that image out of my head and try to find my Happy. I think about everyone's colors. Mrs. Pendrick would be creamy yellow, icing pink, powder blue. And Mr. Hicks would be something easy too, like golf-course-turf green. I try to think about how I would paint them if I still painted. And just like that, Happy has left the building. Like Leah did.

"It's her junior year." Dad leans forward, his not-giving-an-inch stance making my stomach knot. I already know his colors: muddy brown, gray black, the color of pissed. "We need to get her back on track."

"We understand that." Mr. Hicks folds his hands again like a tent. "But this is going to be a very hard year for Allie."

It *is* going to be a hard year. And no meeting is going to change that. So instead of listening to them, I close my eyes and call to my mind the sound of Leah's ballet shoes shuffling against the floor. Eight weeks after, I can still hear them, but who knows for how long? Right now, I'm so grateful for the soft slide, slide, slide that is so real and strong that it fills me with unreasonable hope. Maybe she hasn't left me. Maybe it didn't happen. Maybe she'll forgive me.

"Maybe we could keep just two of the AP classes?" Mom suggests.

I open my eyes and pray I'm not crazy. It's hard to know if you are. Nobody really thinks they are. But I can almost hear Leah laughing with me—so like her to laugh when I'm in the hot seat and she's not.

Mr. Kispert takes out my portfolio and lays it on the table next to a brochure from the Rhode Island School of Design. The requirements are highlighted in crime-scene-tape yellow. "Allie should keep her AP Studio Art class. I'll supervise her. She'll do fine, and she needs it to work on her application."

Reading upside down, I can make out all the things I need to do to make that happen. Last year it all seemed easy. Now each step feels like a mountain I'm not equipped to climb. Mr. Kispert looks at me and winks. I smile back, even though I feel like a complete fake. I can't do art anymore, and I don't know how to tell him.

Mom puts her hand out to take the brochure, and it shakes. *Please don't let Dad notice. Please.* Dad grunts and takes it instead. "I'm not giving up on my daughter. Even if you guys are."

"Nobody's giving up on her," Mr. Hicks says. "We just want her to be okay."

"She wants to go to RISD. How do you expect her to get into a top art school if you don't give her the right classes?" His voice strains, and for a second I think he's going to cry, which I've never seen him do—except when we buried Leah.

"David, please." Mom says.

He slams the table hard. "Goddammit, Karen, this is what you do, what you always do. You give into the girls." He clears his throat. "Her. You give into her."

Mom's eyes well at Dad's obvious stumble. They've been calling Leah and I *them* or *the girls* for so long. It must be hard to adjust, but seeing Dad struggle with the math makes me feel horrible. We did this. We cut his regiment in half. Maybe his heart too. I want to reach out to him. I want to tell him I'm sorry. That I didn't think she meant it. That I definitely didn't—until I did. But that's a cop-out. Truth is, I don't remember most of that night.

Dad's voice sounds like he's surrendering. "What do you want me to do, Karen? Let her fail? That's not exactly going to fix her, is it?"

Everybody gets quiet. I can feel the silence like a noose around my neck. Dad's pain radiates off him. Mom's shame makes her sink into the chair. Mr. Hicks and Mrs. Pendrick sit, waiting for the right thing to say to heal this family. But there isn't anything to be said after all this. After what Leah did and what I almost did.

I close my eyes and wish Leah were here. I wish so hard, I can almost feel her holding my hand. Sometimes she did that when Mom and Dad fought. Sometimes she held my hand and I'd play with her silver flower ring, the one she always wore. They buried her with that ring. Mom said she wanted to give it to me, but I wanted Leah to have it. I lay my head on the table, the cool feeling enough to calm me for a minute.

"Jesus, Allie, can you try to focus?" I lift my head to see Dad close his eyes, and I know I've pushed him too hard. He shakes his head like a bull. He does that when he's done. He stares at the ceiling. "Is this how it's going to be now? Are you going to give up?"

And just like that he makes me want to disappear, makes me wish I could be wherever Leah is now, away from him and his shit. Away from everyone's expectations. Away from his stupid war with Mom.

And more than ever, I wish Leah were here. If she were here, really here, she'd stop Dad from being a jerk. She'd make Mom sit up straight and actually have an opinion. She'd take over this meeting and make them stop talking about my life as if I'm not even in it. Leah could totally do that. She was epic.

Until she killed herself.

Mrs. Pendrick clears her throat. "I understand your concerns, Mr. Blackmore. Junior year *is* a very important year. But Allie needs to heal."

We Blackmores? We don't heal. We patch up and make do. We Blackmores move on. It's in some contract that Dad made us sign when we were born. Leah's in breach. Now I'm the one in the spotlight. Thanks, Sis.

"Allie's seeing someone." Dad clears his throat. "A psychiatrist."

Mom nods quickly to show they're on the same page, which has been a ridiculously rare occurrence since Mom's Xanax addiction made the scene. Or since Dad's girlfriend, Danielle, did. The one that has texted him three times since he picked Mom and me up today. I guess she was mad he didn't let her come. To *my* meeting. My head starts pounding. I reach into my backpack and pull out an Excedrin pack and a Gatorade.

"What are you doing?" Mom's face gets red.

"I have a headache," I explain.

"You're supposed to tell me, and I give it to you." She shuffles around in her purse.

"It's just Excedrin." Does she honestly want to become my personal med vending machine? Like a human PEZ dispenser? I rip open the packet and put the pills on my tongue. Everyone gets quiet and looks at me like I just bit the head off a bat.

This is so outrageous. I can't deal with it alone. Leah should be facing this horrible aftermath with me. Every suicide pact needs a fallback for prisoners of war. Apparently.

Dad's hand goes on Mom's. It's a small gesture but so foreign in their full-scale battle that I can't pull my eyes from the spectacle. Mom puts her purse back on the arm of her chair. I'm not sure if I've imagined it, but I think I hear the sound of the pills rattling in their bottles, and that worries me greatly. Now that Leah's gone AWOL, I don't think I'd follow her, but if I'm so solid, why the hell am I wondering how many pills Mom has on her?

"I want to hear how Allie feels," Mr. Hicks says, breaking my reverie.

I swallow hard. How do I feel? I feel like I'm breaking inside. I can't see colors anymore. It's like when Leah left, she took the best of me. I feel like if one of us should have lived, it should have been her. She'd be way better in the role of surviving sister than I am. She'd have better hair too.

"Allie?" Dad prompts. "Mr. Hicks asked you a question. How do you feel?"

Sometimes I feel like I'm no more here than Leah is. Sometimes I forget. I think it didn't happen. I wait for my cell to ring. I think she's going to burst into the room, full of life and pissed at me for having borrowed one of her things. But then I remember. And it's like that night all over again. And I get mad—at her for going, and them for not even knowing that I'm not just mad she went, but also that she didn't take me with her. Like she promised. Like we promised each other.

"Allie?" Dad's voice gets tighter.

But I can't tell them any of that. They don't want to hear about that. Everyone's so sick of death, they want me to lighten

302

the mood. It's up to me. I'm on stage now. Dad's beating the drum. Mom's cowering. My teachers and the guidance counselors are waiting like revival attendees ready to be preached to, ready to clap. I can't disappoint them. So I try to be like Leah. I sit up tall. I "dance." "It's fine." I look at Mom so she'll know I mean it. Mostly. "AP art classes. Everything else honors."

"You sure you can do that, sweetie?" I hear the relief in Mom's voice. She wants to believe it's all over. I guess I can't really blame her.

Mrs. Pendrick's face screws up. "I think this is a mistake."

"I agree," Mr. Hicks says. "But let's do this. How about we move forward with that schedule and keep an eye on you, Allie? That sound okay? We're here whenever you need."

"Perfect." Dad stands.

Mom follows his lead.

I stand too, not wanting to break rank, especially when there's been a break in the fighting. It's not that I think it's so perfect, but I'm playing the part of the foot soldier, as usual. We soldiers march and follow orders. We soldiers act like it's all good. Hup, two, three, four. Even when we're breaking.

CHAPTER 2

I meet Emery outside her house. She's in tiny running shorts and a sports bra, letting her island-girl skin take center stage. Muscles look better in tan than white. They just do. But Emery's long legs and tight booty would be fierce in any color. She gathers up her long, curly hair in a ponytail, then makes a messy bun and asks. "So, how was it?"

"Fine." I get one last look at my cell, see no new texts, and stash it in my pocket. "Why are we doing this again?"

Emery frowns. She knows whose text I'm waiting for. The same one I always wait for. The unspoken issue between Emery and me that I need to get over—Max. I'm glad she doesn't confront that monster but instead simply says, "I've gotta get in shape. You know Mr. Carbon doesn't cast fat actresses."

It's not like Emery's even close to fat. She's not in the ZIP code of fat. She knows this. So do I, but I also know that she's right about the drama teacher at our school. Leah used to say that he picked out the girls who gave up their ambitions over the summer for ice cream and pizza.

"Okay, but why am *I* doing this?" I ask.

"Because you're my best friend and you're supporting me."

"More like being left behind." Once we get going, Emery will lap me for sure.

"I'll stay with you this time. I swear."

True to her word, Emery starts slow. At first I feel like I can do it. I can run the six miles she's got mapped out for us. "You just want to run by Taylor's house. Admit it," I pant between breaths.

"So what? I look hot when I run."

She's right. She does. Her hair stays in place. Her face stays the same perfect olive color. Her muscles propel her forward. She travels across the landscape more than she runs. Watching her do anything physical is like watching Leah dance.

We round the corner. "So tell me," she says, her breath even.

"Mr. Kispert was there."

Emery glances at the house we're running past and the thin woods behind it. On the other side of those trees is my yard. My backyard with my studio. The one Dad had built for me. At the time I was ecstatic. It felt important, as if he saw me— really saw me—and he knew I was special. But now, I get it. It wasn't a gift. It was an obligation. A promise I made to be the talented daughter who would make him proud.

We pick up the pace, and I am grateful to be moving away from all that, at least for now. My good mood sours as soon as we pass Max's house. His car is parked out front, meaning he's home. And he didn't text. He didn't check in to see how I was, even though he knew how hard today would be.

Emery reads my mood like a psychic at the county fair. "You know how he is."

"Whatever." This time I increase the pace, as if tiring myself out will prove I'm over him.

"Maybe you need to broaden your field."

I concentrate on my legs, which are starting to feel like lead. I tell myself to keep going. I tell my legs to push off like Emery's do. I tell myself that if Leah were here, she'd race me to the end of the street, beat me, then taunt me the rest of the way.

She's still so with me, I can almost hear her saying, *You're slow, Baby Sister. Sloppy Seconds.*

So I start racing. I sprint to the end of the street. Emery's long legs outpace me without even a struggle. I bend over and hold my side, try to catch my breath. Breathe. Breathe. Breathe.

A group of guys jog our way, keeping in a tight formation, teammates in training. They're too far away to see which team. My heart skips a little. I try not to hope Max is with them. As they get closer, I see they aren't the swimmers but baseball players.

They mostly ignore me as they pass, which is totally cool. Except one of them doesn't. Nick Larsons stops, comes closer. Nick Larsons—part baseball player, part artist. I'm not sure the exact proportions of each. He has a tight first-baseman build and warm hazel eyes. He paints more realistic than I like but still decent.

Emery gives me an approving look and then takes off running alongside the baseball team, faster than she and I were running but still not even a challenge for her.

Nick looks at me like he's so glad to see me. He actually looks happy that I'm here, which, in a way, surprises me. "Hey, Allie. What's up?"

I don't answer, just start running again. "I'm slow. You can go ahead."

He runs next to me, easy jock strides, all muscle and strength. Everything I wish I were. He turns and faces backward, jogging the whole time. "You taking studio?" he asks.

"Yeah. You?"

He smiles. "Yeah. Can't believe they let me in. Kispert's cool. But I'm in way over my head."

I pick up my speed, and Nick turns so he's running forward again and adjusts to my new pace. "You won't have any trouble with it though," he says.

"You have no idea."

He laughs. I don't.

When we get to the end of the street, I stop again. I motion behind me. "I'm gonna go home. This is way too much exercise for me."

He puts the brakes on too. "Okay. See you tomorrow. I'll look for you."

"Sure thing." I make myself face him, make myself ignore Max, who has just stepped out of his house. It's like I have some kind of Max radar that I couldn't turn off even if I wanted to.

"Is that okay?" Nick trips a little over the words, making me smile.

I act like I don't see Max standing in the driveway, watching me. I act like I want to flirt with Nick, like it means something to me. "Yeah. More than okay."

Nick's turn to smile. Sweet. I wish I could make my heart skip knowing I made him smile. But I can't. It's his turn to motion behind him. "I'm gonna go catch up…"

"Yeah. Sure."

He jogs away, turning to look at me one more time. I wave, and I tell myself not to turn around. Not to look at Max. Watch Nick, who has that silly smile pasted on his face. He turns on the jets, turbo-ing himself forward.

"So you're into baseball players now?" Max's voice comes from behind me. "That's a completely valid choice. You know, if you don't mind your men a little small."

I still don't turn to face him. "Thanks for your approval. Not that you actually get a say."

He drapes his arms over me, leaning his body against mine. I try not to feel how ripped he is, but I can't. It's not like his body's the only thing I love about Max, but I'd have to be dead not to notice. He whispers in my ear. "How was it?"

Tears spring to my eyes. I want to push him away and run home, pretend that jogging is my new passion. It's not like what he says to me is so profound—it's just that his concern gets inside me. Deep. It blankets me, hugging my ribs hard, massaging my heart. Max does this without even trying. He turns me, so I have to face him. He sees my tears. But it's not like he needed to. Max knows. He holds me against him, and I bury my face in his neck.

"Shh. It's okay. It's going to be okay."

I cry more, not caring. He holds me closer. It's like there's no space between us. I want to turn my face up to his. I want to kiss him. I feel that need in every cell of my body—my Max need. Bottomless and aching and just plain stupid because I know it's not going to happen. Not after that one time last spring. That thought is the slap in the face and the punch in the gut I need to stop the tears. I pull away from him so he won't know—as if he doesn't already.

He wipes one of my tears away with his thumb. His eyes are so intense, I have to look away. "How 'bout I walk you home?" he asks.

I nod. That I can do.